to a different accordion

by

Saxon Bennett

Bella
BOOKS

2011

Bella Books, Inc.
P.O. Box 10543
Tallahassee, FL 32302

Printed in the United States of America on acid-free paper
First published 2011

Editor: Medora MacDougall
Cover Designer: Judy Fellows

ISBN 13: 978-1-59493-242-7

Other Bella Books By Saxon Bennett

Back Talk

Date Night Club

Higher Ground

Family Affair

Sweet Fire

Talk of the Town

Talk of the Town Too

The Wish List

To Darla Sue because she's always there

About The Author

Saxon resides at 35 degrees 55' 43.14 N 94 degrees 58' 3.27" W or thereabouts and most days is grateful. She is the author of a whole bunch of other books most of which she cannot remember the titles to. She's not a serious lesbian. Not to mean she's not serious about being a lesbian, because she is. Serious. About being a lesbian. But she's not a serious lesbian. Meaning she's not serious. But she is a lesbian.

Chapter One—Fishing
To fish in troubled waters—Matthew Henry

"Don't panic. It never helps in a crisis and often hinders any efforts to remedy the situation."

Chase said this as much to herself as to the child. Being prone to panic on her own, she mustered all her sensibilities as best she could and peered down the garbage disposal looking for the tiny puff fish.

Bud shrieked as she sat on the counter, clutching the small glass fishbowl. Annie, a medium-sized, black and white, good-natured-if-a-little-willful dog of indeterminate parentage, and Jane, a black and tan version of her littermate who used a tennis ball as a constant pacifier, danced around barking and howling as if in sympathy with the four-year-old's heart-wrenching dilemma.

The kitchen door opened and Gitana said, "What on earth is wrong?"

Chase looked up from the sink. "We lost the fish. It's down the disposal, but his tail is still flapping around. I think that's a positive sign." She turned on the faucet, letting a little water in so the poor fellow wouldn't suffocate.

Bud put her arms up, reaching out for Gitana who picked her up, kissed away her tears and then went to the door and, opening it, said, "Out!"

The dogs made a hasty retreat. She set Bud on the kitchen stool. "Don't worry." She took the fishbowl, filled it with water and set it on the counter next to the sink.

"What are you going to do?" Chase inquired with trepidation.

Gitana opened a drawer and pulled out the salad tongs. "Rescue Paddington." She stuck the tongs down the disposal and carefully lifted the fish out and deposited him in the bowl. Then she put it on the kitchen island. "See, all better."

Bud shrieked with joy this time. She cooed at the tiny fish and petted the outside of the fish bowl.

"You're amazing," Chase said, bending slightly to kiss her cheek and thanking the powers-that-be that this lovely olive-skinned, brown-eyed beauty, her long hair pulled up in a messy bun, was her partner. She was also grateful that no weird midlife crisis had destroyed their lengthy relationship now that they were both in their forties and such things were possible. They had, after all, survived the unexpected circumstances of Bud's conception—a pap smear turned pregnancy. Having a child had completely changed their lives and Chase liked to think for the better.

"Glad to be of service, but how did Paddington get there in the first place?"

"Bud wanted to do a little housekeeping...there was this green stuff, well, anyway, I let her clean the fishbowl, but during the transfer process from Tupperware to home base we lost him."

"I see." This was Gitana's standard response to all matter of household weirdness.

"How was your day?" Chase asked.

"Not as eventful as yours."

The intercom buzzer rang and Gitana clicked it on. It was Donna calling from the writing studio. Chase still couldn't believe she had a paid personal assistant, but ever since the mystery series she wrote as Shelby McCall—a pen name she rather liked despite her difficulty of becoming this other person who was supposed to have a poise and decorum Chase hadn't exactly mastered as yet—had taken off, Donna had become indispensable.

"Is everything all right? I thought I heard something like bloody murder."

Gitana responded, "It was Bud. She lost her fish down the garbage disposal."

Bud pointed at Chase.

"I did not. You dropped him," Chase said.

Bud shook her head and said in her own language, "Seil."

"Oh, poor Paddington," Donna lamented.

"He's all right, we rescued him," Gitana said, pulling her Day-Timer from her bag.

Donna must have sensed this or heard the flipping of pages. It seemed to Chase that Donna always reminded Gitana of schedules: She invariably drew out her Day-Timer whenever Donna was around. "I've drawn up next week's schedule, did payroll for the office and ordered groceries which will be delivered in the morning. All items being ordered according to the menu that we decided on, including Bud—mind you, those tofu hot dog things are not an easy find."

Before Donna had a chance to go on, Gitana said, "Why don't you come over and we'll coordinate the rest of the stuff?"

"Be right there."

"How did we live without her?" Gitana asked Chase, peering in at Paddington who appeared to have completely recovered from his ordeal.

"We had a lot less going on. All we had to do was buy dog food, get their yearly shots and pick up poop. Our laundry list was short."

"And you weren't a very important author," Gitana said, kissing her neck and sneaking a hand around to fondle her left buttock in order to avoid detection by the child.

"I was important before," Chase said, feeling obligated to defend her earlier works.

"Ah, but moist-mound sagas didn't pay like this Shelby McCall gig," Gitana said, snagging a piece of Swiss cheese from the cutting board where Chase was now chopping broccoli and purple onions for the veggie frittata.

"I wish we could have some prosciutto in it but..." she pointed at Bud, who, despite being under age for kindergarten, carnival rides and complete control of her financial affairs, was a militant vegetarian. She did make exceptions for dairy, having ascertained that no animals were harmed in the making of cheese, butter and milk. Chase was thankful for this because she'd heard that being a true vegan was impossibly complicated, and she was already taxed with the pursuit of protein to insure that Bud did not remain a midget due to her dietary restrictions—which was why Donna was in charge of research, menu preparations and procurement.

"I'm sure she'll grow out of it," Gitana said, sneaking a peek at Bud to see if she was paying attention, but she was still engrossed with the fish.

"I had a green chili cheeseburger with Lacey for lunch," Chase said.

Bud instantly peered at her and wagged her tiny forefinger and said, "Dab, dab."

"What does that mean?" Gitana said.

"I think I'm being scolded." Chase abstained from mentioning in Bud's presence that she'd purchased four more cheeseburgers from McDonald's and had them secreted away in the produce drawer so that she and her willing accomplice could snack on them after Bud and her ethics were safely in bed.

Donna arrived with her massive, heavily bound-in-brown-calves-skin Day-Timer that Bud always eyed with the evident suspicion that it was not an organic plant-based product as she had been told. Donna had the keen gaze of a lieutenant major about to inform her subordinates of the intended battle plan. *Her* laundry lists were as enormous and convoluted as the annotated tax code used by the IRS to entrap the unwary. She set the encyclopedic book on the counter and went to check on

Paddington. She looked at the fish and then at Bud. "Do I need to schedule a veterinary appointment?"

Bud shook her head. "Eh si yako."

"All right, if you're sure." She opened the bible of time keeping. "Okay, now the agenda. Gitana, the people from *Orchid Monthly* are due on Thursday morning at nine. I wouldn't count on a timely arrival at the nursery. It appears these media types have no concept that time is money and that holding up productive working people, the engine that produces the steam that runs this country, is a sin against human nature which strives to be active and accomplish something by the end of the day."

"How do you know that?" Chase asked.

"I talked to a very helpful young woman named Tracey who is on staff at the magazine. If you want to know anything go to the little people, aka the only ones that do anything, and they will know everything."

Chase was always amazed by Donna's research abilities. Her command of knowledge or the attainment of it put to shame even that of Lacey, Chase's best friend and who heretofore had been the Keeper of Odd Knowledge. Chase kept this to herself, naturally, so as not to hurt Lacey's feelings.

Donna continued, "Nora is getting everything set up and is in charge of the staff lottery."

"Lottery?" Chase asked, as she whipped the eggs up on the counter behind her so that Bud would not see the yolks and get all fired up about compassionate consumption.

"We decided that a lottery for the position of helpers in the photo shoot was the only fair way to deal with the situation as everyone wanted their fifteen minutes of fame," Donna said.

"Very egalitarian," Chase said, adding milk to the bowl in the same covert manner.

"Right," Gitana said, noting down the time. Donna had procured a set of interview questions that she had been drilling Gitana on so that she would not be taken unawares by any controversial issues. Chase couldn't imagine what controversial issues were possible in the world of orchids—bisexual orchids? orchids abusing their hosts? earth orchids terrorizing rock orchids?—but according to Donna anything was possible and it was best to be prepared. As the owner and manager of the orchid nursery Gitana would be held entirely responsible if something was found to be awry.

"Now, Chase, you have an online chat with your Shelby McCall readers' on Friday evening at seven—pronto. We cannot be tardy as e-readers are not a patient bunch. I will be onsite so the Luddite need not worry, and for goodness sake get into character so you sound like Shelby McCall, the uber confident worldly mystery writer they expect and not some socially inept lesbian ghetto writer."

Despite her newfound fame and amped-up level of production, Chase was no better with her tech skills than she had been before and her acting skills were practically nonexistent. It had taken Donna months of training for Chase to comprehend the mysterious workings of her BlackBerry at even an elementary level, and despite trying to be in character she most often failed.

Donna continued as Chase, not wanting to fry the eggs until the meeting was completed, started in on the chef salad, cleaning the romaine and spinach and thinking about the nice chunks of Boar's Head hard salami and peppered turkey breast that used to accompany the greens.

"Bud, you have your interview for fall semester at the Albuquerque Academy of Arts and Sciences, providing we can get you to speak a normal language instead of..." With this Donna was at a loss. Despite numerous searches on the Internet, she had yet to discover the origins of Bud's peculiar linguistics. At one point she was certain it was Sanskrit but upon further inspection had vetoed it.

"It's not even Easter yet," Gitana said.

"I know, but there's a waiting list and serious competition. We have to be ready," Donna said.

"She's only four," Gitana screeched. Bud reached out and patted her hand as if to say, don't worry, let them plan and the perverted universe will cast them all asunder.

"But she'll be five in the fall and we have to think of her future," Chase said. She eyed Bud suspiciously, sensing what the hand patting and the doe-like liquidity of Bud's look had meant.

Sometimes she felt like there was a hallway that conjoined their brains. "The universe is not a slave to chance, there is order in chaos."

"Yllof."

"We'll see," Chase said.

"What are you two talking about?" Gitana asked.

"It's difficult to explain. I think we're having a dispute about the nature of the universe."

"Good God, Almighty," Gitana said. She'd taken to swearing great oaths on the seeming comedy of errors that now resided permanently in their lives. Her mother, Jacinda, a devout Catholic, took these oaths to mean a great reverence for the cause and always bowed her head as if Gitana had become the Fatima of Guadalupe.

"It's settled then. We'll get her a speech therapist. I know we can fix this," Donna said.

"Kcuf ffo!" Bud screamed, banging her tiny brown fist on the counter. The reverberation rocked Paddington's watery home and she refrained.

"Don't talk like that, young lady," Chase said.

"What did she say?" Gitana said.

"I can't repeat it."

"How come you're the only one who can understand her?" Gitana asked.

"I don't know. I can't explain it. I just do."

"It doesn't matter. She can't go to school with you tagging along as her interpreter," Donna said.

Chase and Gitana looked at each other and sighed heavily. Donna often ended up as the voice of sanity when it came to making household decisions. The addition of Bud and the change of Chase's writing career had put their quiet little lives into a Star Trekian hyperdrive. Donna, whom Chase had met at a Halloween party before Bud was born—Chase dressed as an Oompa Loompa and Donna as Dorothy—had gone from an unpaid beta reader and researcher to a full-time, well-compensated personal assistant.

"She's right, you know," Gitana said, stroking Bud's brown curls. Bud looked up at her with her exquisite almond-shaped eyes—Gitana's own eyes. Sometimes Chase wished she looked a little more like them instead of being blond and blue-eyed with aquiline features. She looked more like Bud's nanny than her mother.

Chase and Donna stared morosely. "I know it seems like we're selling out her individuality for the sake of the social contract, but she must intellectualize her thoughts in a recognizable language—a common language," Donna said ruefully.

Donna was avid disciple of Ayn Rand's objectivist philosophy—a code of rational ethics that Chase found very helpful. She ran a lot of things by Donna for that reason. Chase hoped this wasn't like Joan Crawford calling that quack Scientologist fortune-teller for advice, but Donna had a way of weeding through the slag pile and coming up with lapis lazuli just when it was needed.

"All right," Chase said. She stared at Bud. "This is going to be hard on both of us. I don't like selling you out, but Donna is right. You have things to say and the rest of us want to hear them. I won't let them do anything bad to you, I promise."

Bud pouted a minute. "Nac yalp htiw meht tsrif?"

"Yes, but carefully. We don't want you ending up in the nut factory. Remember what I told you there is a line."

"What did she say?" Donna asked.

Gitana looked liked she didn't want to know.

"She wants the opportunity to test the mettle of the conformists."

Gitana groaned. Chase put her hand on her shoulder. "It's not easy being different, but you always said that normal is boring."

"I'll make an appointment with Dr. Garcia. We have to go through him first as her pediatrician before we can get a referral to a speech therapist," Donna said, making a notation in her Day-Timer.

"Make sure you find out you find out which bobblehead he's pining after," Chase said.

"I'm on it. I found this online store that sells only bobbleheads and they ship overnight," Donna said.

"Is this bribery really necessary?" Gitana asked. She handed Bud a piece of spinach.

Chase nodded approvingly. Bud loved spinach. Chase was certain this desire had taken root in the womb, as she'd fed Gitana copious amounts of spinach during her pregnancy.

"Of course it is. Dr. Garcia always makes time for her. Do you know how difficult it is to get an appointment quickly unless it's life threatening? Due to the bribery, Bud gets in," Donna said.

"It's like being a big tipper," Chase said, noticing that Bud had now grabbed a handful of spinach. She must be getting hungry, she noted.

"Why doesn't he just buy whatever one he wants instead of waiting for someone to give it to him?" Gitana asked.

"He has a purchasing phobia," Donna said.

"A what?" Gitana said.

"He doesn't like to buy things himself, rather he picks them out and has a neutral party purchase them," Donna said.

"Is he a tightwad?" Gitana asked.

"No. Phobias don't operate like that. He just finds money distasteful," Donna said.

"How do you know all this?" Gitana asked.

Chase started the eggs and pulled the shredded potatoes from the freezer. "His receptionist told us."

"You know about this too?" Gitana said.

"Always go to the little people, they know everything. We bring her chocolate-covered orange Frangos," Chase said.

"Oh, Great God in heaven. You're all corrupt."

Bud piped in, "Puy!"

"What did she say?" Gitana asked.

"She concurs." Chase was setting the table. "Staying for dinner?" she asked Donna as she pulled out plates.

"Sure."

Gitana stirred the potatoes into the eggs. "I feel out of the loop."

"I've got files on everyone we have to deal with. I'll make you copies and then you'll be up to speed," Donna said.

Gitana groaned.

Chapter Two—In the Desert
Life! What art thou without love?—E. Moore

Chase held the dustpan while one of her writing cohorts, Alma Lucero, her lovely wrinkled face and spiky white hair catching the sun, swept up the remnants of an entire china dinner set. The set had been pretty—gold trimmed with tiny pink roses. They were standing in the driveway of Mrs. Givens, Alma's next-door neighbor.

"It was his mother's. He loved it, every fucking piece of it," Mrs. Givens said, leaning over with great difficulty and picking up a piece. "Stupid pink roses."

"It's all right, Evelyn. It's only crockery," Alma said soothingly.

"I suppose you think I'm a horrible person," Mrs. Givens said to Chase. "But then I don't care anyhow, now do I? I suppose I should, but two fits of bad temper in seventy-four years isn't so terrible. I could've been a murderess."

Chase gazed up from the broken crockery and the dustpan to the woman. "No, I think it's the right kind of wickedness, in the sense of being quite correct—thus your behavior is most sensible."

"Are you still reading Dickens?" Alma said.

"Just finished reading *Oliver Twist* to Bud. She loved it."

"Dickens! I stand by *Hard Times* as one of his best," said Mrs. Givens, "or the one I like best. My husband, that miserable little pompous ass, is like Thomas Gradgrind. Do you know what started all this?" She put her arms out expansively, but before she could answer her own question, she caught sight of the fluttering curtain across the street. "That's right, stare away—like I care. You haven't spoken to me in fifteen years, what does it matter now? I can't help it I'm hideous. Don't you think I know I only have four good teeth and I have to strap up and wrap up and hunch over just to get through the fucking day? Do you know what that's like?" She was screaming now.

Chase glanced across the street to see who Mrs. Givens was shouting at, but the curtain had closed. She looked at Alma inquiringly.

"It's Mrs. Bell. They've hated each other for years—something about the theft of tulip bulbs," Alma explained.

Goodness, Chase thought. My neighbors are looking better all the time—though it does help that there's ten acres between us.

"Well, back at it. Do you know how long it took me to do all this, piece by piece in fond remembrance of what each cup, saucer, plate, dessert plate, gravy boat, sugar and cream set and graceful teacups meant to me as I washed and carefully stacked them after each holiday? Those were hard, I liked the tea set, but it had to be done, and now it's all gone."

Chase decided that "Do you know" was Mrs. Givens' way of starting all her tirades. Chase rather liked it. Her mother, Stella, would hate it. Just as she had hated Chase's habit of saying "excuse me" when she couldn't believe what she was hearing. She cured Chase of that. It was a tough love episode, but it had worked. Mrs. Givens and her speech were straight out of Dickens. A character sketch to be dreamed of—a gift from on high. Alma raised her eyebrows as if sensing Chase's brainwave patterns. "I can't help myself."

"So how did it happen, my dear?" Alma asked gently.

Chase hurriedly put the trash can on the side of the garage where she had found it and scurried back so as not to miss any of the story.

"It's the Republicans—those damn miscreants."

"What did they do?" Chase said, wondering how a political party could facilitate the divorce of two elderly people and the destruction of a dinner set.

"Why that bastard, my husband, soon to be ex-husband, is a Republican and it's his fault and you know what he did?"

"No, Evelyn, we don't," Alma said.

"I had the audacity to ask the bastard, that would be Eugene, to go out to the mailbox and post a letter—a letter to my poor sister. She's married to a worthless, shifty, 'maybe I'll get a job when one comes along that pays six figures...' Six figures, my ass. I wouldn't pay that low-life six cents. I send my sister, her name is Marge, encouragement. I go to Smith's and steal quotes from the damn Hallmark cards. Sis thinks I'm a literary genius. I send her checks. Small amounts, mind you, I've got to squeeze it out of Mr. Tightwad, which I do by watering down his soup. He has soup every day, every damn day. I put in twice as much water as is required and he has one can for two days and the stupid bastard doesn't even notice. Ha!"

Chase was mesmerized. Mrs. Givens' tirades didn't exactly make sense or follow proper semantics but they were priceless. She wondered if she'd ever get to this stage of convoluted sentence structure.

Alma looked over her shoulder as Bo's bright green Pacer pulled up in her drive. When he got out she motioned him to go in the house. He nodded.

Good going, Chase thought. Mrs. Givens wouldn't take kindly to a set of balls coming over right now. Bo went inside before Mrs. Givens could see him.

"As I was saying, the Republicans did it. Mr. Pompous Ass thinks all the country's woes are the Democrats' fault. I say now how can that be when the Bushies, that's what I call them, they're just like a bunch of Moonies, exchanging those silly orange sheets for a blue blazer and a red-striped tie, have had their filthy greedy paws on the purse strings and the deregulation schemes for eight fucking years."

Alma and Chase both nodded. They were Democrats. It wasn't like they didn't know that both sides were a bunch of crooks, but Democrats seemed less likely to round up dissidents and put them in camps than the talk-radio-listening Republican freaks. Besides it was sort of assumed that most creative people were Democrats. Chase wasn't excited about being a donkey. It didn't seem a good choice for a mascot—an armadillo would be better perhaps, so the NRA would have more difficulty killing it.

"So that was it?" Alma asked.

"The straw that broke the camel's back. He won't speak to me and my kids don't speak to me either but that's been going on for a couple of years. I'm kind of used to it, but children really should respect their elders." She pointed a bony, horribly gnarled finger at Chase. "Do you respect your elders?"

"Right down to word choice," Chase replied, fascinated with the finger. How did she even write a check with a forefinger like that?

"Good."

"Why don't your kids speak to you?" Chase asked. Alma gave her an almost imperceptible headshake. Chase knew what it meant, but she couldn't help herself. She just wanted one more story.

"Because I won't go to the doctor."

"Why not?" Alma asked.

Ha! Chase thought, she's just as engrossed as I am. Chase couldn't believe Alma had never told her about Mrs. Givens. She was fabulous.

"They're trying to kill me—all of them, the doctors, the specialists and my ungrateful children and to think, I lay in agony thrusting those little squish-faced bastards out of my vagina—it's like a Saint Bernard trying to get out a cat door. It's not pretty."

Chase winced, having been banished from the delivery room because she was so stressed out before the whole thing got started that now she could only imagine the pain and agony that Gitana had gone through as Bud came out the cat door.

"That's right, little missy," she said, pointing the gnarled finger at Chase. "It's not pretty, remember that."

"So how are they trying to kill you?" Chase said.

"With medication."

"Medication?" Chase said.

"For my rheumatoid arthritis. I've been like this for years. I take care of myself. I don't want their pills. That is what killed my friend—the only friend I had," she looked over at Alma, "Except for you."

Alma touched her arm. "And I am your friend."

"I wouldn't mind being one," Chase said, surprising even herself with her forwardness. It wasn't just curiosity or her endless search for fodder, it was something more. Mrs. Givens was honest.

Mrs. Givens smiled at her. She did only have about four teeth, but Chase didn't care. "Come for tea on Friday and bring that little urchin of yours. Alma told me about you being a parent and I like to frighten little children."

Chase laughed. "Oh, I don't think you'll scare this one. I think you will fascinate her with your stories."

"All right then, it seems the rest of your artistic miscreants are arriving—go and write something subversive that'll piss off the Republicans. Tell that spiky-haired one that her web stories make the good people apoplectic and I heartily enjoy the stories."

Jasmine and Delia, two more members of the writing group, stood in the driveway waiting for them. Chase practically skipped over to Alma's house.

"That was very nice of you," Alma said. "You will show?"

"Of course. I'd cancel anything to have tea with her and I promise I shan't ever write anything bad about her. In fact, I might try to keep her out of my stories out of respect."

"Oh, don't do that. She'd be pleased if she were in one."

"Really?" Chase was delighted.

Delia and Jasmine watched them as they came over and Mrs. Givens slowly made her way back to her front door.

"Who's she?" Jasmine asked, eyeing Mrs. Givens.

Chase thought she saw something like greed in her countenance. Jasmine's lesbian detective series, thanks to Chase's intervention with the publisher, had come along nicely. She was now one of Sappho Sisters' best selling authors. "She's mine."

Jasmine pouted. "She's so perfect. Can't I just use part of her?"

Alma frowned at them and then smiled. "I'm sure Mrs. Givens would be quite pleased to have you both over for tea. However, I do not approve of the two of you acting like she is some kind of prize to be apportioned out and stuck in a manuscript." She opened the front door and they went inside.

Chase smelt coffee. Bo had been busy in their absence. "You're correct. It's downright shameful," Chase said, looking contrite for all of five seconds. "What are you going to do with her?" she inquired of Jasmine.

"Oh, I have the perfect spot for her. I needed someone like her, but I couldn't get the character right until now. And you?" Jasmine asked.

"Future reference. I'm taking Bud over for tea."

Jasmine flounced down on Alma's distressed, greatly distressed from years of use, brown leather couch. "I wish I could go."

Jasmine had picked up the art of flouncing from Lacey, her "life partner" as they called themselves, who also happened to be Chase's best friend. She now knew three flouncers, she realized, as Bo came in and flounced down next to her. He was a good-looking guy with his cleft chin and aquiline nose.

"I think she's really creepy," Delia said.

Alma smacked her with the manuscript copy that Delia had been passing out. "That's not nice."

"She reminds me of my Aunt Edna," Bo said, glancing over the copy.

Finding the couch too crowded, Chase went to sit in the burnt orange-colored easy chair that was no longer easy as the leaning back mechanism was broken and had been broken for years. Alma's idea of decorating was comfortable old furniture, a few water color paintings of aspen trees in fall, a portrait of a Hopi Indian in full dance dress and an oil painting of Chaco Canyon with an amazing thundercloud sky. Chase liked that one the best. When Bud got longer legs she planned to take her there and hike around the ruins.

Delia brought out the coffee on a tray and set it on the badly watermarked oval coffee table. She sat down next to Bo and retied her shoulder-length hair with a woven hemp and bead hair band. She looked like Violet Baudelaire preparing for an invention, thought Chase. Chase was reading the entire Lemony Snicket series to Bud as bedtime stories. Gitana didn't necessarily approve so they pretended to be reading *Anne of the Island* by L.M. Montgomery. They'd already finished it, but Gitana wasn't one for counting pages.

It still blew Chase's mind that Delia had gone from philandering butch to monogamous femme. She'd grown out her spiky-hair, although as Mrs. Givens had mentioned, she'd not changed her Facebook photo as she thought her butch image sold better. Now, she wore wide-legged organic cotton trousers and girlie tops as Chase called them, fitted things with hip lines. She still didn't have good manners, but Chase was certain they would eventually show up. At least Graciela, Delia's live-in girlfriend and Gitana's sister, was still mostly the same except that she was entirely devoted to Delia in a way that Chase had never thought she'd see. The former Lothario was now the picture-perfect monogamous partner with a real job. She sold real estate to gay couples and did quite well at it. "How's the husband?"

Delia smiled. "Wonderful as ever."

"They don't even fight," Bo said. He'd recently broken up with Boyfriend 103.

"You're just bitter," Delia said, handing him a cup of coffee.

"That's all right. Mr. Right will be coming along shortly. Besides, I write better when I'm single," Bo said.

For Chase it was the opposite. She couldn't write if there was domestic strife in the house.

"How is E-rotic Editions coming along?" Alma said. She took the cup of coffee Delia handed her.

"Fucking great! We just signed the hottest new erotica writer on the web so far. She was doing her own stuff, but we convinced her that all of us banding together will give us more exposure."

Delia and Bo did a high-five. They had had the wild idea to start an e-press and market erotica. Bo had the computer skills and Delia was the sales person. She could talk anyone into anything. It reminded Chase of that Pet Shop Boys' song, "You've got the looks, I've got the brains, let's make lots of money."

"What's her name?" Jasmine asked.

"Get this, Lolita Loveheart," Delia said.

Bo rolled his eyes.

"It's better than Hard N. Fast," Delia said.

"Are those their real names?" Jasmine said.

Alma's jaw dropped, her usual savoir-faire shattered by Jasmine's naiveté.

"Have you been doing your assignments?" Delia snapped.

"Diligently," Jasmine said, holding up two fingers declaring her oath. "Lacey is delighted with my progress."

"Then you should know better," Delia said sharply, like she was reprimanding a silly child.

"What assignments?" Chase said.

"I'm proofreading all the incoming erotica. Then Lacey and I practice the logistics to see if they're physically possible. It's a win-win situation."

"Are you paying her for that?" Chase said.

"Of course. She gets fifty bucks a story, more if it's a longer one, plus the fringe benefits of the research," Delia said.

Chase suddenly wondered if she was old school. Did Lacey and Jasmine, newbies to the fold, know more about sex than she and Gitana? She might need to pilfer some of their stash.

"That appears to be a fair proposition," Alma said. She circled a few words in the manuscript that Delia had given them all. Delia and Bo were the editors for a printed volume of erotica that was coming out and the group was dealing with some of the more troublesome stories. Those stories, once they got them straightened out, had taught Chase a thing or two, but as yet she hadn't had had the courage to try out any of the moves on Gitana.

"You should know a pen name when you see one," Delia continued to upbraid Jasmine.

"I never really look at the cover page," Jasmine said.

"Which might be an asset," Alma suggested.

"Why's that?" Bo said, pouring himself more coffee from the carafe.

"Hard N. Fast already sets the reader up for a certain kind of story and if it doesn't live up to the preconceived notion of the reader it could be a letdown," Alma said.

This sent Bo and Delia into spasms of laughter. "Letdown," they gasped.

Alma exchanged looks with Chase.

"Why is it that erotica can be so absurd sometimes? It's like dirty jokes. Sex should be sacred and special," Chase said. "Not something to be hurled about like a sweat-befouled jock strap."

"That's really beautiful," Jasmine said, reaching over to pat Chase's hand.

"Good thing you're not writing the introduction," Delia said, once she'd composed herself. "You're getting kind of prudish in your old age."

"No, I think she's getting more Proustian," Alma said, circling another word in the manuscript whose title's meaning still eluded Chase. It had something to do with bumping donuts.

Chase would have taken this as a compliment except she knew Proust had stopped having sex long before he caught a cold and died. She turned back to the manuscript and savagely crossed out the second and third paragraph of a particularly offensive sex act.

On the drive home, Chase wondered when exactly she'd stopped thinking about sex. Was it when she turned forty? Was she experiencing vaginal dryness? When her primary care physician had asked her this, Chase had immediately conjured up an image of her vagina having turned into the Kalahari Desert.

Writing moist-mound sagas had forced her to keep sex in the forefront. She had to in order to keep her characters rolling toward the roll-in-the-hay moment. Mystery novels required less sex and more focus on creating a plot that kept the reader guessing. Chase now spent her time thinking about convoluted murders and deceptions rather than the soft pink folds of the nether regions, about guns, knives and power tools instead of breasts and excited nipples, about brilliant evil people instead of gentle lovers united. Maybe she should take a look at Jasmine's homework and see if it produced rain in the desert.

When they went to bed later that night, Chase tried to think sexy thoughts as Gitana snored slightly. She remained conscious for an additional five minutes before the sandman caught her by the ankles and dragged her off to la-la land.

In the morning as she lay in bed waiting for the coffee maker to go ding indicating it was ready, Gitana was showering. Chase contemplated joining her, but by the time she unraveled herself from the bedclothes—she'd taken to cocooning in the night so that in dreams she felt like she was wrapped tightly in a shroud—Gitana was dressing, and any possibility of sex was waylaid by the oncoming buzz of the day.

Chapter Three—Knowing
Let knowledge grow from more to more.—Tennyson

"How did it go?" Chase asked, as Addison hopped into the water-tower-green Mini Cooper that Chase, with her newfound wealth, had splurged on. She had pined after the little cars when they'd first come out, but it had taken much counseling with Dr. Robicheck, her therapist, to get her past the fear of driving anything less fortified than her tank-like Hummer. Upon minute investigation the Mini Cooper was proved to be a safe car according to industry standards. She would never sacrifice her family's safety for her desire to possess something fun to drive, but she was concerned that the purchase of a sports car could be indicative of a midlife crisis. One the other hand, she was only forty-two and still had her period so she considered herself pre-middle-aged. She hoped this wasn't denial.

"I don't think I got the job." Addison, who was eleven, had

applied for the job of newspaper editor for the Albuquerque Academy of Arts and Sciences, the same school Chase was hoping to get Bud into.

Chase pulled out of the school parking lot and onto Tramway Boulevard. The parking lot was thankfully mostly empty because it was after school hours. She picked Addison up occasionally when her mother, Peggy, was busy with Stella catching criminals—they were the twenty-first century PI version of Cagney and Lacey. "Why do you think you didn't get the job?"

"I don't interview well," Addison said, staring out the window.

Chase had never had a job other than writing and the only interview of any kind had been a query letter—in her case three of them before she got the job of being an underpaid dyke writer. Now, things were different. She got paid more, but there was also a lot of pressure to produce so she considered herself more a part of the working public than before. This interview thing interested her.

"How exactly does one interview badly?" Chase studied her little friend. She'd first met Addison McFarland when she was seven. She had had braids and glasses then. Now her brown hair was cut in a pixie and her soft brown eyes had contacts. She was going to grow up to be rather pretty with her upturned nose and pert lips.

Addison held up her pinky, which had suffered much cuticle damage.

"Ouch. You didn't do it during the interview?"

"No. I did it before, but it was bleeding so bad I couldn't shake hands so I appeared either impolite, haughty, uncultured or all three. Look at this." She pulled out the liner of her blazer pocket, which looked grotesquely bloody. "I had to stick it in here."

"I see." Chase suppressed a gag and turned on Central Avenue and headed toward Stella's, where she would pick up Bud and Peggy would pick up Addison.

"And then I was so flustered, I didn't present my curriculum vitae in a confident manner."

"You have a curriculum vitae?"

"Of course." Addison started in on her pinky again.

Chase slapped at it. "Don't. I'm sure you have a first-aid kit in your backpack—put a Band-Aid on it."

Addison obeyed, digging around until she pulled out a gallon-size plastic bag that contained other smaller bags with every conceivable item for ministering to the body.

"Wow. I'll never have to worry about accidents as long as you're around."

Addison did smile at this. "I am always prepared. I should have told the principal about that."

"You know what? I bet she already knows that. I hesitate to bring this up, but at your pre-adult stage, actual grown-ups do cut you some slack." Chase turned onto Central and headed toward Four Hills.

"I don't want slack." She put the Band-Aid on her pinky.

"I know but sometimes getting a break comes in handy. Many of my gifts of fate have come from someone who gave me a break and I don't think less of myself—I think I've been granted a chance that I have to make good on." She turned on Mountain and headed up the street to the Banter residence and the black iron gates that guarded the place. Everyone had to buzz in now or have the code because of her mother's new profession. Stella and Peggy ran a successful private investigating agency that had taken off during Gitana's pregnancy with Bud.

"Have you been reading those inspirational books again?"

"What gives you that idea?" Chase said.

"Like you don't know." Addison returned the plastic bag to the depths of her backpack. She'd gone from the red one of her earlier years to a dark brown leather one. "Oh, I got a present for Bud the other day when our class went to the Explora museum to see the dinosaur exhibit. Did you know we've got a ton of dinosaur fossils right here in New Mexico?"

"Actually, I didn't. Wouldn't it be cool to find one?"

"Let's dig up all your property and see," Addison said.

"Not on your life." Chase tapped in the code at the gate. She parked the car out front. Stella's Crown Vic wasn't in the drive and neither was Peggy's Mercedes.

"Cool," they said simultaneously. It meant they got to spend some time together. Chase missed spending time with Addison, but they both had more obligations now and those easy days were past.

Rosarita, one of the few people that Chase trusted with her, was watching Bud. They found them on the living room floor amid a flourishing city of LEGOS. They had built a mini Athens it seemed.

"That looks like the Parthenon. I didn't know that was possible with LEGOS," Addison said.

"LEGOS have come a long way since we've played with them," Chase said, not meeting her gaze.

Rosarita openly acknowledged that she thought Bud was the cleverest child on the planet. She didn't appear to be nonplussed by Bud's architectural abilities. "We see it in a picture and she builds it."

"See, she saw it in a picture book," Chase said, moving toward the bar to get a bottle of water for her health and a Red Bull as an energizer. She desperately hoped that Bud wasn't teaching herself Greek but quickly chided herself—Bud couldn't even read yet. She tousled her daughter's hair as she passed by, noting that the Pharos Lighthouse, one of the Seven Wonders of the Ancient World, was sitting outside the city limits. "That was located outside Alexandria, not Athens."

"Citeop esnecil," Bud said.

"I suppose."

"What did she say?" Addison asked.

"She explained that in the land of make-believe anything goes."

Addison laughed and followed Chase to the bar. "Are there any bar snacks?" By this she meant the peanuts, pretzels and rice thingy-jiggers Stella kept behind the once-white leather bar that had now been replaced by a tasteful mahogany one. The living room, which had been completely white, had been redecorated when Bud arrived. As Stella, Chase's mother, put it, babies and white things don't go together. "Besides, I don't want her growing up with kitsch, I want intellectualism." So the living room and great portions of the house now resembled an

English country house complete with reproductions and some original pieces of nineteenth-century furniture. Bud went to a house that could have played well in Trollope or Dickens or an Austen novel. Chase was sometimes alarmed at how comfortable she felt in this house.

Chase pulled out the canister of snacks and two bowls. "You know that if you ever go to a bar that you don't eat this kind of stuff from the communal bowl."

Addison looked at her mortified. "I'd never thought of that."

"Same thing goes for any kind of potluck. It's a germ paradise."

Addison was as fastidious about germs as was Chase. They both carried copious amounts of hand-sanitizer gel upon their persons. Chase had Bud so well trained that after any outside event she automatically put her hands up to be cleansed. Once, when Bud was two, they'd been waiting in line at the supermarket and Bud saw the baby in front of them sucking on the handle of the shopping cart. She'd gotten so hysterical that Chase had to take her outside to calm her down. After that Chase made sure to stay away from small children in the grocery store. Gitana didn't understand this particular behavior because Bud had sworn Chase to silence over the event. She still didn't know how a toddler could swear an adult to silence, but she'd done it.

They got their drinks and snacks and sat on the couch. Bud put the last Lego where she thought it should go and went to sit between them. Rosarita got up slowly. "I go start dinner." Bud blew her a kiss. "Oh, my sweet mija."

Bud stared at Addison.

"What?"

Bud didn't say anything but kept staring.

"All right, it's in my backpack. Go get it," Addison said. She shook her head. "How does she know?"

"Because you always bring her a present. Rue the day you don't. It might get ugly."

Bud dug around in her pack and pulled out the Rubik's Cube.

"How does she know what thing in there is her present?" Chase said. She was secretly jealous of the fact that Bud was privy to the contents of the amazing backpack.

"All I can figure is that she knows what I have in there so anything different must be her present." Addison sipped her Red Bull.

Bud stared at the multicolored cube and then up at Addison. It appeared she didn't want to just play with the thing—she wanted to know how it worked.

"Like this," Addison said. She messed up the colors and handed it back to Bud. "Now, you put all the same colors back together again."

Bud nodded.

"I used to love these when I was a pre-adult." Addison, having grown four years older, now considered herself an adult. Other than not being allowed alcoholic beverages, the vote and a driver's license, she was.

They watched Bud. She stared at the cube, turned it around a few times, stuck her tongue out in concentration and then set her little hands to work. Chase was hopeless at puzzle things. She watched in utter astonishment as Bud put the cube right. Bud screamed and clapped her hands in delight.

"How'd she do that?" Chase asked.

"I don't know, but it used to take me quite awhile and sometimes I couldn't do it and I'm not stupid."

"Maybe she just got lucky," Chase said hopefully. Her heart palpitated. She told herself it was the Red Bull.

"I'll try it again. Only this time you don't get to see me do it," she told Bud.

"That's a good idea. She could have watched how you did it and then mimicked it," Chase said, nodding her head convincingly. It's possible, she thought.

"That's still quite a task for a four-year-old." Addison rearranged the cube, mixing up the colors very thoroughly. "Okay, that's better. It would take me a while to undo it." She handed it back to Bud.

Bud studied the cube for a moment and once again stuck out her tongue and wrinkled her brow.

"See, she's having trouble," Chase said, relieved.

Then with mythic speed Bud fixed the cube.

"Well, now that was amazing," Addison said.

Chase bit her lip. "She..." but she couldn't figure out what to say.

"I'm going to time her," Addison said, taking the cube Bud held up. She turned around again and mixed up the colors. She handed Bud the cube, held up one finger and set her watch. "Go."

Bud's little hands worked their magic. Chase inwardly groaned.

"Fifty-nine seconds," Addison said, astonished.

"Well, that's enough of that. Why don't we pick up the LEGOS before Grandma gets home?" No one moved.

Addison was as engrossed as Bud. She now had her notebook out and was logging times. "I'm going to input this into my Excel program and make a chart." The gleam of research covered her face. "I want to see what the record is."

Chase sat on the floor and stared morosely at the LEGO rendition of Athens and then over at her daughter who was making a mockery of the Rubik's Cube. "Let's not."

Addison looked down at her quizzically, then her eyes narrowed. It appeared she recognized the pattern. "You're trying to hide it. Why? Bud's intellect is awesome. I'd have thought you'd be ecstatic."

"I don't want her to end up as some lab rat being probed by Mensa freaks."

"Oh. I hadn't thought of that. This can just be our little secret. When she goes to school there will be lots of smart kids so it won't be as obvious."

"Oh, I don't think so," Stella said, from the entryway of the living room. Her mother was just as sneaky now as she had been when Chase was a child. No wonder she was a private detective, she had the stealth of an Indian scout. She'd make Zorro seem a klutz.

"Are you tutoring her on the sly? She's four," Chase said.

Stella came over and took the proffered cube. "I don't have to." She messed it up and watched as Bud fixed it. "Very good, my little darling." She patted Bud's head. "And don't worry, the Mensa freaks will have to get by me first."

This made Chase feel better. Her mother made Genghis Khan look like a pansy.

"Addison, your mother will be here shortly. I was rather hoping we might finish up that game of Scrabble so that I could recover some of my pecuniary losses," Stella said.

Addison raised her eyebrows and then cracked her knuckles.

"I'm off then." Chase scooped up Bud and her cube.

When Gitana got home Bud was sitting at the kitchen bar while Chase prepared tofu chili dogs. She wished she'd had the foresight and stealth to purchase beef hot dogs and slip Bud the tofu ones. No matter the method, tofu was tofu and her carnivorous tendencies seemed to pop up with greater frequency the longer she remained a hypocritical vegetarian. She dreamed about meat, ate copious amounts of it whenever she was away from Bud and longed for the day when she could shuck the whole thing off. In the meanwhile she checked for signs that Bud's resistance to flesh might be waning by running her by the deli every time they went grocery shopping just to see if something might catch her eye and undermine the veggie demon inside.

"Hello, my little furry ones," Gitana said, as she patted the dogs' heads and gave them dried duck treats that were supposed to be healthier for them. Chase found herself sniffing the treats and thinking about duck with orange sauce.

Bud held up her cube and crowed, "hctaw, hctaw!"

"Where'd you get that?" Gitana said.

"Addison gave it to her," Chase said. "You know what, maybe we should put it away and Mommy can tell us about her day." She snatched the Rubik's Cube and stuffed it in the first place that came to mind, which was the freezer.

Bud stared in horror and then screamed bloody murder. The dogs leapt up and Gitana calmly suggested she give it back.

"We shouldn't give in to her. It's bad discipline," Chase said, stirring the baked beans and trying desperately to ignore Bud's wailing.

Bud stopped wailing long enough to say, "Feiht!"

"I am not. You've played with it enough."

"What did she say?" Gitana asked, stroking Bud's unruly curls. She'd stopped crying and was now glaring at Chase.

"She is accusing me of appropriating her property."

"You did. Give it back to her."

"All right. We'll compromise. You can have it until dinner. Deal?" Chase said. She stuck out her hand.

Bud glared at her but shook on it. Chase gave it back.

"How was your day?" Chase inquired as she chopped up onions and pickles. If she put enough stuff on the poser hot dogs they might taste better. She watched Bud out of the corner of her eye while Gitana pulled a Dasani from the fridge and sat down next to their daughter. Bud seemed oblivious to everything and now distrustful of handing the cube over to anyone over the age of thirty. She quietly manipulated the cube herself. Gitana didn't seem to notice her nimble little fingers putting it right.

"Not bad. We're getting the newsletter for our customer base ready. That really was a brilliant idea on Donna's part. I think it will get the orchid lovers all jazzed for spring." She glanced over at Bud.

"Because the orchids start to bloom soon and that's the best time to get them, right?" Chase said, in an effort to distract her.

"Uh, yes. Does she know what she's doing?" Gitana said, pointing at Bud.

Chase cut open the buns and put them on plates. "Oh, she's just playing around with it." She didn't meet Gitana's gaze.

"I don't think so." Gitana held out her hand. "Can I mess it up for you?"

Bud looked suspicious but handed it over. Gitana turned away from Bud and messed up the cube. Chase wondered how she knew to do that as if she intuited that a four-year-old could follow her moves and mimic the return sequence. She handed it back.

Chase sighed heavily as Bud's fingers brought the cube right in record time. She held it up in triumph. Gitana groaned and put her forehead down on the bar. "What are we going to do with a genius child?"

"She's not a genius. She's just light on her feet and a quick learner," Chase said, wishing she could snatch the cube from Bud.

Gitana sat up. "When are you going to stop living in denial?"

"I don't know what you're talking about. We're going to have trouble getting her into the Academy because she's such a whiz at linguistics she created her own language, complete with grammatical rules and semantics."

"She hasn't, has she?" Gitana looked mortified.

Chase smiled. Now that they'd stopped living in denial they could discuss it. "No. At least I don't think so. I just want her to have a normal childhood. It's not her fault that some freaky dude with a skyrocketing IQ was the sperm donor."

"I know." Gitana held out her hand and Chase took it.

"We can do it. We always do," Chase said, more to herself than Gitana.

"Maybe Donna can do some reconnoitering and we can bribe our way into the academy," Gitana suggested as she absently took the cube Bud offered. She messed it up.

"I thought you didn't approve of bribery," Chase said.

"Desperate times call for desperate measures."

Chase smiled.

Chapter Four—Speech

Mend your speech a little, Lest it may mar your fortunes.—
Shakespeare, King Lear

Chase, Gitana and Bud sat in the waiting room of Dr. Evangelina Aragon, the illustrious speech therapist that Dr. Garcia had recommended after he'd confirmed that Bud was still definitely odd. Upon leaving Chase had muttered, "Well, that was a complete waste of a bobblehead." But they'd gotten the referral they'd needed.

Bud was leafing through a magazine called *The Scientific Mind*. Her eyes appeared to be scanning the lines and it suddenly occurred to Chase that she might actually be reading. She felt conflicted—on one hand that was amazing, on the other it was terrifying.

"I'll be right back, I have to go to the bathroom," Gitana said. "How about you?" she asked Bud who shook her head no.

Ever since the pregnancy Gitana's bladder had shrunk

to what she was convinced was the size of a thimble. She kept saying she was going to have it looked at but never got around to it. What she didn't know was that Chase had had Donna make an appointment, knowing that when the receptionist called to remind her of the appointment Gitana would go because she thought it a form of social injustice to waste other people's time. Chase sat smugly recalling this.

When Gitana had gone, Bud said, "I can talk right." She didn't look up from the magazine.

Chase was astonished. "What did you just say?"

Bud looked up nonchalantly, "Gnihton."

"You did too."

"Evorp ti." Bud went back to her magazine.

Chase looked around. The waiting room was empty. Should she tell Gitana? Had she imagined it? Oh, this was horrid. She stuck her forefinger in her mouth, making for the cuticle, but Bud slapped her arm. Chase put her hand in her lap.

"If I keep my trap shut, will you talk right one day?" Chase asked.

"Sey."

"All right then," Chase said. She breathed a sigh of relief. She hadn't imagined it after all.

As Gitana returned, the receptionist called their names. "Perfect timing," Chase said. She felt so good she almost skipped into the office. Gitana looked at her queerly.

Dr. Aragon sat in a wingback chair of soft brown leather. She got up and shook their hands. "Please take a seat. Bud, you sit here next to me," she instructed in a soft melodious voice, the kind of voice Chase thought made you feel comfortable, like instead of dissecting your child's linguistic skills she was going to read you a story with a guaranteed happy ending.

Bud looked at her suspiciously but obeyed. Gitana and Chase sat in the other two identical brown leather wingback chairs. The office was definitely brown, right down to the mocha-colored walls, and once again, as she had the first time she'd been in Dr. Robicheck's office, Chase felt like she was sitting inside a walnut. Dr. Aragon's office was more study than speech therapist's office, which did serve to waylay some of Chase's fears.

"So Bud, why don't we have a little chat?" Dr. Aragon said.

Bud sat stoically quiet. "Oh, I see. But you do talk?" This was more ascertainment than question. "Maybe talking makes you nervous?" This was more taunt than question. Chase felt certain Bud would break. She did have a bit of a temper. But Bud sat quiet.

Gitana intervened. "Come on, sweetie, the doctor can't help you if she doesn't know what's wrong. Just say a few words. Why don't you tell her about Paddington?"

Chase watched as Bud's face got red. This was insulting. Maybe this would be just the thing to break her. Maybe now she'd tell them all to piss off and that she could talk just fine and maybe she'd even use a big word. That would be the best, Chase thought. She'd often dreamed of the moment when Bud would burst forth with a Faulknerian vocabulary. It might have occurred except that Gitana broke the spell.

"I thought this might happen, so I brought this," Gitana said, pulling out a small tape player like the kind hotshot business guys used to dictate memos.

Chase and Bud stared at each other in mutual outrage. "Did you inform her that she was being taped?" Chase said, her civil libertarian ideals raised to their full ire.

"Chase, we're trying to figure out what's wrong," Gitana said.

"I know, but it's illegal to record someone without their knowledge and consent," Chase replied.

Dr. Aragon interjected. "That will be very useful." She put her hand out for the tape recorder but as it was about to change hands, Bud leapt out of the chair and snatched it. She ran to the open window and pitched it outside.

"Bud!" Gitana said, completely mortified.

And then the tirade began, Bud started garbling so fast that even Chase couldn't reconstruct what she'd said, although she did catch the occasional swear word. Bud resembled a tiny and very pissed off Napoleon Bonaparte.

Gitana smiled and then laughed. "I thought that might work. I did not, however, think you'd throw it out the window. What if you hit someone below?"

Bud's eyes got big. She stopped her tirade and went to peer out the window. She visibly sighed and then turned on Chase, "Uoy did siht."

"No, I didn't. She did," Chase said, indignantly pointing at Gitana.

"Well, something had to be done. We can't go on with only you understanding what she says," Gitana said.

"On driht nosrep!" Bud screeched.

"She doesn't like when you use the third person," Chase said.

Dr. Aragon, whom they had completely forgotten about as they discussed family politics said, "Why you ornery little elitist. I know what you're up to." She gazed pointedly at Bud, who shrank back a little. She inched toward Chase. "And you two need to cut the cord," she said, indicating Chase and Bud. "That's part of the reason she talks like this."

"I don't know what you mean," Chase said, scooping Bud up and putting her on her lap. They both looked anxiously at Dr. Aragon.

"You know what I mean. You're the only one who understands her, up until now, and that's how come you two are so close, because you have a secret language, and whether either of you are willing to admit it, you both like it."

"I think you're right," Gitana said, agreeing with the doctor in such a way that Chase knew they were doomed. "But what is Bud up to?"

"It's Pig Latin," Dr. Aragon informed her.

Gitana looked puzzled so the doctor explained, "It's English backwards, which is really an accomplishment for a four-year-old because it means that she has to know what the word is as well as know how to essentially spell it in order to reverse it. I'll give you a demonstration." She wrote the phrase "third person" on a piece of paper in Pig Latin and underneath wrote it the correct way.

"Oh, I get it," Gitana said. She eyed Bud and Chase suspiciously. "Did you teach her how to do that?"

"Of course not!" Chase said petulantly.

"Then how do you know what she says?" Gitana accused.

"I don't know," Chase said, not meeting her gaze. "I just do."

"Are you dyslexic? Or ambidextrous?" Dr. Aragon asked.

"Well…" Chase countered.

"When you chew your cuticles on your right hand and have to bandage your right-hand fingers I see you use your left hand quite adroitly, and then there's that right-hand turn in traffic that you confuse with the other right, meaning left," Gitana said.

"Ah ha!" Dr. Aragon said, like she'd caught Chase with her hand in the till extracting twenty-dollar bills. "It's spatial dyslexia."

"Thanks for outing me," Chase grumbled at Gitana.

"It's nothing to be ashamed of," Dr. Aragon said. "Except you have to go around the block more than the rest of us."

"Nac ew og tey?" Bud said.

"I hope so," Chase said.

"In a minute," Gitana replied, not realizing that she'd understood what Bud had said. "Does that mean Bud is dyslexic?"

"Not necessarily. We won't know, of course, until she starts reading, but most likely she does it to amuse herself," Dr. Aragon said, contemplating Bud, who scowled at her. "She'll talk when she's ready. I'd wager she's ashamed of her limited vocabulary and won't talk until she's amassed one large enough to astound people, her parents included. It's pride more than anything else."

"Ssip ffo," Bud screeched and hopped off Chase's lap like a snake had bitten her behind.

"Bud! You apologize," Chase said.

Bud scowled at the whole room. It appeared she thought them enemies and Chase hoped she wouldn't make a run for the window to escape her captors.

"It's fine. I insulted her and that's good. It means it's true. Give her a little time and she'll do it when she feels it's right," Dr. Aragon said. "Here, this is an armistice gift," and she pulled out a small pocket Webster's dictionary from her desk drawer. She handed it to Bud. "For your vocabulary lessons."

Bud inched toward her and then slowly put out her hand.

"Say thank you," Gitana said.

"Knaht uoy," Bud said grudgingly. She gently put the small book in her jacket pocket and then kept her hand on it as if she were afraid that like a gangly kitten it might jump out.

"Keep me posted and we'll meet again in a month," Dr. Aragon said. She leaned down so she could look straight into Bud's eyes. "Study hard."

Once outside, Bud made for the bushes where she'd thrown the tape recorder.

"It's okay, Bud. We don't need it," Gitana said nervously.

"But it's littering and we don't litter, do we, Bud?" Chase said, completely ignoring Gitana's vigorously shaking head.

Bud emerged triumphantly holding the tape player, which appeared to have suffered no real damage. She smiled at Gitana, who looked mortified. Bud opened the tape player. There were no insides, let alone a tape. Bud and Chase both gaped at her. "You lied to us."

"I'm sorry, but I had to do something. Remember, desperate times call for desperate measures. I saved Paddington; that's got to count for something," Gitana said, backpedaling as fast as she could.

Chase looked at Bud, who stared up at her, apparently looking for a clue as to the next course of action. "Well, she did save the fish. Now, what we can learn from this is that sometimes people behave like politicians who distort the truth for what they feel is the good of the people and sometimes it works and other times you end up in a posh prison. So we're going to let her off with a light sentence like you get to stay up later on a night of your choosing and watch anything on television you want excepting violence, sex, autopsies and animal cruelty."

Bud rolled her eyes. "Bunk."

Gitana glanced over at Chase to see if that was a real word. Chase, not wanting to attract attention, nodded slightly. Chase knew that when Bud was in bed they'd dance around in circles in utter glee. It was starting. At the stoplight before they entered the freeway she looked in the rearview mirror to see Bud, her diminutive hands thumbing through the pocket dictionary the doctor had given her. She breathed a sigh of relief.

Chapter Five—Fame

Contempt of fame begets contempt of virtue.—Ben Jonson

Donna pushed Chase through the door of Borders. Chase was dressed in a white turtleneck under a tweed blazer and khaki Land's End trousers with brown penny loafers. Her nightmare had come true. "I can't do this."

"You have to. It's part of the package," Donna said. She looked the picture perfect version of a personal assistant dressed in a nicely tailored gabardine business suit.

"But no one's here and I'm going to feel stupid sitting at a table for two hours with a stack of books like an unwanted goldfish at the pet store," Chase whined.

"I don't think so." She pointed. There was already a line of people queued up at the table, which was next to a life-size cutout of Chase pretending to be Shelby McCall dressed in a similar outfit and holding her latest book. This being two different people, the Chase Banter of reality and the persona of Shelby, was really starting to get on her nerves. No wonder she was such a mess—a bipolar writer with two personalities. Freud would have loved it.

The cutout had been Donna's idea. "It makes a statement." The choice of outfit was also Donna's idea. "We want you to look kind of English-American, like a combo of Patricia Cornwell and a hip Agatha Christie."

This made no sense as Chase had long blond hair, blue eyes and sculpted features. She looked more like one of the women in a Victoria's Secret ad than a mystery writer. But that too had worked in her favor. People seemed comfortable with this look, according to the comments they left at the Shelby McCall website. They said things like "You look just like what I had pictured."

Donna was pleased. Good god that woman was a marketing genius. Chase dreaded the day she would lose her, as some bigger fish would inevitably snatch her up, but then she remembered something from a John Donne poem about fish and netting all you can to have the pike give you something that sickened your soul. She hoped being a fish in this environment would not poison her soul.

The bookstore manager, whose name was Naomi, trotted up to them and vigorously shook Chase's hand. "Ms. McCall, we're so glad you've chosen our store. I just finished *Expiration Date* and I thought it was brilliant."

Enthusiasm seemed to bubble straight from the woman's close-cropped brown hair. She wore makeup but still looked like a sister. Straight women had short hair too, Chase told herself, but her gaydar was beeping away. At least she wouldn't be asked about her husband and children. That was one arena Chase preferred to ignore, but it lurked. Ariana, her editor, had suggested she keep her sexuality under wraps, and Chase's agent, Eliza, a buxom businesswoman of fifty-five, definitely saw the "sexuality liability" as a problem that had to be contained.

The first time Chase had been flown to New York to meet Eliza P. Newman the woman had seemed calculating. At the airport a limo driver had picked up Chase, who, thanks to her mother, was dressed to the nines in an Armani suit and five-hundred-dollar Italian leather shoes. Eliza's office would have intimidated anyone. Chase gathered her wits and remembered everything Donna had taught her. They'd watched movies and television programs with power figures and glassy offices. They'd quizzed Stella on etiquette and Stella, who now had big clients, took Chase with her a few times to meet these people, referring to Chase as one of her junior assistants. Now the efforts of the dress rehearsal were about to be tested.

The minute she'd entered the office, Eliza had sized her up like she was a horse who might be purchased. Eliza adored horses, according to Ariana, and all metaphors pointed in this direction, including the woman's office—a combo of chrome, glass and saddle-colored leather with horse-head bronzes. Chase half expected her to strap a set of pistols on her and demand a demonstration of Chase's shooting ability. Instead, Eliza turned her around, stared her up and down and said, "You don't look like a lesbian. In fact, your good looks are going to be an asset. Please take a seat."

Chase resented that comment and barely refrained from saying. "And you look like Mr. Toad in *The Wind in the Willows* so you don't have any room to talk." She sat down and waited. One thing she'd discovered about these New York power types was that you didn't have to talk much. They talked for you.

"Do you think I'm a lesbian?" Eliza asked.

Chase hated this line of questioning and her patience was thinning. Watching her tone, she politely said, "Is this like that question where a woman asks her husband if she looks fat in this dress and no matter his response he's screwed?"

Eliza burst out laughing. "You're right. But your assumption is that I am a straight woman."

"Are you saying you're not?" Chase countered.

"What I am saying is that whether I am or not shouldn't be a question that anyone would ask."

"I get it. I will be a very private, almost a hermit-like-kind of author. That shouldn't be difficult. I don't particularly like people," Chase informed her.

"But you will have to make yourself known if your books are

to sell. Reviews, book signings and interviews—how will you handle that?"

"You're going to tell me and with some coaching I will be successful," Chase said tartly. She might as well capitulate to the whims of the publishing world because there wasn't much choice. She'd already made up a vocation for Shelby McCall and tested it on an overly inquisitive rich woman who sat next to her in first class on the plane.

"Okay, here's a question. What has Shelby McCall been doing for the last twenty years of her life? College, of course, will have taken up some of it. What about the rest? We can't tell them you've been writing dyke fiction for the last fourteen years."

"I've been an epistemologist working for the Illumination Institute," Chase informed her.

Eliza narrowed her eyes and pursed her lips. Chase wondered if this occupation would work as well on her as it had on the woman in plane. She'd pretended she knew what that was and then asked what kind of bugs Chase studied. "It's about word origins and coming up with new ones when necessary." The woman nodded and didn't talk to Chase the rest of the ride.

"What's the Illumination Institute?" Eliza inquired, as if this might be the hand that brushed away the house of cards.

"It's a building in the middle of nowhere that has been vacant for years and no one knows who owns it," Chase countered.

"That'll do."

And with that Chase was handed over to the woman who would coach her for the next five days on how to behave in a proper fashion so as not to create any debacles detrimental to her future success as a bestselling author. It had really been most tedious.

Now, she was doing her first-ever book signing. How hideous, she thought as she made her way to the table stacked with books. The first few customers were nice and she remembered to scrawl Shelby McCall on the title pages instead of Chase Banter. Then, as if she were back in Eliza's office, with the swish of a hand the house of cards fell flat: The first error occurred.

"Whom should I address it to?" Chase calmly asked in her most polite voice. She tried not to glance at the line and wonder how much longer this would last.

"Sign it to Carol."

And before Chase had gotten the "C" written, the woman said, "I really think there is a definite lesbian undertone, rather a bit too much, shall we say butchness in each of your protagonists. Where do you suppose that comes from?"

Chase bristled. She contemplated the well-coiffed, well-dressed snot and smiled sardonically. "I think my protagonists tend to be..." She got stuck.

Donna must have sensed something was awry and came over. "Is there a problem?"

"She thinks my protagonists are too butch," Chase said, taking up the pen again. Donna glanced over her shoulder while Chase signed the book, "To Carol, the snotty homophobe. Happy reading, Chase Banter, lesbian extraordinaire."

Donna smiled pleasantly at the woman while she snatched the book from Chase and substituted another. The woman looked at her puzzled. "That one has a tiny tear on the title page. I wouldn't want you to have a defective product. I really think that Chase's characters tend to be strong, very self-sufficient women who have set high goals for themselves. I don't think those are necessarily lesbian tendencies, do you?"

"I suppose not," the woman said, smiling curtly at Chase and taking the book.

Then there was the mishearing and subsequent misspelling of a name. Donna had remedied that by quickly supplying yet another book in its place and then the woman had the audacity to ask for the ruined book as well. Donna handed it over pleasantly enough, Chase thought. Maybe she knows that it only takes royalty money out of our pockets. Chase remembered as a moist mound writer that every book sale was precious. Shelby might be a hotshot with books to waste, however it didn't make the insult go down any less easily in Chase's world. She was beginning not to like Shelby.

With half an hour to go, two of Chase Banter's avid fans made a beeline for the table after seeing her. While Chase

Banter never did book signings, her publisher made sure there was always a comely photo of Chase on the back cover. Had Donna not fended the women off with the offer of a complete set of Chase's lesbian works signed by the author and mailed out immediately God-only-knows what could have happened.

There were a few other missteps, but they were minor in comparison. The coup de grace occurred when one young woman, a writer herself, asked about Chase's characters, how she came up with them, etc., and Chase made the mistake of saying that they talked to her in her head and she wrote it all down. Afterward, she realized that she sounded like a schizophrenic.

The interminable afternoon ended at last. The bookstore manager gushed over her sales performance. "I'm going to tell regional and I'm sure we can get some other sessions."

Chase glanced warily over at Donna, who nodded.

"That would be great," Donna said. They shook hands and left.

Donna drove her home after they stopped at the convenience store—where Chase bought two bottles of Dasani and a five-pack of Mentos, which she stuffed in her blazer jacket. She slumped down in the front seat of Donna's '57 primer gray Volvo. Donna was in the process of securing a lease on a shiny black Volvo coupe that they would write off on the business account. "Why can't I just drive the Hummer? It's a nice-looking car," Chase had said.

"Because the Hummer, despite being a biodiesel, is not politically correct and has the potential to create an unpleasant scene with your green readers, and the Mini Cooper is too recognizable," Donna had replied. Chase lapsed into a disgruntled silence.

"It wasn't that bad. We just need to work on some skills," Donna said, as she entered the freeway. Chase sipped her water and looked dully out the window as the Sandia Mountains turned the watermelon color they were named for. "Like what kind of skills?" She could only imagine—a stint with Toastmasters, a debate class through Continuing Ed at the university or a holistic tongue practitioner who specialized in foot-in-mouth syndrome.

"No, I think you'll really like this," Donna said, as if she'd read Chase's mind.

"What is it?"

"It's a group I checked into because I thought it might be necessary," Donna said as the Volvo wheezed its way up the canyon. The mountain sides were still covered in corn silk-colored grasses—the result of winter dormancy.

Chase glared at her. "So you anticipated that I'd fail."

"Not exactly, but there was a possibility and I wanted a contingency plan. Remember *The Black Swan*." It was a book they'd both read about the impossibility of predictions. "'Invest in preparedness—not in prediction.' I did not predict you'd fail, but I prepared in case you did."

It figured that she would wind up with a philosophical private assistant, Chase thought glumly. "So what hoop of fire do you have planned?"

"According to my research you suffer from SUP."

"What does the weather have to do with anything? I like all the seasons in their manifestations of time and growth." That was almost John Donnean, Chase thought.

"That's SAD. SUP means Socially Unacceptable Proclivities," Donna said as she honked the horn to prevent a tractor trailer from running them off the road. She rolled down the window and yelled, "You stupid cake sniffer!" using a term used in the Lemony Snicket series. They'd all decided this was more appropriate than using the F-word in Bud's presence. Chase wasn't certain how it would go over in school if Bud called someone that, but it wasn't truly offensive. Sniffing cakes wasn't a crime after all.

"Oh, great, more sessions with Dr. Robicheck," Chase muttered, even though she still saw Dr. Robicheck biweekly. Adjusting to her new life as Shelby McCall was proving to be a difficult transition. As Chase Banter, life was neurotic but at least it was real. Shelby's life was nothing but one huge sordid lie.

"No, there's another way—a more helpful way. SUP can

be the result of genetics, biological makeup and environmental experiences."

"So I can blame this on Stella?" She had been getting on better with her mother; still, it was always a good idea to have ammunition in the arsenal, just in case.

"I think in your case it's a product of your bipolar disorder and environmental experiences. Stella is well-adjusted."

"And I'm not?"

Donna raised an eyebrow and they bumped along the horrid dirt road that led up to the fortress that was home. Chase got out and opened the gate, scowling from the book-signing debacle and Donna's idea for remedying it.

Donna took her up to the house. "I'll find out the schedule for the next available meeting."

"As in group? I don't do groups," Chase said.

"You do now." Donna tooted the horns for the dogs and left.

Annie and Jane leapt at her as she entered the sunroom.

"I love you too. You don't care if I'm socially unacceptable."

Chase flopped down on the couch, which was really a futon bed that they'd moved from the den after they'd purchased a new Natuzzi leather couch and love seat courtesy of a hefty royalty check from that fucking bitch Shelby McCall and her snotty readers. Chase contemplated if disliking her wealthy persona was a bad thing. She'd have to run it by Dr. Robicheck. The dogs licked her face and she smiled, wondering what she would do without her family. She gathered up their Jolly balls and played a few rounds of fetch, soiling the cuffs of her blazer and getting dirty paw prints on her pristine white turtleneck with complete abandon. Book signings were stupid.

Annie and Jane, tongues extended, finally gave up and went to lie under the juniper tree that Jane had personally trimmed so that all the lower branches had been removed. The juniper resembled a lone tree in the Kalahari.

Chase went inside to change and lick her wounds. When Gitana and Bud came home from the orchid nursery they found her at the kitchen bar with three packs of Mentos unwrapped and grouped together in sets of three. She'd already consumed two packs. Bud sat down next to her and looked concerned.

"It didn't go well?" Gitana asked, rubbing her shoulders and kissing her cheek.

"Complete debacle." She related the whole horrid experience while continuing to suck on Mentos.

Gitana gave Bud a pointed look that the child seemed to grasp immediately. "I think a shot of tequila is a good idea right now." She pulled the bottle of Patrón from the kitchen cupboard.

Before she could assent or decline, Bud had brushed the remaining Mentos into her small but able hands and made for the bathroom.

"Hey, those are mine," Chase said, as she heard the toilet flush.

Gitana poured her a jigger with a slice of lime. "Drink this."

Chase did as she was told, grimacing but complying. The phone rang and Gitana picked up. "It's Eliza."

Chase groaned.

"Heard it didn't go well." Eliza's voice crackled over the line.

"Are we on speakerphone? You know I hate that. Who all is there with you?" Chase asked, envisioning a conference room full of disgusted people with I-told-you-so-looks on their faces.

"Oh, lots of people."

"Great, an audience to my failure." Chase heard the speakerphone click off.

"Relax, it's only Pepe and Peaches." Those were Eliza's chihuahuas, or "rats on ropes" as Chase referred to them. Donna told her that was not politically correct. "A dog should not be shorter than a cat and besides, I've met them. They were the meanest cusses on the planet," Chase had responded. "Did they take the Mentos away from you?"

"Bud flushed them down the toilet, but I did manage to get two packs down," Chase replied.

"Did Gitana get you a shot of tequila?"

"Yes." Obviously, these had been Eliza's express orders to them. Chase could almost see the complicit smile on Eliza's face.

"I've got good troops. Tell Gitana to send another shipment

of orchids—the most expensive ones available—and what does Bud want?"

"She's currently collecting dictionaries," Chase told her, watching as Bud nodded furiously.

"Consider it done. Now, I think Donna's idea about joining the SUP group is a great idea. I'll expect a progress report in, say, two weeks' time."

"Don't cut me any slack or anything," Chase grumbled.

"I won't. Ta-ta."

Chase banged her head on the counter and Gitana poured her another shot. Bud went to her cubbyhole and pulled out her collection of dictionaries. She currently had the pocket dictionary the doctor had given her, the Merriam-Webster's *Collegiate*, an Oxford one they'd found at Thrift Town that had the inscription of Christ Church on the title page and an enormous encyclopedic one with pictures—also a Thrift Town find—that was so large she had trouble lifting it.

"Eliza will probably send her the *OED*," Chase said. She swigged the jigger of tequila, another gift from Eliza. "I can't believe all this graft and bribery."

"You bribe the pediatrician," Gitana said. She opened the freezer and studied the contents. "Let's have those lasagna rolls with that soy meat stuff," she said, as Bud looked up.

"That's with cheap bobbleheads."

"Bud and I have a larger responsibility," Gitana said, digging around in the freezer for the faux meat.

"And what's that?"

"Keeping a bestselling author on track," Gitana said.

Chapter Six—Confessions
May confession be a medicine to the erring.—Cicero

"I can't do this," Chase said, as she stood in the auditorium of the Musical Arts Building at the university, a circle of chairs with a small round table full of coffee mugs and carafes at its center. She hadn't wanted to be early, but neither did she want to be late. This felt like she imagined going to an AA meeting would, having never been there herself but having seen enough "group" things in movies to get the gist.

"And why not?" a voice said, coming out of the blackness of the bleachers. It was an older woman with short, black, spiky hair and dressed in a pink sari. Chase stared at the red dot in the middle of her forehead. "What, you've never seen an Indian woman before?"

Chase fumbled. "Of course I have."

"Yeah, right, in a movie, I suppose." The woman handed

Chase a tray of sugar cookies and pointed to the table. "In my country they call these digestives. What an appetizing name. 'Would you like a digestive?' It makes it sound like you need a laxative. No wonder you people call them cookies."

Chase just stood and stared. She smacked Chase on the back. "It is more than evident why you're here—your gift for speech seems impaired. Here, let me get a pair of vise grips and we'll see about your tongue. Or did you leave it at home? And back to the original question, if you can't do this—with your limited skills I suggest you learn."

"Are you the instructor or coach or whatever?" Chase blurted, her tonguetied-ness worsening.

"Oh my, you will truly be an inspiration if we cure you. I am Lily Hirack and I'm going to offer you the opportunity to become just as fake at social conventions as the rest of the fuckers on the planet. This is the Hindu way of earning points so I won't have to come around again and again."

Lily Hirack had the singsong lilt of the Indian and said the word "fuck" in such a way as to make it perfectly acceptable. That only compounded Chase's inability to speak.

"Now, while we wait for the others we should get a head start. What do you do for a living and why is it imperative that you learn to lie?"

"I thought I was going to learn to be more socially acceptable or at least learn to filter my inappropriate thoughts and rephrase them so as to appear normal."

"Wouldn't that be nice," Lily said, pointing at a chair and indicating that they should sit. She poured them both coffee and waved her hand over the milk and sugar.

Chase took her coffee and hoped the others would show up soon. She looked around, avoiding Lily's intense gaze.

"I would guess you're an intellectual of some sort—someone outside the mundane which is why banality eludes you."

"Shouldn't we wait until the others get here?" Chase suggested, not wanting to repeat her confession.

"You won't get to talk when they get here."

"But I thought these were people who don't talk well and need coaching," Chase said, befuddled. If she had thought therapy and the writers' group were difficult this was like running a psychological marathon.

"Ah, but there you are wrong. People can talk endlessly about their problems: They just find it difficult to cure them. So, chop-chop—what do you do?"

"I'm a writer and I recently failed at a book signing so they sent me here."

"Now, see that was a good answer. An improvement already," Lily said, tapping the table with her forefinger like she was gently ringing the bell at the front desk of a hotel to alert the clerk of her arrival.

"How do you figure?" Chase added a copious amount of milk to the coffee and stared dubiously at the digestives.

"They look worse than they are," Lily said. "Take one."

Chase obliged.

"To answer your question—it was a good answer because it was informative and concise. You are a published writer, so we don't have to ask that question. You immediately identified the cataclysmic event and you've indicated you have handlers."

Chase didn't exactly like the idea of having handlers, but she supposed Lily was right. She and her success were a commodity that several people made a living off. "So what do I do now?"

"You learn the art or rather two arts—the first being polite convention and the second being the creation of a screening device." Lily picked up a biscuit and snapped off a piece. "Look at this biscuit—see two parts. This part—the larger one—is the real you, the things you think, the things you feel, how you perceive the world. This smaller piece is the social acting part of you—think of it in Shakespearian terms, the actor playing one role to his fellow actors and the other who speaks with the audience telling them what's really going on or what he's thinking."

"The soliloquy." Chase was glad they were using her patois to discuss the pitfalls of the outer world. She was reading Richard Russo's *Empire Falls* and the protagonist Miles was a nice guy who thought bad things sometimes—the things he really felt but didn't say when people pissed him off. This made sense to Chase—only she usually said those things.

Lily pitched the biscuit bits into a nearby garbage can. Chase followed her example. Thinking of the things as cookies hadn't helped; they were disgusting.

"You lied about the digestives."

"I did. But under social convention rules of protocol you're not supposed to say anything."

"But I don't want to eat it, so what am I supposed to do?"

"I would discreetly slip it into a napkin and then throw it away." She demonstrated, using a second cookie.

"It's not like you can do that with a whole dinner," Chase retorted.

"No, with that you have two choices—you can buck up and swallow quickly or feign food poisoning." Lily studied her.

"You can't feign food poisoning. That would be rude—unless you're at a restaurant, in which case it's entirely plausible."

"You're getting it."

Just then a young woman entered, pulling another who would have dug her heels in if the floor hadn't been so slippery. "I'm telling you it's not that bad. Lily is so nice, tell her, Lily."

"That it's not so bad or that I'm nice?" Lily said, smiling coyly at Chase as if to say watch this.

"Both," the woman said. She wore a Grateful Dead T-shirt with tight jeans. Her long dark hair was tied back in a ponytail.

"I'm telling you, Isabel, I don't need this. I'm fine," the other woman said. She couldn't have been more different from her friend. She had a blond pixie cut and wore a dark blue tailored business suit.

"You failed an interview for a job that you could have gotten. You were more qualified than that peckerhead—and don't tell me it was sexist because it wasn't. Most of upper management is female. You blew the interview because you can't talk to save your soul."

Well, Chase thought, her friend doesn't seem to suffer from SUP. She could talk the pants off a priest. Oh, shit. See, that's the kind of remark that definitely needs to stay inside, Chase told herself.

"You should talk. You can't even order a Diet Coke without choking, never mind lunch," the blond woman retorted. "Or how about the debit machine at the grocery store or anywhere else for that matter."

"I have a waitress phobia and I'm technically challenged."

Chase could identify with the debit card phobia as she had the same problem, which was why she used cash. Gitana didn't like her carrying wads of cash around, but Chase told her that muggers assumed that no one had cash anymore as it had become an archaic monetary unit. In fact, it almost freaked out cashiers when she used it, like they had forgotten what to do with it.

"You two stop arguing and sit down," Lily instructed.

Chase was disappointed. So much information was pouring out in the process of the argument.

"Oh, hi," the Grateful Dead woman said, as if she had just noticed Chase. "I'm Isabel Montgomery and this is my friend Darlene Lewis."

"I'm Chase."

"Darlene, I concur with Isabel. Fucking up a job interview is cause for concern," Lily said, waving her hand toward the mugs in lieu of a verbal offer of refreshment.

Isabel poured them both coffee and sat back as if all her work was done for the day. "Where are the others?"

As if summoned, Sandra Martin and another woman who introduced herself as Marsha Martin arrived. Chase wondered if they were sisters. They were tall, thin, blond and pretty in that suburban kind of way.

"We're not sisters," Marsha responded to the unasked question. "I was married to her brother."

"I warned her about what a prick he was, but she wouldn't listen. Love and loins will do it every time," Sandra said, shaking her head.

"How was I supposed to know marriage was only about sex and sandwiches?" Marsha said defensively. "I won't make that mistake again. I'll be a lesbian first."

"The sex is supposed to be better," Sandra said.

"Please, ladies, sit down. We have a new member, Chase Banter. I'd like to start the session," Lily said, once again using gestures instead of language to indicate her wishes. Chase thought she might try that. There was far too much noise in the world. Perhaps they should adopt Neanderthal hand signals and lay off the ubiquitous banality of words.

The Martin women did as bade. Sandra poured coffee and Marsha declined. "Jesus fucking Christ, not that again."

Marsha glowered. "The ability to abstain shows control."

Lily made a clucking noise. "Not only do you two say inappropriate things, you conduct yourselves in a rude manner in group situations."

Chase winced. She did the same thing. These people were her kindred and not the people of Prince Edward Island that Anne of Green Gables chose as kindred spirits. Perhaps Donna had been correct—she needed this group, if anything, to learn what not to do. Her perspective was getting clearer by the minute.

"What?" Sandra said, not altering her already annoyed tone.

"Infraction number two." Lily took a pad from the table. She dug about for a pen. Chase picked it up off the floor where it had fallen and handed it to her. "Tone of voice."

Sandra took a deep breath and sweetly said, "I am at a loss as to what you are referring to."

"That's better." Lily pointed at Chase and nodded. Chase took this to mean that tone of voice was her first lesson. It must have been because Lily went back to ripping the Martins a new asshole. Chase had often wondered what that cliché actually meant. Shouldn't it be something along the lines of a *bigger* butthole, not another one? Because logistically where would you put the other asshole? It wasn't like there was a lot of room down there and if you were going to put it somewhere else in the body, where would that be—the middle of your hippocampus?

"You are having some sort of disagreement, ignoring the decorum of group dynamics and taking the Lord's name in vain. Religious people find this unacceptable. What if Chase here were an ardent Christian and took great offense at what you had said. You're not, are you?" Lily asked, suddenly aware that she might be adding her own infraction to the list.

"Not exactly," Chase hedged.

"You don't have to be shy," Isabel said. "I'm an agnostic."

"It's a little more complicated than that," Chase said. She

wasn't exactly a practicing Catholic, although she did believe in superstitions such as sprinkling Bud with holy water every morning and getting dirt from Chimayo to cure ails, but other than that she was suspicious of the church. The security of God, the sense of having his protection like an insurance policy against the potential disasters that the universe had a tendency to throw at a person, and the healing powers of faith made her feel safer, but she despised the papal machinations.

"You do not have to share your politics or your religion with us. In fact, those are topics that should be avoided in group situations because you are bound to meet some finger-pointing fanatic who is just itching for a confrontation," Lily said. "Today we will start with Chase and then move on to Isabel. That was the order of arrival so there is no need for concern over favoritism." She looked at Chase, who related the story of her book-signing debacle and then, seeing as she was in confession mode, also admitted her debit-card phobia and her hand-sanitizer obsession.

Lily smiled at her. "That was very good. Let's see what the group has to say."

"I think you should have told the misspelled-name bitch to fuck off," Isabel said.

Darlene smacked her shoulder. "That's not a good start."

"She took advantage of the situation," Isabel retorted. "It was deliberate."

"And how do you know that?" Sandra piped in. She was evidently still miffed with the other Martin and was now taking it out on Isabel. Chase thought this unkind.

"I'm a librarian. I know things and I understand treachery. Had she not asked for the misspelled-name book it could have been an honest error. But since she did, Chase probably didn't hear it wrong, rather the woman intended the mistake to happen. As for the homophobe lady, well, enough said on that."

"I think you're right," Marsha said.

"She'll probably sell the book on eBay as new and autographed by the author," Sandra said, nodding at her sister-in-law. The pack has regrouped itself, Chase thought, recalling Annie and Jane's behavior. The dogs sometimes fought with each other, but then some outside threat would arrive and they would become a pack again.

Lily studied them. "Let us look back on this discussion and check for infractions."

Isabel spoke first. "I shouldn't have advised Chase to tell the lady to fuck off, but I'm fairly certain that's how Chase felt."

Lily studied Chase. "Did you?"

"Not only did I want to tell her to fuck off, I wanted to tell everyone there that I was a writer, a solitary creature who didn't appreciate being a chimp in a monkey suit set up for their inspection."

"I don't get it," Darlene said, her brow furrowed.

"How many times have I told you about metaphor? A chimp in a monkey suit means that she's one creature made to look and act like another," Isabel said.

Darlene pursed her lips and Chase wondered if she got it even now. She liked Isabel already and hoped she could find out what library she worked at so she could stop by and visit further with her.

"Ah, but that is what you all must be if you are to become socially acceptable," Lily said, pouring herself more coffee.

"But what if we don't want to be a chimp in a monkey suit?" Darlene said. Chase could tell she was reliving her failed job interview.

"Then you can continue to make a social ass of yourself. I suggest you make a trip to the zoo and take a look at a chimpanzee's ass before you decide on your course of action—the suit is an improvement," Lily said, adding sugar to her coffee.

Chase wondered what a hopped-up-on-caffeine-and-sugar Indian woman would be like.

"Let's go to the zoo and take a good look at that ass," Isabel suggested.

Chase was certain that Lily would think the idea preposterous but thought it funny all the same. It would make the point, but she highly doubted that group sessions went on field trips. To her surprise Lily agreed.

"We'll take my van in case someone loses their nerve," Lily said, looking pointedly at Marsha.

As if bidden to substantiate her cowardice, Marsha said, "But what about Isabel's turn?"

"I forgo for the good of the community," Isabel quickly said.

As they all stood in front of the chimpanzees' cage, Chase found herself quite naturally repelled and she was glad that she had been born a homo sapien. She did have to shave her legs and she was keeping an eye on her menopausal mustache, however she was certain that her behind, even when not clothed, did not look like that.

"I hope I don't suffer some kind of reincarnation snafu or retribution and come back with that ass and fur to boot," Isabel said.

Chase smirked. She looked over at Marsha, who stared in horror. "I don't want to be like that."

"Then what are you going to do about it?" Lily said.

"Lie like hell," Marsha replied.

Darlene nodded. "When my boss, who conducted the interview, asked me about my disciplinary philosophy, I should have reiterated her policy instead of telling her that I thought redirection instead of punishment was a better policy."

"Exactly," Lily said.

"You could still implement your policies after the fact," Sandra said.

"Look at politicians. They do it all the time and have done so throughout history. Hell, the politics of Rome in the BC's does not differ that much from the present," Isabel said.

Chase studied her closely. She'd have to make a point to curry favor with Isabel. She wasn't necessarily good at making friends, but Isabel's gregarious nature would make up for her reticence. Fellow booklovers were a rare commodity.

"So you're basically teaching us to lie," Marsha said.

"Not really. I'm teaching you screening—Machiavellian practices sprinkled with anarchy," Lily replied.

Chase glanced over at Isabel, wondering. Chase had yet to

meet anyone who had actually read Machiavelli's masterpiece, *The Prince.*

"Machiavelli has been grossly misinterpreted," Isabel snapped.

Chase smiled. She thought the same. He'd been a statesman and he'd had all his property confiscated by that same state, yet he went on to write a dissertation on how a state and a sound-minded sovereign might rule his conquered territories. Chase could never understand how this had resulted in Machiavelli being turned into the embodiment of evil—whether it was the conquering part or the intrigue necessary to politicking. Alexander the Great had used similar methods and had been a brutal leader and soldier. All Machiavelli had done was to write a treatise while he suffered reduced circumstances.

"You are quite right there, Isabel. He was a genius at performing the necessary. You have to be smart about how you say things—rephrasing with an eye to compassion for your listener. If you shock or dismay your audience you get nothing. If you're smooth and subtle you may just get what you want," Lily said, eyeing the ice cream stand.

Still surprised that in the course of one afternoon she'd met two people who'd obviously read the book, Chase piped in, "So we're not lying, we're maneuvering the world to our making in so far as that is possible."

"Precisely. Now let's go have some ice cream. I think we've seen enough ass for one day," Lily said.

When Chase returned home, Gitana was sitting in the garden reading to Bud, who appeared to be politely listening to *Green Eggs and Ham.* Seeing Chase, she ran toward her for an embrace, as well as, perhaps, to escape early childhood literature.

"How'd your group-thing go?" Gitana asked, closing the book after noting the page number.

"We went to the zoo and looked at the hindquarters of the chimpanzees," Chase said, studying her sleeve, which had chocolate on it.

"Ass," Bud said.

"And had ice cream," Gitana said, staring at Chase with the she-said-another-real-word look.

Chase pursed her lips as she studied the stain. Definitely a Spray-n-Wash job. Since Bud's arrival her laundry skills had improved to the point that she was becoming a veritable chemist. The household tasks she'd once done to take her away from the creative life when she was stumped had been removed once Donna started doing the shopping and organizing and Merry Maids took over the cleaning. The laundry had become her only outlet, and as with most of her pursuits she approached it with the thoroughness of a Dickensian washerwoman.

"Ooz?" Bud asked, looking up at Chase and taking her hand. Chase sensed that Bud wanted to get away from story time.

"It was a field trip because we were learning how to function in a more socially acceptable way and to understand…" Chase got stuck. To understand that being part of a group made one have to wear a monkey suit?

"It will probably take a few more sessions to really understand how things work," Gitana said, getting up and taking her other hand. "Let's go make some dinner. We're proud of you, though."

Chase gazed lovingly at Gitana and then down at Bud, who was smirking. How a four-year-old could smirk like some smart-aleck adult mystified Chase, but Bud had it down to a fine art.

Chapter Seven—Novelty

Human nature is greedy of novelty.—Pliny the Elder

Bud was once again smirking as they stood in the yoga studio awaiting their first lesson. Lily had proposed that everyone in the group take a class in something completely out of their comfort zone. Ideas had been thrown around. You could do it with someone and you had to do it for at least six weeks. "No bailing out," Lily had said firmly, her lilting voice oddly at variance with American slang.

The Martins had chosen a watercolor painting class because according to them they were as unartistic as a pig with a paintbrush. Isabel had chosen river rafting because she was not athletic. Darlene chose belly dancing because she was inhibited. That left Chase, who could think of nothing or rather nothing the class would agree to with the exception of mother-child yoga. They'd used a continuing ed catalog from the university because the classes lasted six weeks and supplied an inexpensive way to try something new.

Bud looked odd in her yoga pants and pale blue top. She resembled a midget contortionist in a freak show. Chase didn't look much better. She felt acutely like an athletically dressed soccer mom in black stretchy pants and a long white T-shirt that Gitana found frumpy, telling her she had a nice rear end and shouldn't be averse to showing it. They rolled out their mats like the others. Bud sat cross-legged on hers and took up the lotus position. It occurred to Chase that she had been practicing. She mentally ran through the voluminous books in their library and suddenly remembered the yoga book that Gitana had purchased just after her pregnancy to limber up and reverse some of the damage that Bud's arrival had occasioned.

The group of mother-child yoga students was an odd mixture of hippie and suburban. Some children wore tie-dyed shirts and play shorts while the suburban mothers sitting on the opposite side of the room with their rather whiney children had on Title-Nine wear. Chase and Bud had gone to Target and purchased the stretchy pants on the sale rack in the sports department. Chase saw no sense in spending money on a six-week experiment. She didn't foresee yoga as a lifelong pursuit. She'd seen the strange and painful-looking poses of the dedicated. She was satisfied with simply touching her toes.

Their yoga teacher turned out to be a handsome young man with dark hair pulled back in a ponytail and sporting a goatee. He was tanned with a long and limber-looking body. Chase swore she heard a collective intake of breath on the part of the straight women. Chase caught a glimpse of a possible other lesbian mother and her heart quickened—a kindred spirit. This yoga thing could be a boon after all. The woman, who had shoulder-length wavy brown hair and a round happy-looking face complete with dimples, smiled complicitly in her direction before patting the hand of her son, who was anxiously awaiting some kind of activity. Bud glanced at the little towheaded boy with interest. Chase's parental hackles went up and then she remembered: Bud wouldn't be dating for many years—in her thirties if Chase could manage it.

The teacher's name was Paul and he'd been practicing and teaching yoga for fifteen years. "I want to impress upon you that this is not a competition but rather a coming into a growing awareness of your body and its abilities. If at any point you feel you are not comfortable with a particular pose you should stop and rest."

Uncomfortable, as in a hamstring removing itself from its bony attachment, Chase thought. She looked over at Bud. She was politely listening, but Chase could tell she was ready to get started. Bud was mostly about learning through the experience of trial and error. Chase looked around and noticed the other children squirming. Then, as Paul seemed to sense their irritation at having to sit still, he demonstrated the first pose, which was lying on one's back, hands at the sides, palms up. This seemed easy enough, Chase thought, and then the contortions began. All the poses had strange names, which Bud seemed to already know, because as Paul explained the name, its pronunciation and then began his demonstration, Bud was already in position.

A brunette woman with an ungainly two-year-old leaned over and whispered, "Has she taken a class before?" She seemed to be implying that while Chase was as uncoordinated as her two-year-old, Bud had the grace of a yoga master in training.

"Not that I was aware of," Chase said, trying to arch her back so she resembled a pissed-off feline about to attack—the cat pose.

Paul walked around the room adjusting people's poses until he came to Bud, whom he appreciatively studied, ignoring Chase altogether despite her misshapen cat pose. "My little one, you have found the golden path already."

Bud smiled demurely.

After he left, Chase hissed, "You're such a show-off."

Bud cocked her head and raised her eyebrows as if to say, "You could have studied as well, but you didn't. Hence you look like an idiot whereas I have the grace of the ages."

"Some people find overachievers insufferable megalomaniacs."

Before Bud could snidely respond there was a scream from the back of the room and a young woman dressed in expensive yoga clothing had leapt up clutching her child and grimacing.

Chase wondered if her hamstring had pulled its anchor.

"Look!" She pointed at the floor near the sink with the dripping tap. Chase knew at once what the problem was. The yoga class was located in the basement of the Student Union building. The Northeast Heights had a horrible roach problem—which Chase had always found amusing as wealthy homeowners waged battle on the orange-backed menace that invaded their yards and houses. They were attracted by water and the dripping faucet was perfect. "Kill it," the woman screeched, staring pointedly at Paul.

"I can't. In addition to teaching yoga I'm also a Buddhist monk. We are forbidden to kill any living thing lest it be an ancestor awaiting reincarnation," Paul calmly said. "We must learn to live with them as they with us."

All the other women had now snatched up their children. Chase was about to do the same when she discovered that Bud had disappeared. Chase looked around frantically. The woman with the dimples and the young son touched Chase's elbow. "She's over there." She let go of her son's hand and he raced toward Bud.

Chase stared uncomprehendingly as Bud handed the young boy a stack of Dixie cups and pointed at the offending insects. She demonstrated, coming up behind the cockroach and quickly plopping a cup over it. The boy followed her example and in no time the colony of cockroaches was ensconced in a flower-covered world of paper. Bud looked up triumphantly. "Yurt!" She held out her hand for the boy to shake and then went back to her yoga mat.

Chase clapped her hands and then plucked Bud up in her arms. "You said a word, a real honest-to-God word. Your first-spoken-in-the-company-of-others word in real English."

The suburban woman who'd commented on Bud's uncanny ability concerning yoga was perplexed. "Her first word was yurt?"

The woman with the dimples, who had introduced herself as Lou when they exchanged names, laughed. "Considering the occasion I'd be proud. She just captured a rogue invader using a policy of containment rather than destruction."

Paul knelt down and smiled at Bud and her new friend

Peter. "Good work." Chase liked it when grown-ups got on a kid's level. It was the height of politesse, like getting up when an elderly person needed your seat on a train or a bus. Her own polite behavior had only been thwarted once. When waiting in the doctor's office for Gitana, she had attempted to help an elderly man get up out of his chair. It seemed the thing to do at the time, but she had underestimated his girth and while trying to help him up she'd ended up in his lap. He didn't seem to mind having a pretty blond woman there but his wife did.

The women resumed their yoga positions with wary eyes turned toward the paper cups and their unwilling occupants. Only during the short session of meditation was their vigilance forced to a stop. Chase thought meditation was kind of silly for a room full of kids until she discovered that meditation worked like a drug on tired children. Bud curled up next to her while Paul made soothing conversation to get them in the zone and then silence ensued. Chase tried to quiet her mind, only to discover that it refused to be still. Her thoughts had become a cat's cradle of conflicting ideas—like two actors on a stage doing a monologue at the same time.

"We're supposed to be concentrating on being completely empty," she told her mind.

"Like that's ever going to happen. Let's use this time to work out that scene at the warehouse you've got coming up," her mind replied.

"That's not what meditation is supposed to be like. It's a time of no thinking, a blue space where I can find peace and harmony—a oneness with the universe."

"That's bullshit. If you don't want to think about the book, then let's think about sex."

Sex *was* a topic that had been popping up a lot more lately. Since Bud's arrival her and Gitana's sex life wasn't what it used to be. Chase, having never been the instigator, had depended on Gitana to keep the hearth fires warm. Now, it seemed, they were so busy and seldom alone except at the end of a hectic day that making love or rather making time for love had gotten bottom-shelved. Listening to Delia's and Bo's erotic short stories had made her think about sex. And now in the middle of a roomful of mothers and children she was thinking about it again instead of clearing her mind. It was horrid and she couldn't have been more relieved when the whole thing came to an end.

After class, Lou and Peter came over. Bud and Peter then went to help Paul slip pieces of the flyer for the yoga class under the paper cups so they could relocate the cockroaches. Paul had them put the nasty creatures into a plastic bag, telling them he would take them someplace nice where they could make a new home.

"Do you really think he means that? We had a dog once that had taken to killing cats and my father told us he took him to a nice farm where he would be happy. Come to find out much later, he'd taken him to the pound," Lou said.

Chase thought about this for a moment. She put Japanese beetles into gallon-sized clear plastic bags and baked them in the sun to kill them after she'd meticulously picked them from her spinach and lettuce before they had the chance to destroy her entire crop. She did this without Bud's knowledge, knowing it would traumatize her. She suffered some pangs of guilt, but justified it by telling herself that for the sake of the helpless and indefensible lettuce and spinach plants, she was forced to remove an evil entity from the universe. Besides she was almost certain that the destructive insects of the world were the product of God's nightmares and thus could justly be eradicated. "If it were me, I would let them burn in the hot parking lot after class, but knowing that guy," she pointed at Paul, "he will find a good home for them."

"Like the Republican headquarters," Lou said.

Chase laughed. Maybe Lily was right—it wasn't that difficult to make friends. It helped that Chase despised the Republican Party, but what if she hadn't? She wouldn't have to say anything to the contrary. She could do as Lily said—smile and nod.

"Have you ever noticed that parents have the uncanny ability once you've reached a certain age to reveal truths that destroy the myths they created for you as children?"

"Like the dog story?" Chase queried.

"Yes. I mean why tell you these things so much after the fact that it makes absolutely no difference. I was happy with the myth," Lou said, watching as her son poured the last cup of cockroach into the bag.

Chase, suddenly remembering that Lou might be gay, tried to think of a way that Lily would approve of to find out. Finally she said, "Lou, I don't know how to ask this but…"

"Yes, Chase, I am gay," Lou said as if sensing Chase's trepidation.

"This is so amazing—you're the first other gay parent I've met. How are you and your partner handling it? I have a thousand questions."

The look on Lou's face made it more than evident that Chase had once again screwed up. Lily had told the group before she sent them out like untrained dogs loosed on an unsuspecting public that they would initially fail and here it was. She let out a sigh. "I'm sorry. Did I say something to offend you?" God, she hoped Lou's partner wasn't dead—a horrible car accident or cancer or any number of terrible deaths—leaving this poor woman with a child and without help and support. Chase's face must have been the picture of regret for Lou touched her arm and smiled.

"No, I'm not offended. I'm just another single parent who had a partner that decided being married and having a child wasn't what she wanted after all. The hard part is that she is Peter's biological mother and he can't understand why she left us. Luckily, he sees me as just as much a victim and his only ally."

Chase was crestfallen and Lou saw it. "Don't worry. We're getting along fine."

"If you ever need help or a babysitter or car repairs or anything," Chase stumbled.

"You're a mechanic?"

"Well, no. I'm a writer, but when a person needs car repairs you also need other forms of transportation and with just the one of you…" Chase trailed off. She was making a mess of this and she was going to have to report this to her SUP group.

"You're Delia's friend," Lou said, obviously delighted. She smacked her forehead. "Hello? Chase Banter! I've heard all about you."

Chase was taken aback. Oh, God, what had the queen of

smut said about her? "What did she have to say?" she asked, with evident trepidation.

"Nothing bad. She admires you. She said you are talented and have a gorgeous wife and that she is in a monogamous relationship with Gitana's sister, which I found rather miraculous considering..."

"Oh." Chase was relieved. Those weren't bad things but rather facts. That Delia had stuck to the facts was a wonder in itself. "So what do you do?"

"I own the Erotique."

"Oh." Chase said. She was using that word a lot. She could hear Lily telling her that she was doing a poor job at making conversation.

"I can see you've never been there. Delia does a lot of promo work in the online message board at her website. Reading erotica lends itself to buying some of the delights that we sell. You should really stop by. It's a tasteful place," she added, perhaps sensing Chase's discomfort.

"I see." Chase chastised herself. That response was not much better than the "oh." Lily would be truly disappointed with her lack of garrulity. She could see it now, Lily in her lilting English saying, "So you, the woman of words, have turned monosyllabic." Chase contemplated not telling her but then decided being dishonest would not secure her success. "I will do that. I might learn something." She was even more astonished by this remark.

"That would be wonderful. It's especially good for spicing up long-term relationships—not that it applies to yours. It's just that sometimes as we are inculcated more and more into mainstream society we as lesbians seem to lose some of our sense of self. Our store is designed to rekindle that sense through a combination of sexuality and sensuality."

This suddenly made sense to Chase. In her new career as mystery writer she had, in essence, ceased to be a lesbian writer. She had turned tail and joined the mainstream, forgetting her past and her allegiances. "I know what you mean. Being accommodated has broken our ranks and with the lure of acceptance we have let our sense of community wane."

"Very eloquently put. Come by and we'll have coffee," Lou said, as the children, faces flushed, approached them.

Chase smiled as Bud put her hand out to shake that of Peter, who with equal solemnity, grasped her hand and shook it.

"You'll be coming back?" Chase asked anxiously.

"Of course. I would not desert you in this bastion of soccer moms." Lou smiled.

In the car Chase grilled Bud about Peter. "So you two seemed to be getting along splendidly," she baited.

Bud didn't look up from her *Merriam-Webster's Pocket Dictionary.*

"What did you two talk about?" From what Chase could see Peter had done most of the talking.

"Ffuts."

"Like what kind of stuff?" Chase realized she sounded like a neurotic overprotective parent of a well-endowed teenager. And this was the look Bud gave her—a mixture of annoyance and sardonic innocence. "I know you're only four, but it's never too early to be cautious around the opposite sex."

Bud rolled her eyes.

"All right, I'll leave it alone, but if he tries anything…"

Bud sighed in exasperation and went back to studying her dictionary.

Later that evening when Gitana arrived home she found Chase sitting cross-legged surrounded by a pile of books. Bud was painting the orbs of her model of the solar system.

"What are you two doing?" she asked as she kissed the top of Bud's head. Bud looked up sweetly. Gitana studied the model. "I'm glad to see you're including Pluto. I think it was extremely unkind to demote a planet to a cluster of debris like that."

"Ditto," Bud said.

Gitana glanced over at Chase in a meaningful way. They'd decided that it was best not to acknowledge when Bud used the linguistic mode of communication of the country they inhabited. They had used this same method with the dogs. Jane, as a puppy, had refused to eat unless she was hand fed. Worried about her nutritional needs they had succumbed. Then finding themselves short of a dog-sitter they had to resort to putting the dogs in the kennel while they went on vacation. Jane had returned from the experience with kennel manners—meaning she grabbed at treats and was suddenly able to feed herself. They'd broken the grabbing, but they counted each day that she fed herself. They didn't praise her. They pretended not to notice and the psychology worked. Jane was now a self-respecting dog and not a coddled puppy.

Gitana glanced at the book titles. She picked up *The Memory Board*. Chase was marking passages with sticky notes on *The Well of Loneliness*. Chase put the book down. "I feel like I've lost my sense of lesbian identity. I tried to count how many lesbian thoughts I've had today and I came up with two. Only two. That's downright disgraceful."

"What were they?"

Chase glanced away. "One was academic."

Gitana smiled slyly. "And the other?"

Chase glanced over at Bud, who appeared to be absorbed with getting the rings straight on Saturn. "I was folding underwear and, well, you know it made me think of things."

"What kind of things?" Gitana inquired, running her forefinger along Chase's collarbone.

Chase blushed profusely. "We'll discuss that later."

"I certainly hope so. What happened to inspire this sudden reclaiming of your identity? Did the Pink Mafia pay you another visit?"

"No, but had they been more astute they could have."

Chase thought back to when the Pink Mafia had accosted her. It had happened shortly after the publication of her second mystery. She'd pushed the memory aside for a year or so now, but as anyone who has received a visit will attest, the experience is unforgettable. It's not that they threaten to sew your vulva shut, only that they remind you of your duty to behave in a fashion acceptable to the high standards of lesbianism.

Chase had been in Office Max replenishing her notebook and pencil lead supplies when two women dressed like FBI agents, including the dark sunglasses, had approached her. They were a tough-looking duo.

"Ms. Banter, a word please." One of the women guided her back to the binder section, which was devoid of other customers. The other one pulled out the yellow gate that the personnel used to block off the aisle when a forklift was in use.

Chase frantically reviewed her list of indiscretions. She had promptly paid the parking ticket she'd gotten in Santa Fe. She'd immediately purchased Bluetooths when the hands-free ordinances had been instituted in Albuquerque. Both dogs were current on their rabies shots and she had refrained from looking up how to make bombs on the Internet despite the need to do so because one of her villains had used a bomb.

Unable to contain her panic, she blurted, "What have I done?"

One of the large women, the one with the black crew cut, took her glasses off to reveal penetrating blue eyes. "It's what you haven't done."

This sent Chase into a review of her current procrastinations. "Well, I have been meaning to replace that gutter and fix the hole in the stucco or there's my lapsed magazine subscriptions and I really did misplace the electrical bill," she blathered.

The other woman sniggered but did not remove her glasses. This revealed her dimples. Her blond hair was cut short as well. She was of a slighter build but taller than the other woman. "We don't care about that."

"I can't think of anything illegal that I've done."

"You've violated the code." The woman with the black crew cut glowered.

"Which is?"

The blond woman handed her a laminated card. Chase quickly read it. "You've violated rule number three."

Chase looked at the card again. "I've shunned my duty to the cause? How?"

"You've deserted us by becoming Shelby McCall. Don't

think we don't know about that," the woman with the black crew cut replied.

Chase had enjoyed having a pen name then, especially given the success of her first two mysteries. In addition to helping her to create her persona of trousers and blazers without feeling a complete hypocrite—well, at the time she hadn't thought that she was a hypocrite—it gave her a certain amount of anonymity in her life as Chase Banter. When she handed over her Visa card, no one said any of the socially unacceptable and ignorant things that were guaranteed to pierce an artist's tender heart and psyche. Like "Hey, are you that mystery writer that lives around here?" Or "I only read real literature. You know, like Jane Austen and Harper Lee." Right. As if Austen hadn't essentially been a romance writer and *To Kill a Mockingbird* wasn't in large part a mystery novel, Chase thought smugly.

"I don't know what you mean," Chase said, trying to buy some time. She looked around desperately for one of the red shirts that indicated the presence of a sales person.

"Lesbian books—your books are necessary to keep the flame alive. We can't have it like it was before, where women were scrambling for the few available books that had lesbians in them. What if Beebo Brinker hadn't come along? Or Rita Mae Brown hadn't written a few books before she bailed to write novels about fox hunting that do not contain even one lesbian character. We started her career and this is what we get." The woman with the black crew cut glowered again. She moved forward, backing Chase up against a shelf of hard plastic binders of various colors. She pointed her finger at Chase's chest. "We will not allow that to happen again."

The blond woman pulled the finger down. "Let's be diplomatic about this. You will continue to write lesbian novels—at least one per two-year cycle. That's fair. And do not cheat us on page count. Books are expensive and less than two hundred and fifty pages will not be acceptable." She pulled a sheet of paper from her inside breast pocket and handed it to Chase. "These are some issues we have decided need to be addressed through the medium of fiction."

"Who is 'we'?" Chase inquired, hoping it wasn't something

like the freaky right wing triumvirate that was supposedly threatening to take over the world through the financial control of all available resources.

The blond woman whispered, "The Council for the Continuation of Lesbian Culture."

"This is a joke, right?" Had Lacey hired these women to come and yank her chain? She had also been adamant about Chase continuing to write lesbian fiction, whining at her, "You can't just abandon us."

The blond woman lowered her sunglasses to reveal nearly black eyes. "Do we look like we're joking?" She cracked her knuckles.

"Maybe not," Chase said.

"We'll be going now. Just remember: We're watching you and we expect results," the woman with the black crew cut said.

Chase snapped back to the present. Bud had finished painting Saturn's rings and now was looking expectantly at Gitana. Every afternoon they played what Chase referred to as Extreme Croquet. Bud had seen croquet in a movie and then pleaded for a set for her birthday. Chase had tried to explain that they needed grass and that seeing as how Bud's birthday was around Thanksgiving that they couldn't play then even if they had grass. Bud remained adamant and they ordered a set online. The day it came, Bud took it outside and set up an elaborate course atop snowdrifts, off rocks, around the garden and through a tree grove. It was absurd. But she got everyone to play that day and it turned out to be more fun than playing on grass because it was far more challenging. Thus Extreme Croquet was born.

"Is it time?" Gitana said mockingly.

Bud pursed her lips as if to say, "You know it is."

"Can I beg off? I've got some work I have to do right now," Chase said, leaping up.

Bud gave her the stink eye.

"It's important," Chase said.

"Yrev?" Bud inquired.

"Yes."

Bud nodded. Gitana took her hand and called out behind her, "Don't get too lost. We'll be hungry soon."

"I won't." Chase went to her writing studio, taking the dogs with her as Jane had a habit of stealing balls during Extreme Croquet, making the game even more extreme. The dogs settled on the couch with their chew bones while Chase rifled around in her desk drawers until she found the laminated card and list that the Pink Mafia women had given her.

Chase read the mission statement again: "We, the duly elected Committee members, are dedicated to the care and feeding of Lesbian Culture, the maintenance of our collective identities and the common causes that unite us as a people."

Chase sighed heavily. They really did need a writer—a speechwriter. Just who had "elected" them, anyway? And who had drafted this credo, which was part dog food label and part Declaration of Independence, with precepts that had been lifted from the Hippocratic Oath and the Boy Scouts?

"Precept #1: Do no harm." That was good as far as it went, Chase thought, but then her mind delved deeper. Did this include not dating converts—as dating a straight woman becoming gay or, to be politically correct, realizing her true sexuality, could and did usually cause harm, as it had in the case of Lacey and Jasmine? That had broken up a marriage, albeit not a good one. And Delia had been instrumental in that because she'd first seduced Jasmine. Had the Pink Mafia visited her?

"Precept #2: Be clean, diligent and kind." The diligent and kind part was simple enough. But clean? Did that mean hygienically clean, clean of drugs or linguistically clean?

The third one—the rule they said Chase had violated and for which they had deemed she owed reparations—was just as she remembered: "Do not shun one's duty to the cause."

She looked over the list of issues they'd given her. Again, who were they to tell her what to write? Still, the topics weren't bad ones—combating homophobia, overcoming fear to realize one's true identity, spirituality within the pagan community, family relations including stories with children and, Chase was glad to see, fur kids. It was the last category, though, that caught her attention. They wanted a novel about a lesbian commune.

Chase's seemingly dormant or rather taking-a-vacation-on-the-island-of-Lesbos muse popped her head up from the lounge chair where she had been drinking a piña colada. Chase assumed she was just getting ready to wave down a waiter for another shrimp cocktail when she heard her fairly scream, "Let's do that one!"

The Muse of Commercial Endeavor twirled around in her ergonomically correct office chair and threw a silver-plated letter opener at the Sacred Muse of the Divine Vulva, as Chase had always referred to her, who ducked just in time for it to miss her.

"Ladies, that's enough."

"We'll see about that!" said the Muse of Commercial Endeavor. She got up from the chair in a fury and was coming toward the Muse of the Divine Vulva with a stapler.

Chase, deciding that Divine Vulva didn't stand a chance against a loaded stapler, stuck out her foot and tripped Endeavor. She dropped the stapler as she flew into Vulva's lap face first.

"Oh, I like that," Vulva said.

Endeavor scrambled away from her. "Don't touch me, you pervert."

"Homophobe," Vulva said, taking a sip of her drink and finishing off her shrimp cocktail.

"Both of you stop it. Let's have a nonviolent discussion about the pros and cons of doing this book."

"Which I think we should call *Living with Lesbians*," Vulva said. She'd never been good with titles.

"That's just what I mean. You have no marketing sense. That title makes the book sound like a self-help book for coping with lesbians," Endeavor said.

She was right, of course, Chase thought. Endeavor was always right. Endlessly right. And when it came down to it, right was tiresome from time to time. Couldn't she write two novels like she used to? Her mystery series wasn't as challenging as it had been in the beginning because she was familiar now with the style and the readers' expectations. Maybe writing a lesbian book would freshen her up a bit. Endeavor was beginning to cramp her creative juices like she was a lemon being squeezed dry.

"You know what, I'll write both."

"You can't do that. It's a stupid waste of time," Endeavor said.

"Oh, do shut up for once. I need a break and I want to be relaxed for the next novel. I'll write better and most likely quicker because I'll be more motivated and not piss around so much. That's how I worked before you came along," Chase said. She smiled warmly at Vulva, who fairly cooed. "Ready to come out of retirement?"

Vulva hopped up and rubbed her hands together. "When do we start?"

"Right this minute." Chase turned on her computer.

Chapter Eight—No

And whispering, "I will ne'er consent," consented.—Byron

Lacey stood in the doorway of the writing studio. The dogs looked up at her sleepily—after ten in the morning they were out of commission until Gitana returned home at three. Chase was cursing under her breath: The auto-control on her tab mechanism had taken to blocking the text on the right and she didn't know how to fix it. Donna would have to do it later, but it irritated her and an irritated writer did not do her best work while being irritated. Good God, even her thoughts were messed up—using the same word three times in one sentence was considered a felony in the editorial department.

"What's wrong?" Lacey asked.

"My tabs are fucked up and I can't fix it."

Lacey leaned over. "Have you saved this?" She pointed at the computer screen.

"Yes." Chase leaned back. Lacey's breasts were dangerously close to her face. Ever since Lacey had become a lesbian or, as Lacey put it, "discovered her true persuasion," her propensity for close personal contact had blossomed. If she sat next to you, it was always so close your thighs touched. When she hugged you goodbye, it was full body contact. If you said something cute, she stroked your cheek and gazed at you lovingly. It was downright creepy, but Chase didn't want to hurt her feelings. They had been friends or, as Lacey put it, "BFFs," best friends forever, since they were children. At least Lacey wasn't insisting that her entire life be rewritten to accommodate her present identity— something like "I dated this guy but it was really a brainwashing of my lesbian sensibility by the all-invasion patriarchal culture of gender-difference in the mating arena." *That* Chase could not handle.

Lacey moved the mouse around, clicking it and frowning until she corrected the situation. "How in the..." she stopped and glanced in the direction of Bud, who appeared to be fiddling around with Chase's old laptop. "I mean how on earth did you do that?"

"Like I know. I must have hit a weird key." Chase did not have the stunning typing skills that one would expect of a writer. She had only recently learned to write on the computer rather than in her marbled composition books, and typing and composing didn't always jibe—especially if she was on a roll. At the end of the day, Donna went through and fixed the snafus. This system worked extremely well because they didn't end up with a slew of proofreading at the end. "But thanks."

Bud, it appeared, had come out of her concentrated trance and looked up from the computer. "Ciao." She waved at Lacey, but the motion was more "go away" than "welcome!"

Lacey's head whipped around. "Was that Italian?"

"That particular greeting has more than one meaning, you know," Chase said, giving Bud a disapproving glance for being rude. "And I think Bud was aiming for the other end."

Bud glowered and jabbed at the laptop. She did have a point. Chase was often cranky when she was interrupted from her writing. Bud had probably learned it from her.

"What is she doing?" Lacey asked as she peered at the screen of Bud's computer.

"She's writing a story." Chase beamed at her. If Chase couldn't win a Newberry Award for her novels the next best thing would be for her amazing child to do so. She hoped Bud could pull it off before she turned twenty. The world appreciated the merits of the young far more than the seasoned.

Bud nodded.

"It looks like gibberish to me. Are you sure she isn't just playing around? And why isn't she typing with both hands?"

"Because she's four and her hands are too small for the keyboard. The tech industry doesn't make keyboards for toddlers," Chase said blithely.

Bud looked smug.

"Well, if it's a story, what does it say?" Lacey challenged.

Chase got up and went to the second desk that now graced the studio. She said, "May I?"

Bud turned the laptop so Chase could see it more easily. "It says 'Once there was a blue bear that wandered the forest searching for others like her—big and blue and round. She searched for a long, long time and could find no one. She sat down under a big tree and began to cry great big tears and when they hit the soft forest floor they grew into blue bears. The more she cried the more bears there were until her tears were of joy rather than sadness.'"

Bud looked up at her, seeking approval. Chase smiled broadly. "That is a fabulous story. I love it and I think it's very philosophical." They both looked at Lacey.

"Are you sure she's not an alien?"

"Lacey!" Chase admonished.

"I've never met a kid who's as creepy smart as she is," Lacey said, studying Bud with apparent suspicion—like if she looked long enough and hard enough Bud would turn light gray and her eyes would become large and slanted.

"She can't help it she's smart. Look, you've hurt her feelings," Chase said, pointing at Bud, who stared at Lacey with doe-like eyes.

"Oh, I'm sorry." Lacey reached out and gave her a hug. "Can

I bribe my way out of this?" she asked as she released Bud and dug in her enormous Coach purse.

"New purse?" Chase inquired. The thing must have cost seven hundred dollars.

"Yes, isn't it nice?" She finally located the item she was looking for. It was a red iPod a little larger than a wallet. "You can download entire audio books or podcasts or just music if you like and you can look stuff up—it hooks right into the Internet." She handed it to Bud.

Bud looked at it in wonderment. Chase instantly coveted it. Bud saw this and held it close to her chest. "Knaht uoy."

"Oh, I got one for you too," Lacey said, digging out another one and handing it to Chase. Hers was lime green. Donna could give her lessons and she liked the idea of looking things up. She still meant to visit her potential new friend, Isabel, at the Main Library to do a little research. She loved libraries and she was hoping Isabel would show her the ropes of their operation, which had always been one of her secret fascinations.

"Do you like them?" Lacey asked.

"Well, of course. But I'll need lessons," Chase said, noticing that Bud was already fiddling around with hers. She studied Lacey for a moment, suddenly aware that Lacey didn't drive nearly forty miles from Albuquerque into the boondocks of the East Mountains to hand out iPods. "What's the catch?"

Lacey moved a stack of papers from the couch and sat down. "Why does there have to be a catch?" She looked around at the scuffed furniture and old leather chairs. "You know, I could order some furniture from the Pottery Barn and really spiff this place up."

"We like it this way," Chase said. Bud looked up from her new toy and nodded. "Now, what do I have to do?"

"Well, there is a small favor I have to ask and believe me I wouldn't do it if I wasn't desperate, especially now that you no longer write lesbian fiction, but we need qualified and published panelists."

"As a matter of fact, I *am* writing lesbian fiction again now. I'm doubling up."

Lacey leaped up and raced to where Chase was sitting at her

desk. She hugged her so forcefully it nearly knocked both of them to the ground. "That's fabulous. I mean, I know you need to write for serious cash, but your dyke fans miss you. I know they do. I check out the blogs and they bemoan the loss of dyke writers. I try to tell them that they need to help support these authors by purchasing books. Somebody has to pay the bills."

"Panelists?" Chase asked once Lacey had resumed her post on the couch.

"Yes, we're setting up a public discussion panel on the future of lesbian fiction. We've got Jasmine, P.H. Kinjera, she's the dyke philosopher, kind of like a younger version of Mary Daly, Delia, of course, taking up the erotica end, and Ellen MacNeil, who does first-person humorous coming-of-age stories. I'd like you to cover the romance end."

Chase sat stunned. "You've arranged all this?"

Lacey blushed. "Well, I've had some help."

"Who?"

Bud's iPod was now playing Vivaldi, *The Four Seasons* concerto. She had managed to download already and Chase was duly impressed. She looked sheepish and turned down the volume. Chase found it odd that a four-year-old was fascinated with classical music, but she was glad Bud didn't have a penchant for *American Idol* and dance to it in front of the television like other small humans.

"Your mother." Lacey picked up a book on Emily Carr, a Canadian artist who painted forests. Chase had read a biography on her and discovered that she was a much-ignored artist who had done the same kind of work Georgia O'Keefe had. It had been research for the art theft part of her latest novel, *The Thief.* Chase had chosen one of Emily Carr's paintings in hopes that it would spark interest in this amazing but little-known artist.

"Stella?" Chase said incredulously.

"She *is* a private detective. She located P.H. Kinjera and Ellen MacNeil. P.H. is flying in from San Francisco and Ellen is coming from Louisville. They're going to stay at the house. They seemed thrilled."

"They're staying at Stella's house?" Chase's imagination was ablaze with the horrid possibilities.

"Well, it's certainly big enough and hotel rooms are so impersonal. I thought we could take them up to Santa Fe on the train and show them the sights. They've never been here. You know, the little sand houses commonly referred to as pueblo-style adobes—the planning committee must have stock in ristras. God, you've seen one you've seen them all, but they seem to fascinate tourists. I have no idea why. We'll take them to see the Native Americans selling jewelry on the plaza. Now, those are some hardworking artisans that could use some financial support as well as recognition. Don't you think?"

Chase's mind swam. This couldn't be real. Bud had moved on to Handel and seemed delighted with her new toy. Perhaps she was dreaming and the music was her alarm going off.

"Let's go over this again: You want me to be on a panel, my mother is putting up two lesbian writers and we're going to do a little sightseeing with people I've never met before and you bought me this souped-up iPod as payment?"

"There could be other incentives if need be," Lacey said, looking around again to see if they were lacking some crucial item in their immediate environs. She noticed Bud plunking away one-fingered style on her computer. "Eureka" crossed her face. "And I know what it is."

"Lacey," Chase said.

Lacey interrupted her, "Please, please, please. I'll send Bud to Harvard or the Sorbonne, all expenses paid, anything—an expedition to the Antarctic."

Bud looked up at this. "No!" Chase said. "And in case you've forgotten Bud has a hefty trust fund, courtesy of the malpractice settlement of Bud's conception that Stella and that skank family lawyer of ours, Owen, obtained to provide for her care, feeding, electronic devices and education."

Bud brought out her small Curious George coin purse, looked inside and then turned it upside down and raised her eyebrows.

"You don't get your allowance until Saturday. And if I remember correctly you owe me money for letting Jane pop my exercise ball."

Bud pursed her lips and gave Chase the stink eye. She went back to downloading her classical library.

"How'd that happen?"

Chase was secretly relieved that their domestic issues had diverted Lacey's attention. "Bud has boundary issues. Jane was displaying an overly keen interest in my exercise ball due to its size. Bud couldn't stand the pining and gave in. Jane dribbled it down the hill and then attempted to bring it back up the hill and popped it in the process."

Bud put her hands up in mock resignation, as if to say, "Dogs these days."

"Well, anyway about the panel…" Lacey put on her best pleading face.

"I'm not good at stuff like that and if Eliza finds out, she'll kill me. I'm supposed to be divesting myself from the lesbian stuff."

"I've thought of that. We'll put you behind a screen."

"Oh, that looks good. I'm on a panel about the state of lesbian lit and I hide behind a screen."

"You've got a point there." Lacey stuck her face between her hands and closed her eyes, apparently deep in thought. "I know, we'll put you in disguise."

"What, like glue on a fake mustache?"

"No, that might offend the menopausals in the audience. You know how sensitive they are about facial hair."

"Oh, my God, this is not happening," Chase said, her voice gaining several octaves.

Bud made some clicking noises on the computer and then called out. Chase flew over, immediately petrified that she'd hurt herself. Lacey followed. Bud pointed at the computer screen. She had taken a picture of Chase and run it through a magazine cover program. It showed Chase with her hair turned strawberry blond and tied up with seductive stray hairs loose about her shoulders. Then she had added on groovy square glasses and a low-necked frilly dress shirt.

"That's fucking brilliant! Oh, sorry about that, Bud." Lacey put her hand over her mouth.

Bud shrugged and pointed at Chase, who shot her a dirty look. "Mi ginog ot raews."

"You are not," Chase said.

"What did she say?"

"Something about a similarity in our lexicons."

Lacey's brow furrowed and then she looked at the computer image. "All right, then, this is going to work. No one will recognize you."

"I'm not dying my hair and dressing like that," Chase said indignantly.

Bud giggled.

"C'mon, you've got to do it for the cause. We'll use temporary dye and I can fix your hair like that and get you some real girl clothes. You'll be the star of the show. There's nothing like a hot lesbian writer to stir up support, not to mention sales."

"You're going to make me prostitute myself," Chase said. She looked at the clock and prayed Gitana would show up to save her as Bud clearly had turned traitor. It was five minutes to three. She studied the dogs sitting out on the deck. They would pick up the sound of the Land Rover's engine long before Gitana pulled up in the drive.

Lacey's eyes narrowed. "What do you think those book signings are all about? You'll do it for straight people, but you won't help out the women who started your writing career. How crass is that?"

Chase flinched. Lacey did have a point. It was rather ungrateful.

The Muse of the Divine Vulva popped up. "She's right, you know. Besides it will help with sales. If you sold more of your dyke books, you-know-who," she pointed at the Muse of Commercial Endeavor, who was sulking in the corner after the last altercation, "would leave us alone for a while."

I'm fucking surrounded, Chase thought.

"Just do it. You could get some good material out of the deal," Lacey prodded.

That was another point. Chase had been out of the loop. She'd need to recharge her lesbian batteries if her cast of quirky characters were to evolve properly. She certainly didn't want a flop on her hands. This book needed to come out fresh and exciting or her audience would think she'd lost her touch.

The dogs heard the Land Rover and darted off the deck

toward the front gate. Chase relaxed. Surely Gitana would see the madness and get Lacey to see the futility of such a project. Gitana came up to the writing studio and poked her head inside. Bud jumped up with glee and pulled her inside, screaming, "Ees, ees!"

"What is this all about? Hello, my lesbian sister," Gitana said. Lacey had taken to calling her friends "my lesbian sister," informing everyone that they were part of a long-standing, reaching-back-to-the-time-of-Sappho, tribe. Chase absolutely refused to do this. Converts were like ex-smokers—zealous in their new cause.

Bud pointed at the screen. Gitana leaned down. "Wow, who's that?" She smiled lasciviously.

"You know damn well who it is," Chase said petulantly.

"I'd date her if she wasn't already taken," Gitana said, winking at Lacey, who smirked.

"She wants me to go in disguise or rather dressed like a prostitute," she said, darting a look in Bud's direction. She didn't want to have Bud looking up the word in one of her many dictionaries. "To do this lesbian panel to promote dyke things."

"Dyke things, you make it sound like it's going to be a promo show for..." Lacey glanced at Bud, who was changing Chase's shirt on the computer, apparently studying color schemes. She lowered her voice, "Sex toys."

"I think you should do it. Lesbian voices and images are getting sucked up into mainstream culture. We're losing ourselves," Gitana said. She stroked Bud's hair and took a quick look at her color choice.

"I thought that was the whole point of gay liberation," Chase muttered.

"No, it's not," Lacey said. "We want to be part of mainstream culture as ourselves—as a recognized entity, not as some fringe group to be tolerated in the I-know-a-lesbian-and-she-seems-normal talk at dinner parties." She flounced down on the couch and punched one of the worn blue pillows. "It makes me so mad. Here I am trying to do my best to improve the situation and you won't stand by me."

Gitana raised an eyebrow at Chase.

"Oh, for fuck's sake, I'll do it but under protest."

"Chase," Gitana admonished, pointing at Bud.

"It's a hopeless cause. She already swears in her own tongue. We'll just have to brief her about not doing it in public."

Lacey leaped up and gave Chase another bone-crushing hug. She kissed her on the lips and said, "I love you. I'll get everything set up." She patted Bud on the head and then said, "You're brilliant and you'll get a payoff."

Bud smiled.

Chapter Nine—Persuasion
And make persuasion do the work of fear.—Milton

"I think this panel idea is great," Jasmine said as she lounged on the sagging couch in Alma's living room.

Bo poured the coffee and automatically handed the milk to Chase so she could cut the steaming black liquid.

"I'm totally stoked and I've already got an outfit picked out," Delia said.

"I can only imagine," Chase said, taking a sip of her coffee and rolling her eyes at Alma, who smiled congenially.

Delia crossed her legs and adjusted her gauzy long skirt. Chase wondered how long this Stevie Nicks-a-la-mode-Tinkerbell stage was going to last. She'd learned the other day during their study session on natural history with Bud that moths were kindred to butterflies, differing in body type and nocturnal habits but like them undergoing what was referred to as a complete metamorphosis in that the adult did not resemble the larvae in any way. Clearly the former butch had undergone a complete metamorphosis. Chase hoped never to undergo such a radical change.

"It's tasteful yet accentuates my various still-nubile accoutrements so as to inspire lust and thus book and ebook sales as well as advertising—if we can get those kind of people," Delia said, giving Bo the eye.

"I'm working on it. I can't help it if these fags are picky graphic artists who insist on perfecting their icon," Bo said defensively.

There was a crash outside and then other crashing noises and then a child's squeal of delight. Chase glanced out the window to assure herself again that Bud was wearing her safety goggles.

"Bud is helping Mrs. Givens smash a twenty-four piece dinner set," Alma explained.

Jasmine opened a roll of mint-flavored Mentos and handed one to Chase, who eagerly took it.

"I can only have one," Chase told her. Jasmine nodded, sticking the roll back into her messenger bag as if it were a moonstone to be protected from eager thieves.

"And why is that?" Bo asked, peeking out the window. Chase could see Bud lifting a dinner plate over her head and smashing it down.

"She's bonding with Mrs. Givens. She saved up her allowance to buy that dinner set," Chase said rather proudly—like Bud was helping the poor and perpetually deprived rather than assisting an elderly woman to smash plates, cups and saucers for the pure enjoyment of it.

Jasmine, who had been just as interested as Chase in Mrs. Givens as a character study, pouted and then said, "I don't get it. Bud brings her a dinner set and then they break it. Whose idea was that?"

"It was Mrs. Givens' idea, but it was Bud's desire. It was a pretty ugly dinner set," Chase said.

"Do you think that's a safe thing for a four-year-old to be doing?" Jasmine asked petulantly.

"Who are you, OSHA? She's wearing safety goggles," Chase said.

"Children, I've invited Mrs. Givens for tea on Sunday afternoon and you can both come listen to her stories, which I'm sure she would be delighted to share with you—both of you," Alma said. Chase and Jasmine stuck out their hands and shook and simultaneously mumbled apologies.

"The only reason I brought Bud was that everyone else was booked. It was her suggestion to get the dinner set. I didn't put her up to it," Chase said.

"I'm sorry. I know you would never do anything so underhanded and self-serving as using your child to further your artistic career," Jasmine said. She screwed up her face. "Would you?"

"Jasmine!" Alma admonished.

"Well, you know, you guys are always telling me I'm gullible, so I was just checking."

"You don't suspect someone and then tell them that," Bo said.

"It's a good thing you have Lacey and us to watch out for you," Delia said, topping off all their coffees, which had grown cold.

Jasmine pursed her lips. "Is there a book or something?"

"About what?" Bo asked. He was a hands-on kind of guy. In Bo's eyes, you figured stuff out—you didn't look it up.

Delia was pretty much the same, although Graciela had purchased the *Joy of Cooking* book for her and she was devouring its contents and becoming a good cook. Chase had noticed Graciela's expanding waistline. Chase, having now reached her forties, was watching hers. She'd purchased a Wii system and she and Bud ardently played Outdoor Adventure, which was an exercise game on a sensor mat. Bud always kicked her ass, but all the jumping, running and reflex training made her sweaty and seemed to keep off the ten extra pounds that turning forty was supposed to deliver around your middle like an unwanted present.

"She wants a manual on how not to be gullible," Chase replied.

"Read more thrillers," Bo suggested. "When you can figure out what the characters can't then you'll be better versed in the evils of the world."

"I like that," Jasmine said cheerfully.

"Or you could go to Chase's SUP meetings," Delia said, with a smart look on her face.

Chase blanched. "How do you know about that?"

"Graciela reads your message board and saw the card with the name of Lily whatever-her-name on it and the dates and times of your little get-togethers."

"That's a violation of privacy," Chase said, glaring at her.

"Don't put something somewhere so everyone can see it," Delia retorted.

"Eop," Bud said, as she entered the room.

Chase forgot her irritation and smiled at her. "You're right. It's like the purloined letter."

Alma patted the couch next to her and Bud nestled in between her and Jasmine. "Don't tell me you're reading her Edgar Allen Poe as bedtime stories," Alma said.

"No, we read it in the garden at midday so we, myself included, don't have bad dreams."

Bud took the proffered bottle of water from Jasmine and sipped it greedily. "Drah krow."

"I'm sure it was," Alma said, patting Bud's hand.

"You understand her?" Chase said.

"Of course, we've had lots of pleasant conversations," Alma said. Bud clasped her hand and smiled angelically. Alma was another one of the trusted circle that Chase allowed to watch Bud when schedules got tight.

"I know it's a kind of Pig Latin, but I can't wrap my brain around it. I'll just have to wait until you decide to speak lowly English with me," Bo said, handing Bud the tray of chocolate chip cookies.

"Only one," Chase said. Bud gave her a dirty look.

"So what do you guys talk about, molecular biology?" Jasmine said tersely.

"You're as bad as Lacey. It's not her fault she's ahead of herself," Chase said, contemplating the cookies and then remembering that according to her doctor lower caloric intake was as essential as exercise in staving off the ten pounds that lurked around the corner.

"Tsiega togib," Bud said.

"Your vocabulary is getting quite advanced. It's just about time, isn't it?" Alma said, putting her arm around Bud, who gave a deprecating shrug.

"What did she say?" Jasmine inquired.

Delia, who had jotted down the syllables on her notebook and translated them, said, "I don't think you're going to like it but realistically speaking it's true."

"What!" Jasmine demanded.

"She called you an ageist bigot," Alma said, taking a cookie and handing it to Chase. "We'll go for a walk around the park when we finish up here."

Chase nodded and took the cookie. No one had yet noticed her concern about calories except Alma, who like herself didn't want to squander all the time she'd spent accumulating knowledge to have it wasted by a premature death due to unhealthy habits. Chase hoped she'd grow up to be just like Alma.

"You know," Bo said, putting his forefinger to his lips, "Your SUP group could prove very useful. So the basic mission of the group is to teach you all to be more socially tactful, correct?"

Chase nodded. "It's more like lying but social lying so as not to stick out in a group by saying something inappropriate— like when a woman at my book signing told me she was from Trinidad, Colorado, and I said isn't that where they do all the sex changes."

"I can see where that was not a good thing to say," Alma said.

"So, it's not like your particular social skills are necessarily being eradicated, rather they're being subsumed when you're successful," he added. He sipped his coffee, meditatively.

"I know where you're going with this," Delia said, her eyes gleaming.

"You've lost me," Jasmine said, absently handing Bud another cookie.

Chase was about to object to that when it dawned on her what Bo was proposing. "Oh, no. Absolutely not."

"What do you mean? It's perfect," Delia said. "Your freaky buddies will ask the most inappropriate questions we'll ever come across, hence we will be well-steeled for the real thing."

It appeared Jasmine had now got it. She also moved the cookie plate away from Bud, who was putting forth a hand to partake of yet another. "You want us to expose ourselves intentionally to people who ask embarrassing questions?"

"Yes," Delia said, as if Jasmine already agreed with the scheme.

"I'm not doing a practice run. The real one is going to be horrid enough," Chase replied.

"I don't think it's such a bad idea. I mean, think about it, the real performance has the potential to turn out, shall we say, less than ideal, but if you could practice and overcome or at least confer with each other as well as pick your group's brains you could learn a lot," Alma said. She got up and went into the kitchen, leaving the others to mull it over. She returned with another bottle of water and handed it to Bud.

"Thank you," Bud said quietly.

Somewhere it registered in Chase's brain that Bud had done something odd, but she was too busy bailing water out of her frightened EGO canoe to acknowledge it.

"I think it's a good idea," Jasmine said firmly.

"Ha!" Delia said. "You're outnumbered."

"It's my group," Chase said. She scowled.

"Chase..." Alma said.

"All right, all right. But I'm going to have to ask and it's not guaranteed they'd go along with it. Besides, won't it be antithetical to the group's mission?"

"No, it won't. It's like a reverse Pavlovian thing," Delia said.

Bo and Jasmine looked quizzical. Chase rolled her eyes. "Don't even bother. I will ask them." She glanced over at Bud, who had that hopped-up-on-sugar look. Alma saw it too.

"Perhaps we should go for that walk now. Any other takers?" Alma said.

The others made their excuses and left.

"I can't believe I'm going to do this," Chase told Alma as Bud clamped her hand in hers and pulled her to the door.

Alma grabbed a faded canvas hat and her sunglasses. "It'll be good. Trust me."

Chapter Ten—Preparation
Semper paratus. Always prepared.—Lord Clifford

The writers group arrived first. Lily Hirack enthusiastically welcomed them to the auditorium of the Musical Arts Building. She took Alma by the arm as if, upon first meeting, their kindred spirits had already embraced each other. Bo glanced around and Chase wondered if he was formulating some boy-porn story centered in a gymnasium. It still seemed odd sitting on fold-up chairs in the center of an auditorium.

Delia was ecstatic. "Look, she's got it all set up," she said, pointing to the long table with a pitcher of water and five glasses, one in front of each of the chairs.

Chase studied it dubiously. She still had misgivings about the whole panel thing. Lily, after quizzing Alma as far as was polite for a first meeting, brought the group together.

"So, Chase has been a great addition to our little group,

not to mention her neurosis is of particular interest to me as a behavioral scientist. I'm planning on writing a paper with the working title of 'Writers with Bad Manners,'" Lily said, smiling broadly. "If it's all right with you."

Chase tried to keep the alarm out off her face. "Sure."

"Ah! See, you *are* improving. I know you're mortified and you lied...pretty well too," Lily said. "And don't worry, I was only kidding."

Chase let out a long breath.

"But that you should not have done. Just move the conversation along. Laugh at my little joke and pretend that it wouldn't bother you in the least. See, if someone thinks you are not, how do you say, fazed, then they are no longer interested in tormenting you," Lily said. "Now, please be seated. I hear the others arriving. Isabel will be serving refreshments. She has a waitress phobia so we're doing a role play in hopes that by playing both sides of the menu game she will overcome it. She's actually getting quite good at it. My only fear is that she will consider it as a second career."

"She's a librarian," Chase added.

"I hear myself being spoken of," Isabel said as she walked into the gymnasium. She was followed by Darlene, who was looking rather pleased with herself.

"Ah! What is up?" Lily said.

"I got the job. Peckerhead was caught falsifying docs and Mrs. Philson brought me back in and this time I answered all the questions correctly."

"How cool is that," Lily said, taking her hand and pumping it enthusiastically.

Sandra and Marsha Martin came in. Marsha glanced nervously at the panel. "See, lesbians," said Sandra. "So if you have any questions about sex or recruitment practices, now is the time."

Marsha turned beet red and glared at her.

"Now, this, this is my prodigal child—the worst one. My paper about her I would call 'Misfits and Misgivings.' She is like the puppy you can never train—always piddles in the corner," Lily said, shaking her head.

"I'm Sandra and this is my ex-sister-in-law Marsha. She is bi-curious," Sandra said, coming over to shake their hands. Marsha followed suit, not meeting Delia's gaze or Jasmine's. "Delia gave me lessons and I have to say that it really helped me," Jasmine said. "But I know how difficult it is making such a leap."

"I'm not gay," Marsha said.

"She's in denial. I'm making her watch reruns of *Ellen* so she can see what it looks like to others," Sandra said.

"I wouldn't worry about Delia's conversion talents. Her philandering days are over," Alma said, gently taking Marsha's hand and shaking it.

Bo piped up. "Do I get to be the philosopher or the coming-of-age storyteller?"

Chase leaned over, incredulous. "Oh, I don't know. Let's do a pros and cons list. Alma—amazingly smart, worldly, classically educated and you…"

Lily cleared her throat and stared pointedly at Chase who, like an errant child, immediately changed her course. "And you are great at telling stories about seduction and first times."

Alma raised her eyebrows in true appreciation. "I think the group has done wonders for you."

Bo, not appearing to understand the nuances of what had just transpired, said, "I think it'll work better that way. I honestly don't know much about lesbian philosophy."

"I didn't realize there was such a thing," Marsha said, stealing a glance in Delia's direction.

"Mary Daly is the best-known philosopher and she raises some very interesting points," Isabel said.

Chase wondered how many books Isabel had read. Her knowledge base appeared to rival Chase's. Isabel was definitely giving off kindred spirit vibes.

"You've read it, of course," Isabel said, looking at Chase, who nodded.

"Oh, for fuck's sake, what hasn't she read? You should see her damn house. There isn't a room without a book in it," Delia said, disgustedly, as if Chase's predilection for the written word was some sort of sexual perversion.

"What's your average?" Isabel inquired as she served up coffee and tea with the efficiency of a wide-hipped, tight-jeaned, full-mouthed, friendly-gal-kind-of-truck-stop waitress who would retire wealthy.

Lily now raised her eyebrow in interest.

Chase was embarrassed lest Isabel think her a slacker or the others think her a freak. She cleared her throat and took a sip of water.

"In this case a simple answer carries no social stigma. Either you read a lot or you don't and I'd wager on the former," Lily said.

"Not to mention," Sandra said, "that both you and Isabel are probably fast readers. My mom can read a three-hundred pager in about eight hours. I mean they aren't political treatises or anything but still."

"Roughly one hundred and six a year."

"That's about the average rate for a person who devotes about four to six hours a day reading. Do you use the Mortimer Adler method on some of the books?" Isabel asked.

"Mostly on the research ones. Never on novels, but I don't waste time if it's a bad one."

Delia rolled her eyes. "Thank God for small wonders or you'd have read yourself blind."

"I thought you could only do that by masturbating—at least according to the bishop," Bo said smugly.

Marsha blushed at that. "See, you do need a lesbian," Sandra chided.

Lily cleared her throat and pointed at the chairs that faced the panel, indicating they should sit. "Just because we are making allowances for inappropriate behavior so as to steel our panelists for the general population does not mean that it's carte blanche. Lesbians are not sexual tutors and people's sexual proclivities are off limits."

"What about panel questions? Sexual proclivities are certain to be asked about," Isabel said, her lips curved slightly, revealing a mischievousness Chase found herself rather interested in seeing.

"Only in that context...if it's all right with our panelists," Lily said, studying the group for signs of dissension.

"Mi vulva es su vulva," Delia said, slipping just for a moment into her previously lascivious persona and eyeing Marsha.

Chase smacked her arm. "Married."

"I'm not married," Marsha said, a little too quickly.

"No, but she is," Chase said.

"If you're serious about experimenting, we do have a group of available sex counselors that help with the transition process, including in-home services," Jasmine said as brightly as if she were explaining the virtues of Amway products.

"What!" Chase shouted.

"Lacey set it up. She thought it would be beneficial," Jasmine said, obviously not getting that Chase was outraged.

"And you guys say you don't recruit," Bo said. He took a sip of his coffee and raised his eyebrows.

"So this is what she's doing at the Community Center—running a fucking whorehouse," Chase said.

"Of course not. She is simply helping bisexual or unsexually-manifested women discover their potential desires. No one is doing anything they don't want to do," Jasmine said soothingly.

"Boy, where was that group when I wasn't married?" Delia said.

"Enough," Lily said.

"Inappropriate behaviors," Chase muttered, glaring at Jasmine. She was going to wring Lacey's neck when she got hold of her.

"Now, let's get down to business. The first question," Lily said. She pointed at Sandra, who pulled a notepad from her bag.

She smiled politely at Bo and then cocked her head at Marsha as if in challenge. "This question is for you, Bo."

Bo leaned forward and put his hands together as if to relay his readiness for questioning.

"Do you really feel that coming-of-age or coming-out stories have any place in the current world view of homosexuality—I mean isn't this kind of stuff just giving the newbies something to masturbate to?" Sandra sipped her coffee and then glanced at Lily. "Is that inappropriate enough for you?"

Lily pursed her lips. "Very and for the sake of learning I shall tell you why. First, it's disrespectful because it lacks compassion and it smacks of disinterested bigotry and second..."

Isabel burst in, "And it's a perfect example of Aristotle's Fallacy of the Consequent."

Lily rolled her eyes. "You, be quiet. Erudition thrown out like that is just as inappropriate. Like anyone knows what that means. That is nothing but intellectual strutting."

Delia leaned over toward Chase. "You know what that means, right?"

"Well, yeah." Chase glanced over to see if Lily was listening, but she was still chastising Isabel, who was doing an admirable job of defending herself. "Aristotle wrote that superior people, or rather 'good men,' make the right choices and that's what makes them better than the others."

"There's nothing wrong with that," Delia said.

"Not exactly. See, the category for being a good man making the right choices consisted of male Greek aristocrats and everyone else, especially women, were inherently inferior so treating them that way was perfectly understandable and commended."

"Oh, well, that's totally fucked," Delia said, wrinkling her brow. "So Bo would always be better than me regardless of what I did?"

"Yes."

"Hmmph. Fuck Aristotle."

Bo stopped watching the tennis match of wits and leaned toward Chase. "What should I do?"

"Wait it out, I guess," Chase said, looking at Alma, who sat sagely in her chair taking notes. "What are you doing?"

"Oh, my goodness, there is some worthwhile stuff here— food for thought, shall we say," Alma said, not looking up from her notebook.

Jasmine and Chase stared at each other and started paying strict attention, but Delia had grown bored with it. "Come on. Are we going to answer questions or just sit here and listen to you two blather on and on about your intellectual intercourse?"

"Discourse," Chase amended, but no one was listening.

Lily stopped arguing with Isabel and stabbed a slender brown finger at Delia. "I shall expect you at next week's meeting. You have the manners of a pygmy."

"I didn't think pygmies had manners," Isabel said.

"My point exactly," Lily said.

"And why should I?" Delia countered, winking at Marsha.

"Because you could go much further in your vocation if you had some skills, and if you don't you'll end up alone, dying in a rented room, your bedclothes full of urine and your cat waiting to eat your face off as soon as hunger overwhelms her," Lily said.

Everyone blanched.

"You see why I'm the leader. I started these kinds of groups because I am the master of inappropriateness. I could shock you people right out of your underpants," Lily said, her hands raised to the sky as if she were Moses parting the sea of respectable conversation.

"Holy shit. What time does the meeting start?" Delia said.

"Wednesday at five thirty," Marsha said timidly.

"All right then, let's get on with another inappropriate question," Lily said.

Isabel raised her hand and smiled wickedly. "I have one."

Lily nodded.

"It's for Delia or Chase as I think it applies to both of you. It concerns love scenes. There seems to be an overuse of 'pink folds,' 'slick,' 'suck,' 'thrusting hips'…and so forth. Is it absolutely necessary? I think most readers can imagine what goes where and when."

"They make us do it," Chase blurted. This was one of her greatest panel fears—the love scene explored and judged.

"Who?" Isabel inquired, raising an eyebrow.

"The editors," Chase said as if she were in the thrall of alien masters who had attached electrodes to the tips of her fingers and would zap her if she did wrong.

"Oh, for fuck's sake, lady!" said Delia. "Do you know what lesbian readers would do if they were cheated out of the love scene—they live for those moments. If we just quietly shut the bedroom door on the sex scene, there'd be a fucking lynch mob of angry lesbians."

Lily tilted her head and studied Delia and then she looked at Chase. "She's worse than you are and I think you're pretty bad."

"Thanks for the compliment. You should meet her partner, who is also my sister-un-in-law. Now *she's* a piece of work."

"Well, moving right along," Lily said. She dabbed her forehead with a white linen hanky. "It's Marsha's turn."

Marsha colored a little and then spoke. "This one is for Alma."

Alma looked up from her notebook. "A philosophical question—how nice."

Marsha looked uncertainly at Lily.

"How could yours be any worse than we've already had?" Lily said, shaking her head.

"Go ahead, Marsha," Alma coached.

"Well, it just seems that lesbian culture has waned—what used to be their invisibility was eradicated by a sort of feminist outing of crones, separatists and ardent women fighting for their right to be recognized and that now all that movement has seemed to get for women was more work—they are still bearing children and cleaning the house and, in addition, expected to pull in half the family income. The separatists have seemingly disappeared, crones are in rest homes playing bingo and lesbians are buried under the dross of 'hot,' their whole sense of being tied up in acting out sex scenes for both straight and gay audiences. I mean, is all the culture tied up with the Dinah Shore weekend?"

They all looked at her astonished, none more than Sandra perhaps. "What the hell! Where'd you get all the info?"

"I researched it," Marsha said proudly.

Alma looked thoughtful. "Yes."

They all turned to look at her. "What do you mean?" Delia said.

"Yes, Marsha is quite correct—from what I know. I will turn to the rest of the panel for their opinion," Alma said.

Even Bo seemed to ponder the question, Chase observed, or he was doing a pretty good job of looking like it.

The Sacred Muse of the Divine Vulva appeared and whispered in Chase's ear. "See, you going off to Commercial Land is like leaving the island of Lesbos in exile. We can't keep losing our talent." She looked pleadingly at Chase.

"I think that Lesbian Culture *has* lost its way," Chase said. "We no longer have a cohesive center and have now become a trophy at suburban dinner parties of the caliber of 'Oh, we know a lesbian couple and they're perfectly nice—and their decorating skills—to die for.' Oh, don't forget they are a hard-working bunch of overachievers." Vulva beamed.

"Because we FEEL the need to make up for the one thing we can't change about ourselves—that we are gay," Jasmine screamed. "This whole fucking attitude drives me up the wall."

"Better watch that or you'll end up in SUP class," Delia said. "But I feel your pain, sister," she said, sticking out her fist so she could bump knuckles with Jasmine.

Lily clapped. "Now this kind of stuff will delight your audience. Yes, you are a downtrodden people, yes, you are the Bollywood imitations, yes, you are the indigenous peoples brought into the throng so that you will lose yourselves in a swirl of Othellian possession without love—always the outsider awaiting entrance, knowing this is your due—and yet never allowed in the front hall but only at the kitchen door."

"We're still better decorators," Bo said.

"You are a simply amazing woman. Can we have lunch?" Alma asked Lily.

"I'd love to. Now, let's go have a margarita and toast Marsha for bringing out the best in us all," Lily said, getting up.

"Can we do that?" Isabel asked.

"It's not an AA meeting despite the furniture," Chase said.

"Of course we can. We are free peoples," Lily said, happily leading them out.

Chapter Eleven—Death
Pale priest
Of the mute people.—*R. Browning*

"Can I go get the mail?" Graciela asked, as she rifled through the key rack by the kitchen door. She was dressed in camouflage pants and a black tight-fitting T-shirt.

She hardly looked like a successful realtor. Rather she resembled a mercenary, Chase thought. Great, the neighbors will love that. Instead of seeing us as we are, two sedate women with one child, living quietly in a hard-won garden paradise, they'll think we've finally resorted to establishing that lesbian paramilitary training center they were worried about.

That had been one of the scenarios the "neighbors" had entertained about them when they moved out to Bum Fuck Egypt as Lacey referred to it or, as Chase saw it, a piece of property nestled in the mountains just outside of Albuquerque—along with rumors of a separatist commune and an art colony specializing in Fiesta Ware. Everything related to stereotypical lesbianism had been explored, it seems. It hadn't helped, of course, that Graciela had enlisted several of her friends to help them move and they'd all dressed in combat gear. Nor had it helped that she had announced their arrival by hoisting a rainbow flag atop the studio that Chase, who'd been embroiled in unpacking, hadn't noticed for several days. Chase had been furious about the flag, but Graciela had only laughed. "We were just claiming the place for you. This is now officially lesbian ground."

"Tell me again why you're here?" Chase looked up from her notes. This panel thing was taking up way too much time. She shoved the notes away. She'd just have to wing it. Besides she was already behind on her third novel in the mystery series, as her muse, Commercial Endeavor, was constantly reminding her. The lesbian novel, on the other hand, was coming along nicely, much to the delight of the Sacred Muse of the Divine Vulva.

"To see my beloved niece and my beautiful sister—and you too," Graciela said, gleefully clutching the mailbox key.

Bud coughed. Chase leaped up and grabbed a tongue depressor from the emergency medical kit she kept at the ready. "You've got a cough. I hope it's not strep."

"ON, on," Bud said, pushing her back. "Suoitecsaf."

"Jesus, that's a word," Graciela said.

For some uncanny reason, Graciela was one of the few other people who could instantly translate Bud's speech.

"She's got a collection of dictionaries. She probably has a better vocabulary than the average high school senior," Chase said, not without a little pride.

"Yeah, but what's it going to take to squeeze it out of you," Graciela said, plucking Bud off the kitchen stool and squeezing her until she squealed with delight.

"Don't do that. You could burst her spleen."

"You've got to stop worrying. You'll curse us all with the horrors you imagine," Graciela said, setting Bud back down.

This had occurred to Chase, who was bipolar with a little OCD mixed in, all of which served to make her irrationally superstitious.

Addison came in the kitchen door with the dogs. "Don't talk

to her like that. You know how paranoid she gets about bad luck tied to her cycles and rituals."

Chase pursed her lips. "I don't like being referred to in the third person either."

Addison bowed her head in acquiescence. "I stand corrected. I must be growing up. I'm behaving like the rest of you."

"Not like me. I only play at grown-up," Graciela said.

"Prove it," Addison replied.

"Do you have boobs yet?" Graciela said.

Addison looked genuinely astonished. She glanced down as if she half expected a set of double D's to have appeared on her chest.

"I think she just acted like a twelve-year-old boy," Chase said.

Graciela buffed her knuckles on her chest.

"You win. It doesn't hurt, does it? They don't really say anything about it in the books or on the Internet," Addison said. She glanced at Bud, who'd picked up the mailbox key and was palming it, making it disappear and reappear.

"Does what hurt?" Chase asked, genuinely confused. "And when did she learn to do that?" she said, pointing at Bud.

"Getting boobs, and I bought her a magic book at Borders because she decided after growing up and becoming a virologist she wants to become a magician. She thinks it'll be a good hobby for her retirement," Addison said.

Chase put her head in her hands. Bud used this as an opportunity to pull a scarf out of Chase's ear.

"How cool is that!" Graciela said, clapping her hands.

Addison patted Chase's shoulder. "She can't help it if she's an exceptional child. Remember, I used to make you nervous."

"No, it doesn't hurt when you get boobs and you're brilliant, but you're not nearly as eccentric as Bud."

Bud had left and returned with a small box. She pointed at it. Graciela instantly got it. She put her index finger in it. "Don't cut it off," she teased.

Bud pulled out the tiny saw.

"Where did she get that?" Chase yelped.

"It came with the book. Don't worry. You know, this is all

displacement," Addison said. "It's the lesbian writers' panel thing that Lacey roped you into that's twisting up your knickers. She's not going to cut off Graciela's finger and most likely she won't become the next David Copperfield."

Right then, Graciela screamed. "Ah, it hurts. Look, it's a bloody stump." She writhed around the kitchen. Bud giggled.

Chase looked alarmed. "I thought you said it was safe."

"Relax," Graciela said, holding out her hand. "Now, can we go and get the mail? I ordered something for Delia and had it sent here. She's such a snoop I can't have it come to the house."

"What is it?" Chase asked.

"It's a matching dildo and vibrator set in neon orange—you know like the color of those traffic cones. It's so cool," Graciela said, grinning.

Chase stared at her in utter disbelief.

"I can get you a set if you want."

"There are…" she was going to say children present but glanced at Addison who seemed to be waiting for just that word. "People who have been on the planet less time than we have present, so perhaps we shouldn't discuss your purchases."

"You can look up dildos on Wikipedia," Addison said. "They have a long history."

"Og htiw?" Bud asked, putting the saw set back into the small wooden box labeled Magic Kit.

"No," Chase said instantly.

"Why not? It's just a dirt road with absolutely no traffic. Being this protective is not good. It'll bring Shiva down upon you," Graciela said.

"She's got a point. I'll go with them," Addison said.

Chase was undecided, but the phone rang and it was Donna. The three of them inched toward the door. Chase couldn't concentrate on what Donna was saying and them too. "You can go, but be careful. I mean it."

Donna gave her the rundown on her hair appointment for the trim and, as Lacey put it, "just a few highlights" and for the shopping trip that she'd coordinated with Lacey. Chase need not bother with that detail, she said. They'd pick out the suit and she'd only have to show up for the final fitting. Chase jotted down the hair appointment time and went through the panel notes she'd sworn off of one more time while she waited for the mail crew to return. She heard Graciela's gigantic Ford truck pull up in the drive. When they entered the house, she immediately knew something was wrong.

Bud walked right past her, head hung low.

"What happened?" Chase said, panic overriding all other impulses, even the one to chase after Bud.

"We had a little accident," Graciela said.

Addison nodded gravely.

"What kind of an accident?" Chase yelled. "Is everyone all right?"

"Everyone except the rabbit that got run over," Addison replied.

"It wasn't her fault," Graciela declared.

"Whose fault?" Chase asked, looking queerly at Bud, who'd returned carrying four black dress socks.

Addison glared at Graciela. "Hello."

"I mean my fault. The rabbit came out of the middle of nowhere. We couldn't help it."

Bud shook her head. "I did it."

At first the shock of Bud's complete sentence overrode the import of what she was saying. Chase hugged her. "You're talking in normal sentences. What do you mean, you did it?"

Bud looked pleadingly at Addison.

"Do you want me to tell her?"

Bud nodded. She tied a sock around her arm and handed each of them a sock to use as an armband indicating they were in mourning.

They obediently put them on.

"Bud was driving the truck when the aforementioned rabbit made a suicide dash for the front right tire. At least it was quick." Addison sighed heavily.

"You let a four-year-old drive a two-ton truck? Have you lost your mind?" Chase screamed. Then she glared at Addison. "Why didn't you stop her?"

Addison didn't look at Chase. "Because I drove down to the

mailbox. It wouldn't be fair not to afford the same opportunity to Bud. We are both children, thus we share the same status."

"But you're eleven at least and this is the first time you've ever referred to yourself as a child."

"I know. But how can any child resist the opportunity to drive and we both know how to, more or less, from driving the golf carts around at the nursery."

"You drive the carts at work?" Chase was incredulous.

Addison quickly realized her mistake. "I mean, not all the time."

Chase's eyes narrowed. "Is that why those orange cones are set up in the back lot?"

"Yeah, it's a wicked course. Bud usually wins. She never knocks down cones. It seems kids have better reflexes. The bunny thing was just a fluke. We should really go bury it before the coyotes get it," Graciela said.

Bud nodded gravely.

"You are in so much trouble," Chase said. "Bud, you're grounded until you're twenty-five. Addison, you're going to have to sort out the mess I made of the Excel program and you," she pointed at Graciela "are going to pick up as many loads of manure as my garden will hold."

Addison groaned. "But I just got done downloading an entire gig of songs onto your iPod."

"I feel in light of the fact that I will carry with me the guilt of killing a fellow creature for the rest of my life that my grounding is excessive. How about two weeks and I still get to drive the carts?" Bud said.

"Holy Mother of Christ," Graciela said. "She goes from gibberish to huge sentences. Wicked. Look, she feels terrible." She put her arm around Bud, who was starting to tear up.

"Besides you can't ground her until she's twenty-five as she will long before then be a grown-up, and you should let her drive the carts because when she does get her license she'll be an expert driver," Addison said.

Bud looked up at Addison with utter adoration.

"I don't understand how we got to my doling out punishment for an obvious crime to negotiating the sentence," Chase said.

"It's referred to as plea bargaining," Addison said, opening the drawer that contained the collection of glued-together Popsicle sticks that they used when burying the dead creatures run over by cars—for despite being a busy author, Chase still continued her practice of giving respect to the unfortunate victims of roadkill by preventing the desecration of their bodies by crows and car tires.

"I'll get the shovel. I suppose I'll be keeping it for a while, getting the manure and all," Graciela said, not looking happy about it.

They walked down the road, as the incident had occurred close to the house. "See, we almost made it," Graciela said.

"That is beside the point," Chase said, digging the hole. She got it started and then handed the shovel to Addison, who dug a bit more and then handed off to Graciela.

Bud, looking grief stricken, and wearing enormous yellow plastic gloves, gently picked up the bunny and laid it in the grave. She wiped a tear away and stepped back so Chase could shovel the dirt back on. Addison handed Bud the tiny wooden cross.

"I'll say the benediction," Graciela said.

Knowing her to be heathen and pagan, they all stared at her in astonishment.

"In death, this poor wretched creature will find the safety that in life she or he could not find because of motor vehicles, coyotes, owls, crows, angry farmers and small children behind the wheel."

This started Bud howling in grief.

"For fuck's sake, Graciela, say an amen and get it over with before Bud ends up in the psych ward," Chase said.

"Amen," Graciela said, putting an arm around Bud. "Don't worry, kid, I killed a cow once."

Bud looked up at her in amazement.

"How'd you do that?" Addison asked.

"Cow tipping. Poor thing died of a heart attack," Graciela said. "This won't be the first time I've shoveled manure for restitution."

"Was that when you were arrested that time we bailed you out?" Chase asked, shouldering the shovel.

"Jailbird?" Bud asked. She looked up with mortification at her aunt.

"It was before you were born. I've reformed myself."

They heard crunching tire noises on the road and turned to see Gitana coming. She pulled alongside them. "Oh, my God, what happened?" she said, pointing at their armbands and then seeing the shovel. "Oh, no, not one of the dogs. Please…"

"No, no, it was a rabbit. We just finished the funeral," Chase said, stroking her cheek.

"It was entirely my fault," Bud said.

"What did you do?" Gitana asked.

"I was driving the truck and the rabbit ran out in front of it. I couldn't help it," Bud said, looking mournfully behind her at the grave.

"Oh, baby. It's okay," Gitana got out of the car and held her. Then she stepped back. "You talked in normal English and in full sentences." She scooped her up and twirled her high in the air. "You talked, you talked, you talked." She kissed both Bud's cheeks.

"I think it was the shock of what happened," Addison surmised. "She started doing it right after the…you know, the incident."

"They are all in deep shit for allowing her to drive," Chase added.

"I let her drive down the road all the time," Gitana said quite calmly as they got in the Land Rover.

"What!" Chase said.

"Chase, it's a private road and it's more like four-wheeling than driving. It's not like I'm letting her motocross," Gitana said.

"That'll be next," Chase muttered.

"Dude, you need to seriously relax," Graciela said.

"She's never been able to relax for as long as I've known her," Bud said, quite authoritatively.

Gitana gazed in utter amazement at her daughter in the backseat. Chase pursed her lips. She was going to miss being one of the select few that could understand Bud. Now, she'd have to share her with the world. "Oh, like you've known me forever,"

Chase said, turning to look at Bud, who was holding Graciela's hand.

"My version of forever," Bud retorted.

Chase screwed up her mouth in consternation. She did have a point.

"So what's for eats for the funeral reception?" Graciela said, rubbing her hands together.

"Not rabbit," Bud said.

They stared at her. "I apologize. That was in poor taste," Bud said, turning crimson. "It just slipped out."

"Welcome to my world," Chase said.

Chapter Twelve—Trade

Love the little trade which thou has learned
and be content therewith.—Marcus Aurelius

"I can't imagine how this is going to be a good thing," Chase said, as Lacey helped her try on a nicely tailored linen suit.

"You need to meet more of your kind," Lacey said, nodding at the small Jewish tailor as he wrung his hands. Lacey was not one of his easier clients and she was springing for the suit since Chase had nearly had a coronary when she heard the price.

"My kind? What does that mean?" Chase said, wriggling as Lacey pulled at the shoulders.

"I think it needs to fit snugger across the shoulders," Lacey said to the tailor.

"I like things to fit loose," Chase said, waving off the tailor. He looked entirely too intense with his pins and quick fingers. He had the largest, darkest eyes and the longest nose Chase had ever seen. She wondered then if she was being politically incorrect as to ethnic characteristics, but he was Jewish and he was a tailor.

"What is the point of a tailored suit if it fits like a paper bag?" Lacey said petulantly. She signaled to the tailor to proceed pinning up the excess. Chase suddenly felt like a voodoo doll.

"I just don't think this is necessary. I'm never going to see these people again anyway."

"That's my point. That's the point of the whole panel. We're losing our focus and sense of community. We're not just gay, we're a people, a people lost in the wilderness—no offense, Joseph—of a consumer-oriented, culturally bereft society."

"You're nuts. I thought the whole agenda of gay rights was for our kind to assimilate and now that that has happened you're complaining. Not to mention you've been gay for about four days," Chase said, taking off the jacket at Joseph's behest.

Chase watched Joseph's face in the mirror. He smiled ever so slightly. "So Joseph, how long have you been Jewish—since Moses came along and took you all on that nightmare vacation?"

"So I came to the flock late, that doesn't make me any less gay. You know what your problem is?"

"Gee, I can think of a few things," Chase said. The tailor eyed the rear end of the pants. They were loose-fitting as well. Chase gave him a dirty look. He put his fingers together in an ever-so-slight manner. She nodded reluctantly. It was probably better if he made the decision rather than Lacey.

"Your problem is...you've lost your lezzie," Lacey said, flouncing down on one of the leather divans as if the exertion of saving Gay World had sapped all her strength.

Chase and Joseph caught each other's expressions in the mirror. Their mutual look of incredulity made them laugh and then really laugh.

"Has anyone seen my lezzie? I seem to have misplaced it."

Chase watched as Lacey's face turned crimson and Joseph, his shoulders still shaking, went off to the back room to finish the alterations. She went to sit next to Lacey, who'd gone from angry to pitiful. Chase took her hand. "Come on, don't cry. I didn't mean anything. It was just that 'losing your lezzie' just

sounded so cheesy, like one of those old lesbian novels with the lurid covers."

"I know that, but it is really the essence of it and you of all people," Lacey said morosely.

Chase was truly puzzled. She'd never been a radical lesbian. It really hadn't seemed necessary as she was a hermit anyway. "Lacey, I'm just me, a person who happens to be gay. It's as simple as that."

"But it's not as simple as that when people are still being persecuted all over the planet and people still feel like they have to hide it and people are still getting beaten up," Lacey said.

Chase let out a deep breath. "You have a point." She seemed to be saying that a lot lately.

"A really good point and it's up to people like us to make a difference."

"All right. I'll try to summon up all my lezziness for the occasion."

"Great. Now, I've brought the biographies of all the participants. We can go over them while Joseph finishes the suit. You can do that, can't you, Joseph?"

A muttering came from the back room that Lacey took for assent. Like he has a choice, Chase thought smugly.

"Here we go. Now, P.H. Kinjera is the philosopher, degreed out of Harvard, masters at Emerson, doctorate at Berkeley. She's an expert on feminist linguistics. In fact, she's working on rewriting the English language so it will be woman-oriented."

"What the hell does that mean?" Chase asked, snatching the biographies out of Lacey's hand and glancing down at them.

"Like taking the semen out of seminal and how the Constitution still doesn't include women, at least not by name—stuff like that," Lacey said, taking the paper back.

"Oh, well, that's understandable," Chase conceded. "But the whole of the English language. I mean, is that really possible?"

"She's going to try. Remember, Mary Daly did a pretty good job of it but new fire and brimstone are necessary. You'll like her."

"I think I'm going to be intimidated. We're talking about a scholastic powerhouse." An image of Camille Paglia came into her mind; the thought of having dinner with her made Chase's bowels twitch.

"It's all good. She's very user-friendly and she's a Chase Banter fan. You two will get along just fine." Lacey peeked behind the curtain to see how Joseph was coming along and, Chase suspected, to avoid Chase's glare.

"So what you're saying is that you are single-handedly going to revamp the philosophical, emotional and literary landscape of lesbo-world," Chase said, suddenly grasping the extent of Lacey's monomania.

"With some help," Lacey said, holding up the jacket that Joseph handed her. "Nicely done." She patted him on the shoulder and handed him her credit card. "With ample compensation for the rush job. Whatever you see fit."

Joseph frowned.

"I will not let my evil accountant cheat you. We'll trick him. Add the bonus to the cost of the suit. He'll only complain about my extravagance and the rest is none of his business." She handed the jacket to Chase, who put it on. It fit beautifully.

"You're serious," Chase said, flabbergasted.

"Well, someone's got to do it. Ta-ta, Joseph," Lacey said, as they passed out the door with the carefully wrapped suit.

"I don't see how a dinner party and a panel discussion are going to accomplish that," Chase said as they slipped into Lacey's Subaru.

"But don't you see, this is only the beginning—the bringing together of our people. Think of it—with these speakers we've created a salon, like on the Left Bank when Gertrude Stein and her girlfriend, you know the one with the mustache, oh, what's her name, Alice, brought intellectuals, writers and artists together and now we're doing it with lesbians. And I've got a film crew coming in to tape it so we can put it on the web."

"What!"

"Oh, it'll be all right. Just don't forget to take your meds. I've got some Xanax if things get dicey." Lacey turned up the music and sang along to the Indigo Girls' tune "I Was Only Joking."

Chase was so thunderstruck that she sat silent all the way back to the house. Gitana found her in the same condition when she returned home with Bud. Chase had eaten her way through three packs of Mentos and had to be put to bed.

Gitana stroked her forehead and calmly said, "Whatever it is we will sort it out in the morning. I'll bring you some soup."

Bud sat by her and held her hand. Then she handed her Thomas Wolfe's *Look Homeward, Angel* and looked imploring.

"All right, I guess reading about a nut ball might stabilize me."

She took up the book and didn't realize until later, as Bud lay asleep in her arms, that reading oddly tragic novels didn't exactly make for normal bedtime stories, but then there seemed no real sense of normalcy in her life. Instead of being alarmed by this thought she found it a relief. These past four years of trying to be a normal person, trying to fit into the prescribed roles of parent and mainstream author had been rather a strain. As she closed her eyes, she decided she would do her lesbian best to help Lacey. She would not, however, become a banner-carrying militant lesbian.

Chapter Thirteen—Soul

'Tis an awkward thing to play with souls.—R. Browning

"I don't see the problem with it," Gitana said as she buttered the toast.

Chase stared at her in amazement. "Only that I'm not supposed to do things like lesbian webcam panels in case someone recognizes me. I could become schizophrenic being two writers who are not supposed to be the same person."

"People do not become schizophrenic because of pen names as it is a brain chemistry issue and embracing your lesbian self, something you've always been, would not produce multiple personalities. You are still Chase Banter, the lesbian romance writer, and Shelby McCall, dressed in tweed, the mystery writer," Bud said. She took a piece of toast and smiled sweetly at Chase.

"Thank you, Dr. Freud."

"I wouldn't worry so much about it. You'll be dressed

entirely differently and your hair will be lighter. It's kind of like a disguise," Gitana said, handing Chase a piece of toast and the jar of peanut butter.

Chase looked at it with distaste. She'd suddenly lost her appetite. Reaching around the back of the kitchen stool and into her backpack, she pulled out a fresh pack of Mentos.

"You can't have that for breakfast," Gitana said, pouring Bud a glass of orange juice which she guzzled down, putting her glass out for more. "I certainly hope you're not going to grow up to be a serious drinker."

"They're fruit-flavored. I had bought all the peppermint ones they had," Chase said, attempting to open the stubborn package. Bud snatched them out of her hands. "Thank you. You know how package-challenged I am."

Bud smirked and tossed them to Gitana, who handed them off to Annie, the dog, whom she had trained to bury Mentos packages out in the yard. Annie ran for the door before Chase could stop her.

"That's not fair. You guys act like I'm a heroin addict."

"Mentos have become your heroin," Gitana said. "Do you have any more?" She nodded at Bud, who deftly took Chase's backpack off the chair and began to search its contents, quickly locating the contraband.

"This is a violation of my civil rights," Chase said indignantly.

"People with addictions forfeit their rights because they can no longer be responsible for their actions," Bud said, handing over three more rolls to Gitana. Annie had returned and was given the rest. She eagerly took off.

"I'm so glad you talk now. It saves me from having to explain things," Gitana said, stroking Bud's head.

"I'm not. What does that say about me when a four-year-old has a better understanding of my behavior than I do?" Chase lamented.

"That you have a retarded sense of self," Bud said, taking another piece of toast.

Chase took a desultory bite of hers. "I suppose you're right."

Bud stroked her forearm and looked empathetic.

"I think you should do the video," Gitana said.

"But why?"

"Because—I can't honestly believe I'm saying this—but Lacey is right. We have neglected our duty by slipping into the homogeneity of a culture that pretends to acknowledge our existence when in actuality it belittles and ignores and in some cases harms us. This is the twenty-first century and we still haven't come that far," Gitana said.

"But I'm going to be dressed as a butch tart in a tailored suit and Eliza will somehow find out. You know how connected she is."

"Then tell her ahead of time and suffer the consequences," Gitana said, almost blandly as if it were the easiest thing in the world.

"What about my career, our standard of living?"

"Chase, our standard of living will survive it," Gitana said.

"So you're saying my monetary success is of no account?" Chase said, a bit huffily.

"No, I'm not. I'm saying money isn't everything."

"You sound just like a rich person," Chase replied and then instantly regretted it as she herself was a trust-fund baby and had seldom wanted for anything.

Gitana raised her eyebrows and pursed her lips.

Bud piped in. "The trust fund annuity Owen established for me has no stipulations on its use concerning household expenses," she said.

"Let's see how this dinner thing goes and we'll take it from there. Deal?" Chase said. She looked disdainfully at her breakfast.

"Are you going into town?" Bud asked.

"I wasn't planning on it. Why?"

"I would like to visit my grandmother Jacinda, who is helping with the setup at the church jumble sale, which allows me first access to all literary items. I might be able to get some dictionaries. The *OED* could be out there. And I will need to have an advance on my weekly stipend," Bud said.

"What is a jumble sale?" Chase said.

"Hullo, it's a Briticism for garage sale, but that term would not be appropriate as it is not being held in a garage but rather the church basement," Bud said, taking a third piece of toast. Gitana took in her daughter this time and raised her eyebrows again. "I'm growing," Bud replied.

"How come you've gone from three-word sentences to Virginia Woolfe-length sentences?" Chase asked.

"My lack of vocabulary," Bud said flatly. She pulled out the account ledger she kept in her backpack slung over the kitchen chair. "I think twenty dollars will suffice. If I don't use it I will return it to my account."

"How do you know I'll take you?" Chase said, already pulling twenty dollars out of her wallet.

"Because you love me and you would never let Jacinda down and secretly you're hoping I'll find the *OED*."

"You're right. Let's go. I'll see if I can meet Lacey for coffee and get more particulars on this film thing."

"I'll see you two this afternoon," Gitana said, putting the breakfast things away. "And no Taco Bell for lunch no matter how much you plead and cajole," she said, pointing at Bud.

Bud gave Annie and Jane their departure biscuits and told them to guard, upon which they went to sit under their favorite tree and take in the sun.

As they got in the car, Bud said, "Did you know that most people no longer get enough vitamin D?"

"I did not." Chase started the car and pulled down the drive toward the road.

Bud hopped out of the car and opened the gate, waited until Chase pulled the car through and shut it. The gate opener had gone the way of the garage door opener—neither worked for unknown reasons—so they'd gone back to the dark ages of manual manipulation because getting a repairman up there was like asking for an audience with the Pope.

"Can I drive?" Bud asked when she opened the door.

Chase stared at her in utter disbelief. "You've got to be kidding."

"Actually, I'm not. I will be sixteen one day and with

accelerated driving skills my chances of survival will be greatly increased."

"I'm in my forties and my chances of having a heart attack have greatly increased. You can drive with your mother because she has a calmer disposition, but not with me."

Bud seemed to consider this. "I would miss you if you died," she said and got in the car and fastened her seat belt.

"That's nice to know." Chase started down the bumpy road.

They rode in silence until Chase said, "Why do people suffer from a vitamin D deficiency?"

Bud smiled. "I wondered how long it would take before you asked." Bud turned off the timer on her elaborate watch.

"How long?"

"Two minutes and thirty-five seconds. People do not go outside and have the glorious rays of the sun dance across their skin often enough. That is why, I presume, that Annie and Jane always have a sun bath. Animals seem to inherently know what their bodies need. Women are especially prone to this particular deficit."

"Where did you learn this?"

"It was on the pop-up page of our Internet provider. The article fell under our decided rules of appropriate reading so I opened it."

"There is absolutely no reason for me to doubt your integrity, right?" Chase held great reservations about Bud having access to the Internet, but Gitana had drawn up a set of rules in contractual form that they had all decided on and Bud had sworn to adhere to them.

"Of course not. I am as good as my word," Bud said with some indignity.

"All right. Will you call Lacey and see if she's available for a tête-à-tête?"

Bud started to pull up the number on the iPhone Lacey had given her. Technology, the bane of Chase's existence, was the delight of Bud's. She could do the most amazing things with the computer and she had now become a go-to girl for all the snafus that Chase created in her own tech-world.

"No, wait. I have a new plan."

Bud raised her eyebrows and looked for an instant like a miniature version of Gitana.

"I'll go with you and then when we're done we can go see Alma. I need her POV on this and you can visit Mrs. Givens. I mean, if you don't mind. I don't want to cramp your style," Chase said as she turned toward the freeway.

Bud giggled. "I think that's a perfect idea and if we find the *OED* we'll share it."

"It will help to have another set of eyes. We should run a copy of it and give the illustration to Jacinda. She gets around a lot; maybe she'll find it."

"What about lunch?" Bud said.

"We just had breakfast," Chase said, still feeling the coffee as a turbulent ocean with toast as a raft on top.

"Did you know that peppermint has the homeopathic affect of settling the stomach?" Bud said, digging about in her backpack.

"That must be why I crave Mentos."

"Precisely," Bud said, pulling a pack of Mentos out for Chase's inspection.

Chase went to grab for it and then remembered they were going fifty-five miles an hour. Maybe she really did have a problem. She refocused her concentration. "What do you want for them?"

"I want Taco Bell."

"We can't do that. Gitana expressly forbid it."

"Let's revisit that particular injunction. She said no Taco Bell for *lunch*. The popular assumption of lunchtime is between twelve and one o'clock. She did not forbid Taco Bell at any other time. So if we had Taco Bell at say eleven thirty or one fifteen that would technically not be having lunch at Taco Bell."

"Oh, my god, you're going to grow up to be a Machiavellian. I knew it."

"What she doesn't know won't hurt her."

"Oh, no," Chase wailed. "It's worse than I thought."

"Do you want the Mentos or don't you?" Bud twirled them around.

"All right. This will be our secret, however, and if Gitana does figure it out you're taking the fall," Chase said.

Her cell phone went off and she glanced over at Bud. Chase did not talk on the phone and drive. Bud clicked it on and put it on speaker. Donna was explaining to Bud that they, under no circumstances, were to forget that they had a meeting with the Albuquerque Academy principal at two thirty. Bud stared at Chase in disbelief. Chase pulled the car over at a set of mailboxes.

"What on earth are you talking about?" Chase screamed at the phone. "What meeting?"

Donna's voice was shrill and Chase thought she might burst into tears. Donna had spent the last two weeks in New York with Chase's publisher and had just returned on the red-eye flight the night before. She'd been brought to task on getting Chase to modify her media behavior and had not been the same since. Chase's new book, *Hide and Seek*, a title Chase despised, was due out in May for the summer season, "the best time for trashy reading," according to the New York publicist hired to get the media blitz going. Her name was Myra and she'd also had a go at Donna, telling her that she had to, in Myra's own words, "get that fucking hermit the hell out of the fucking Republic of New Mexicistan, a place that most Americans thought you needed a fucking passport to get into, and get her to start promoting her books like a fucking good girl." Chase's proclivity toward profanity didn't even come close to that of Myra, who used "fuck," "hell" and "shit" in almost every sentence. It seemed the New York people were going to torture Donna until they got Chase to do their bidding. It was really rather savage and underhanded, Chase thought.

"You can't keep doing this to me. I'm your personal assistant." Donna unexpectedly flipped into Myra mode. "I'm supposed to know when you take a fucking shit and now you're not paying attention to the fucking detailed schedule I've fucking set up for you. You ungrateful SOB. I warned you two weeks ago and again this morning on your e-mail which, of course, you never fucking check, and now I'm calling to fucking remind you!"

Chase glanced over at Bud who apparently hadn't paid any attention to the swearing as she had dug Chase's BlackBerry from her backpack and was diligently scrolling through the schedule page. She pointed to the screen and fervently nodded.

"You have to stay away from Myra and the rest of the New York crowd. They've severely damaged your capacity for normal English."

Donna burst into tears or that's what Chase assumed from the horrible gulping noises she heard on the other end. "I'm so sorry. I shouldn't have said those terrible things. I'm positively evil."

"No, you're not. You are absolutely correct. We will have no problem making that appointment, and although I'd like to be more prepared for this meeting I'm sure with Bud's help we will have no troubles. She does speak well."

"Yes, thank goodness or we'd really be fucked. Oh, shit, I've got to stop using that word."

"Don't worry. A couple more days at home in the comforting arms of beloved friends and you'll be good as new. You're probably suffering from jet lag. If not, we'll hire that freaky medicine man guy we met at the Tijeras Art Market and he can cleanse your soul or was it your colon? I can't remember." Chase glanced at the clock. They had to get going.

Donna, being the mind reader she was, said, "I know you have to get going. Gitana told me that you were going to a jumble sale to look for books and I hope you do find the *OED*, although it is highly unlikely. Just don't forget the appointment. Oh, and by the way, Myra knows about the lesbian panel thing but she hasn't told Eliza."

"Oh, fuck. Sorry about that, Bud. How'd she find out about that?"

"I think she has a Chase Banter's favorites link and is keeping really close tabs on you. She thinks it is, as she puts it, 'a fucking top-drawer idea.' She is elated that you are doing something public."

"What about not making my lesbianism apparent to my straight readers? Remember, it's supposed to be a big secret."

"Myra thinks that whole thing is stupid. Lesbians read other mystery fiction and this is good for both your books. Besides, she says that most of the world ignores lezzies, as she calls them, so your straight readers won't have a clue."

"She's probably right. Okay, off we go."

"Don't forget."

"I won't, I promise. I have Bud with me. She's a junior you."

"Tell her I love her."

"Donna loves you."

Bud blew her a kiss.

"Ditto on her end. Ta-ta." Chase spun off the dirt shoulders and headed for the freeway.

"We have approximately two hours to assist at the jumble sale and acquire as many books as possible," Chase said.

Bud nodded, her fingers flying on MapQuest as she researched the fastest route to the academy from the church.

"What are we going to say in your interview with the principal?" Chase said as she merged onto the freeway.

Bud shrugged.

"That's not helpful." Chase popped another Mento into her mouth.

"We'll think of something and if we can't we'll call Gitana," Bud said cheerfully.

"Maybe we'll find a used book on interview techniques."

"We can always hope. We will be in a church and God does work in mysterious ways. And please do not use the holy water stand as a drinking fountain like you did last time."

When they finally found a parking space forty minutes later in the large but very full Church of the Blessed Virgin, Chase had worked herself into a panic attack. The drive had left her too much time to think about the interview with the principal.

"Just breathe," Bud said as she dug around in her backpack for the phone. "I'm going to call Gitana."

"Why don't you ever call her Mom or Mama or one of those other parental names?" Chase asked as she took deep breaths and tried to quiet her palpitating heart.

Bud was dialing the phone. "Because then I'd have to call you 'Dad' and that would be too weird. Besides I find those paternal monikers rather pathetic and belittling. By referring to you and Gitana by those names I'm essentially saying that your complete identity is solely in reference to me which denies you an identity outside of that particular sphere of existence."

"Why do I ask these questions?"

"Beats me."

Gitana picked up. "What is it? Are you all right?"

"You have to stop treating these calls like it's the bat phone. Can't I just call to talk to you?" Bud said.

"Well, yes, of course. But what's wrong?"

"Chase is having a panic attack and although I am aware of the basics of CPR I do not think I have the physical strength to save her life."

"Hand her over."

Bud gave the phone to Chase, who actually was breathing better by then.

"What's wrong?"

"Bud's appointment with the school principal is this afternoon and I don't want to screw it up. Her entire future is in my hands."

"Oh, no, I completely forgot. I would come, but I have that big shipment going out and I can't risk snafus."

"See, I told you it was serious."

"Let me call you right back. Just stay put."

"Okay." Chase meant this until a van pulled up with its entire cargo area loaded with books. Like sale-struck shoppers they gravitated toward the vehicle and offered to help unload it. The elderly lady was happy for their assistance.

"I don't know about the wee one here, but your help would be much appreciated."

"I'll get a cart," Bud said, running for the church basement.

"She's a wee one but a smart one," the woman said.

"So where'd you get all the books?" Chase asked as she scanned the book titles while she unloaded the boxes.

"They were my brother's. He's late now and I wanted his library to go to a good cause. He would want it that way."

"What did he do for a living or did he just like to read a lot?" Chase was already picking books out of the boxes and setting them aside on a piece of newspaper that she'd found in one of the boxes. The woman looked at her queerly. "I'm going to buy these ones...you know, for the wee one."

"Can she read already?"

"Oh, yes. She's a gifted child," Chase said. This was the first time she'd actually said that out loud but like an addict—one who goes to any lengths to get the goods.

"Well, maybe she'll grow up to be an English professor like my brother."

"I hope so."

Bud returned with one cart and Jacinda pushing another. Chase could tell from the color of Bud's cheeks that Jacinda had kissed and pinched them raw, but Bud was good-natured and only rubbed them a little. It was only a matter of seconds before Chase received the same treatment.

"Oh, you two are so sweet, my blessed children, to come help an old woman. You make me so proud," Jacinda cooed.

Chase and Bud looked down at their feet. They were horrid. They'd come to get books. Their charity was a farce. "We're giving the books a good home, surely that counts for something," Chase whispered to Bud.

Bud furrowed her brow for a moment and then nodded. She pulled out her rosary beads and did a few Hail Mary's. "See, it's all better now. Get scanning."

"And she's religious too," said the elderly woman, who Jacinda introduced as Nelda Simons.

Jacinda patted Bud's head.

"You two pick out whatever you want before we put them out and we'll set a good price," Nelda said.

"Yes, we always sell the paperbacks for fifty-cents and the hard covers for a dollar," Jacinda said.

"Oh, I hope they all find homes," Nelda said, putting her hand on her heart.

Jacinda patted her arm. "Of course they will."

Meanwhile Chase was unloading the boxes and Bud was scanning titles. Bud leaned over and whispered, "Can I get an advance on my allowance?"

"The library fund is nonprofit and has its own generous allotment."

"What are we not going to buy so Gitana won't know how much we spent?" Bud said, pawing her way through another box.

"She understands our bibliomania. I'm thinking we'll be creative with the grocery list and I won't go into town as much so that will save on gas."

"Good call."

"Let's get these inside so we can do another load," Chase said, pulling on the cart. Bud followed behind carrying the stack they had so far. She could barely see.

Jacinda came up behind them and relieved Bud of some of her burden. "You don't want a bad back like mine, mija."

"Thank you," Bud said, smiling angelically. That smile could send Jacinda into religious ecstasy.

Once inside, Bud and Jacinda unloaded the books and piled them on long fold-up tables while Chase made loads back and forth, plucking books out as she went along.

On the last load, Chase's cell phone rang.

"What's up?" Chase said.

"It's all set. Donna will go with you. She doesn't know why she didn't think of it in the first place aside from the fact that you should be expected to handle it on your own, but of course you can't and she hasn't slept in two days. Tell Bud not to swear and don't do anything abnormally precocious."

"What are you talking about?" Chase said as she plucked *Rembrandt's Hat* by Bernard Malamud from a stack Jacinda had just set down. She handed it to Bud, who put it in a box they had reserved for their stuff.

"Your appointment at the school. You haven't forgotten already. What are you two doing?"

"We're helping at the jumble sale. What do you think we're doing?"

"Are there books there?"

"There's a few. Grab that one, Bud. Henry James will go quick and we don't have *Washington Square*."

"Oh, great heaven and Mary, it's bibliomania. You're stoned on books."

"I am not. Bud, get that one, we need more biographies, the Albert Schweitzer."

"Chase, stop. Focus. You have to go to the school and you have to have it together. Is Jacinda there?"

"Yes, do you want to talk to her?" She needed to get off the phone if they were going to make it through the rest of the boxes before the sale started.

Chase got Jacinda, who'd moved on to help with the maternity clothes table. "Gitana wants to talk to you." She handed her the phone.

"My daughter, she's very religious too," Jacinda told the women who were helping her fold and display the clothes, referring to Gitana's newly acquired swearing of oaths when the situation warranted it. "She's always giving up great prayers to our beloved savior and saints, especially the Virgin." She lifted the phone to her ear. "Si?"

Jacinda nodded, promised, nodded again, promised again and said, "I love you, mija" and handed Chase the phone. "You must leave in forty-five minutes, go to the school, act as normal as is possible and if you mess this up you will both be grounded for the rest of your lives. I think she means it," Jacinda said, doing a Hail Mary as a precaution.

Bud looked up alarmed. Jacinda came over and gave her a hug. "We can do this. Look for your books and we'll get you out of here or, Great Mother of God, we will all find ourselves in a purgatory not of our own making." She crossed herself and Chase and Bud followed suit, then she set the alarm on the enormous multifunction watch that Bud had given her for Christmas.

It was then that Bud spotted the book in Nelda's hand. She let out a little screech and flew to the box Nelda was unloading. The box was enormous and it had taken Chase, Nelda and Jacinda to ease it onto the cart. Chase and Bud had been so busy unloading the other boxes they'd forgotten about the mother lode of the big box. Chase came over and the three of them peered into the bottom of the box—there, neatly stacked, were nineteen more leather-bound books with *Oxford English Dictionary* embossed on the cover. They were like golden eggs nestled in a cardboard box.

"We'll take those, all of them," Chase blurted. Then, she calmed herself. "What do you want for them? I mean they are certainly worth more than the other hardback books." She didn't want to seem too eager, but she wanted them in her possession before anyone else got ahold of them.

Nelda picked one of them up and gave it a cursory glance. "You want the whole set?"

"Oh, yeah, we might as well. Don't you think, Bud? She collects dictionaries. She likes to learn new words." Chase picked up one of the books and found her hands shaking. She handed it to Bud, who stared at it reverentially, running her fingers along the gold embossing. She had tears in her eyes.

Nelda noticed and stroked Bud's hair. "Oh, mija, you must have these." She looked at Chase. "Can you afford twenty-five dollars?"

"Oh, that's too little for those," Chase said, her conscience getting the better of her.

"I think we need to talk," Bud said, grabbing Chase's hand and pulling her to one side. "We'll be right back," she told Nelda.

"What are you doing? We have to buy those before someone else gets them," Chase said, watching with panic as Nelda unloaded the box.

"Offering too much is going to tip her off as to their worth and maybe she won't want to sell them," Bud whispered fiercely.

Chase looked at her in alarm. She had inadvertently created a maniacal bibliophile. Obsession was a bad thing—even if it was books. "This is for the church and cheating God in a church—his own house, for Christ's sake—is turning your back on God."

"You're not even sure of your faith," Bud muttered.

"I like to hedge my bets," Chase retorted. Nelda was looking at them.

"We, or rather you, will give the church a generous donation to make up for it," Bud suggested.

Chase struggled for a moment and then assented. "All right. Here take the money and pull it out of your purse and make it look like you're spending your last sou," Chase said, giving her the money.

"What's a sou?" Bud said, tucking the money away in her plastic-coated Curious George coin purse.

"Foreign money. It's always in novels—it's a device to indicate the dire straits of the protagonist. We'll look it up in the *OED* when we get home. Quick!"

As they paid Nelda for the *OED* and thirty-two paperbacks, Jacinda's alarm went off. "Mijas, you must go. Hurry!" Jacinda helped them load the car and Bud hugged Nelda, who told her to be a good girl and grow up smart. "You could be the next Nancy Pelosi," Nelda said.

When they got in the car, Bud asked, "Who's Nancy Pelosi?"

"She was the Speaker of the House. I think you might already be smarter, but God forbid if you grow up to be a politician."

"I'd get more funding for libraries and put a stop forever to the banning of books."

"I love you," Chase said.

"Did you like my crocodile tears?"

Chase was pulling out of the church parking lot. "You didn't."

"You wanted them, didn't you?" Bud pulled up the GPS for the academy as they had always gone to the school from the East Mountains not from the South Valley.

"We're probably both going to go to hell for this," Chase said, turning on Atrisco and heading for Central.

"We need to go the other way. The school is on the north end of Tramway. Think of the view of the Sandia Mountains I'll have as I toil in the pursuit of knowledge."

Chase pulled into the parking lot of the latest used car lot and flipped around. "I can't believe you played Nelda like that."

"It was necessary. I had to have the *OED*. It's for my education," Bud said, stroking the volume she'd plucked off the top of the stack. "Look at it. It's so beautiful."

"How much of this playacting stuff do you do?" Chase inquired, suddenly aware that Nelda might not have been the first person to have been treated to Bud's Machiavellian behavior.

"Only when I have to." Bud had the volume opened and was reading the definitions with evident glee.

"Which is?"

"Whenever I want something."

"Oh, my God!"

"Relax. Gitana has radar for it. You're the only one I can sucker punch."

"Great." Chase made a mental note to ask Gitana about the radar thing.

Chapter Fourteen—Consequences
In everything one must consider the end.—La Fontaine

Chase and Bud sat in front of the academy with dolorous faces. They were waiting for Donna, who had yet to appear. They had three minutes until the interview with Principal Melinda Marshall. Chase stared up at the great stone archway that housed massive wooden doors with a heraldic shield on them that had something to do with the original founders of the school. She'd read an account in the brochure but could not remember it. Normally, she would have memorized the entire brochure cover to cover, however, much to her shame, she had been remiss because of all her other obligations.

She had become a distracted parent and in Chase's overachieving obsessive-compulsive world this was unacceptable. Making a mental list of why she'd not memorized the school brochure, she came up with the writing of two novels at the same time and dealing with the dissension and almost all-out warfare between her two muses, the Sacred Muse of the Divine Vulva and the Muse of Commercial Endeavor, each claiming proprietary rights to her imagination, Commercial Endeavor for the sake of monetary gain and Vulva for the salvation of her lesbian soul. Chase had thought this a bit over the top, but Vulva did have a point. Chase had not been particularly lesbian lately, as had been indicated on more than one occasion. What if she really *was* losing her lezzie?

Then there was the SUP group and her retraining in the art of social skills, which had suffered another defeat. Lily, the group coordinator, had been sorely disappointed when the group had been put to the test at a PTO meeting where once again Steinbeck's *The Grapes of Wrath* was about to be banned from the school library along with *Heather Has Two Mommies.* Lily had thought this particular meeting would be a perfect testing ground since it related to Isabel, a librarian who was adamant about censorship, and because Chase and Delia were writers. It was Delia's fault the whole fight started. She said she thought it would be more interesting if they banned Radcliff Hall's *The Well of Loneliness.* Marsha defended her because she'd obviously taken a shine to Delia, and Isabel, getting caught up in the fray, started listing all the books that had ever been banned. She insisted on knowing how the board members felt about these books, noting the reasons why in the past they had been banned and demanding to know did the board agree with those rationales? Chase had done her best to stay out of it until one of the board members, a prissy woman with a pinched expression, got into the demonic nature of homosexuality and how all children with gay parents should be taken away and doled out to proper families. Many unpleasant things were said on both sides and the debacle ended with security being called and the SUP group being escorted off the school premises.

And then there was… Chase would have gone on if Bud hadn't yanked her back from her neurosis. "We have to go," Bud said.

Chase leaned back in her seat and sighed. "I don't know if I can do this."

"We don't have any choice."

At that particular moment, a troop of children a little older than Bud came tromping behind a teacher in single file—their stance almost alike as they trundled past. In their uniforms they looked like Mussolini's Blackshirts and Chase's stomach dropped. "We could homeschool you. I'll hire tutors."

"Then I'll end up being as socially inept as you," Bud said, opening the car door.

"What's wrong with that?" Chase called after her. She still hadn't removed herself from the driver's seat. Bud came around to her side.

"It's a cop-out. I can be a good little soldier and still keep my sense of individualism. That's your problem—you think that if you even so much as dunk a toe in the raging river of homogeneity that you will lose your sense of self. It's not like that. The raging river is the challenge, it's the quest, it's the odyssey."

Chase couldn't remember the grammatical term for three beautifully linked clauses, but Bud had it down. "If I let you go to school will you at least try to win a Pulitzer?"

Bud pulled her from the car. "I will give it my best effort."

"I don't want it to be one of those mean autobiographies that slam the parents."

"Then I suggest you watch your back," Bud said.

"Bud!"

Bud squared back her shoulders, studied the Latin inscription above the massive wood doors, sighed heavily and then marched forward.

Chase scrambled behind her. "Please God, let this go well." They both crossed themselves.

Principal Marshall's office was prominently marked with a gold placard. They walked into the reception area. Chase felt a certain trepidation, which she associated with being called into the principal's office for some offense in her youth. She made her best attempt at looking confident. Bud sat down and looked Pre-Raphaelite angelic.

"Hello, we have an appointment with Principal Marshall." Chase didn't know what else to call her as she didn't know if she was a Doctor, a Mrs. or a Ms. type of woman and she didn't want to get off on the wrong foot.

The receptionist was a kindly looking woman of fifty-something and her gray hair and round glasses gave her the air of someone who would be gentle with small children. Chase hoped this was not a masquerade just to suck people into turning their children over to the educational equivalent of the Gestapo.

"Oh, yes, Ms. Banter, I believe. Melinda is expecting you."

Chase glanced up at the clock hanging behind the receptionist's desk. They weren't technically late—they were essentially right on time.

"Oh, don't worry. You're not tardy. Melinda is just really looking forward to meeting you…and Angelica, of course. Right this way, please."

Chase glanced at Bud for some sign of her take on the situation. Bud furrowed her brow and shrugged.

Before they'd gotten to the office, which was down the hall a short way, the door to the office flew open and an attractive, yet competent-looking woman in her late forties, dressed stylishly in what Chase knew to be an Ann Taylor business suit—blazer and matching trouser set—stepped out. Her hair was dark and cut in the latest above-the-shoulder-but-below-the-chin ragged cut that Chase always found odd because to her this expensive hairdo looked like it was done with the edge of a meat cleaver rather than styling shears, but Lacey claimed it was the height of fashion nonetheless. Lacey had transcended this look and grown her hair out. She now tied it back in a ponytail because she felt this was her true lesbian hairdo—although it was not one of the seven lesbian hairstyles that Lacey had been told about during her initiation into the subculture of true lesbianism. Chase understood none of this—perhaps another sign of "losing her lezziness."

"I'm so pleased to meet you," said Melinda, who insisted that Chase use her first name as she pumped Chase's hand and gave Bud a cursory, however, not unkind look and bade them sit.

"Now, I think you should tell us a little about yourself, Chase, may I call you Chase?" Melinda asked.

Chase wanted to be amiable. "Of course. What would you

like to know?" she replied, trying to think of parental litanies. All she could come up with was, "I feel that being a parent is one of the most important episodes of my life and I want my child to have a good, I mean, an outstanding education."

Bud visibly blanched. "Banal."

"Good word, Angelica."

"You can call me Bud."

"Ah, you have a moniker. We are very respectful of the student's right to call him or herself by a chosen name. If you prefer Bud then Bud it shall be." Melinda marked this down on her record file. Both Bud and Chase glanced at it.

"No, what I meant, Chase, was how do you think the creative process affects you as a parent?"

Chase was silent.

"She means your writing," Bud said, pointing to Chase's stack of lesbian novels topped off by her two mystery novels that sat on the corner of Melinda's desk.

"Oh."

"I am a big fan. Now, Bud, this does not mean that you have no standing on your own. I can already tell that you are well above average and we will leave it at that because brilliance is best encouraged by civility and structure."

"What are you basing that on?" Bud asked.

Chase thought Bud was holding her own.

"Chase's personal assistant, Donna, has minutely documented a CV for you that lists your achievements as well as your Mensa score."

"You took the Mensa test? When did you do that?"

"Addison thought it would be interesting so we did it online. She actually scored higher, but she said that's because I am four. My years of study have not exceeded hers so I don't feel too bad. I don't know what my list of achievements are."

"Your grandmother supplied your reading list."

"Your reading list?" Chase's voice had gotten high and a little squeaky. Bud pinched her and gave her the don't-fuck-this-up-or-we're-dead look.

"I think it's quite diverse and I am aware that some of these books were read to you but that still qualifies."

"Oh, I see, well, that's great," Chase said.

"Now, back to you, Chase. How did you come to be a writer?"

Chase scrambled as the spotlight was now on her. Bud smiled encouragingly. "Well, I used to have these running daydreams as a child and then I just started writing them down and then rewriting them and then..." God, she hoped she didn't sound completely unhinged.

"I remember that you told me once that coming up with stories was like playing a chess game that you were totally in charge of, and so plot was like figuring out the moves and the chess players all had histories and motives and that's what made the story—a combination of strategy and language as well as a good dose of managerial finesse," Bud said.

"Exactly!" Chase said.

"How interesting." Melinda seemed satisfied with the answer and Bud and Chase let out a collective sigh.

"Would you like me to sign your books?" Chase asked. Bud smiled encouragingly. She dug a pen out of her backpack and quickly handed it to Chase.

"I would recommend using the Chancery Cursive script for this particular signing, considering the prestige and posterity of this fine institution," Bud said.

"Good idea," Chase said.

"Oh, I'd be delighted." Melinda scooted the books over. "Here, sit at my desk and I'll give Bud a quick tour of the school."

"I'd love to see the library," Bud said.

They left and Chase got down to business. At Donna's suggestion, she had taught herself calligraphy—so that each reader could choose how he or she wanted the book signed and each one would feel special. This, Donna told her, would give Chase something to concentrate on that was productive instead of focusing on how miserable she was. So far the idea had worked, but they'd only done it for virtual signings that Chase had done online. Readers printed off the inscription and then pasted it in the front of the book. This had been hugely popular and it was all thanks to Donna's amazing, imaginative approach to marketing. Myra could go fuck herself, Chase thought as she carefully inscribed Melinda's books.

When Bud and Melinda returned, they were holding hands and talking amicably.

"All done," Chase said, meaning the book inscriptions and hopefully the interview.

"Oh, it's beautiful," Melinda said, looking at the title page of the first book.

"So?" Chase asked.

"It's all settled. Bud is a shoo-in, but let's keep the Mensa score to ourselves. This does not mean you'll get to slack, young lady. Your teachers will be notified of your abilities and you will be given honors classes as you progress."

Bud groaned.

"What did you expect?" Chase said, frowning at her.

"An outstanding education," Bud said weakly.

"Now, I suggest you have one last joyous summer before the work of your life begins." Melinda shook Bud's hand and then Chase's. "So when does your new book come out?"

"In May. I'll be sure to send you a copy."

"That would be splendid." Melinda beamed.

Chapter Fifteen—Faith

Attempt the end and never stand to doubt;
Nothing's so hard but search will find it out.—Herrick

Having congratulated themselves on their performance with Melinda, Chase and Bud disobeyed orders and went to Taco Bell, where they shamelessly stuffed themselves. When they returned home with Mentos on their breath and a taco sauce stain on Bud's white polo shirt courtesy of Chase, who'd been eagerly reading the packet caption and opening it at the same time so that she had sprayed her luncheon companion with sauce, they were met with complete panic by Gitana and Donna—so much of it, in fact, that their indiscretions went quite unnoticed.

Donna gripped Chase by the shoulders and looked pleadingly into her eyes, "Tell me you didn't fuck it up."

"We didn't fuck it up," Bud replied, as she deftly slid a sweatshirt off the coatrack in the corner and slipped the garment on, thereby covering the stain.

"Bud, great God of mercy, don't talk like that," Gitana said, squatting down to look in Bud's eyes for confirmation. "Really?"

"Principal Melinda is a big Chase Banter fan. She has all her books and Chase autographed them. So we are a shoo-in," Bud said. "She did say that I must not mention my Mensa score."

"Mensa score?" Gitana looked over at Donna, who'd released Chase and was now pouring herself a shot of tequila. She shook her head.

"It's a long story. I think I'll go take a bath," Bud said, opening the fridge and pulling out a squeeze box of grape juice.

Chase suspected Bud wanted to avoid all the adult hoopla and having done her part was making a run for it.

"A bath?" Gitana said, glancing at her watch. Bud usually took her bath right before bed, not before dinner.

"I got pretty dirty at the jumble sale, but we did find the entire twenty volumes of the *OED*," Bud said over her shoulder on her way out of the kitchen.

"You know, I got pretty dirty too. I think I'll go take a shower," Chase said, hoping she could pull the same tactic.

Gitana blocked her way. "I don't think so."

"Well, I should at least get the books out of the car," Chase said, making for the kitchen door. This time Donna blocked her path.

"Tell us everything," Gitana said.

"I'm so sorry I didn't make it in time," Donna interjected. "I saw the Hummer in the parking lot at the school, but by that time I couldn't just go barging in without making you look incompetent."

"Thank you, Donna," Chase said, not knowing if she should be offended or not.

"So I e-mailed Bud's CV to the secretary, who promised to get it to the principal's office ASAP."

"Which she did," Chase said.

"Did you happen to catch the secretary's name?" Donna said.

Chase thought hard, trying to re-create in her mind the small brown wood plaque with the gold lettering that sat on the secretary's desk. Donna stared at her intently as if willing her to remember. "It was Eleanor Raymond."

Donna hugged her.

"Why?" Chase asked.

"So I can send her a thank-you gift," Donna said. She screwed up her face. "Did you notice anything about her desk, like did she have a candy dish or a vase or a fancy pen or…"

"I'll send her an orchid," Gitana said impatiently. "Now tell us what happened."

"It was exactly like Bud said. Really. I signed her books and she gave Bud a tour of the school. Bud took the Mensa test with Addison's help and Bud will have to do some accelerated coursework. That's all."

Both Donna and Gitana looked grossly disappointed. "That's it," Gitana said. She took the bottle of tequila from Donna and poured herself a shot, slamming it back and wincing.

"So let me get this straight, you two have been getting yourselves all tied up in knots for nothing—imagining all sort of horrendous scenarios based on nothing but irrational fears. Is that correct?"

They both looked sheepish.

"Isn't that the kind of thing you always accuse me of?"

Donna studied her fingernails. "I bought you a five-pack of Mentos," she said, pulling it from her bag.

Chase snatched them. "Where were you, by the way?"

Donna glanced at Gitana, who pursed her lips. "She was tied up with something," Gitana said. She poured Donna another shot of tequila. "You should stay here tonight. I think we all need a little downtime—pizza, movie and a few cocktails."

"Yes," Donna said, sighing.

"What happened?" Chase said, eyeing them.

Donna blurted, "I got a speeding ticket—that damn Myra had me on the phone so long I left late and then…" she started blubbering.

"A speeding ticket?" Chase was horrified. It was as if Donna had just been accused of butchering an entire kindergarten class.

"Don't be such a hard-ass. People do occasionally get speeding tickets," Gitana said.

"How fast?" Chase asked, her eyes narrowing.

"It wasn't that bad," Gitana said, patting Donna's shoulder.

"How fast?"

"Sixty-eight in a thirty-five," Donna screeched out.

Chase was speechless.

Donna blathered, "I didn't mean to. I wasn't really aware of how fast I was going until the, you know, red lights started flashing. I'm probably going to have to go to traffic school if I want to keep it off my record."

At this Chase brightened. "Can I go with you?"

They both turned to look at her in amazement. "Why?" Gitana asked.

"Because they give you all sorts of tips on safe driving. It's like getting lessons for free, well, not exactly free. How much is the ticket for?"

"A hundred and twenty-five dollars," Donna said, equally as brightly. "I thought that was a deal, considering."

"It was, considering that at that speed, you could have killed a dog, a child, an elderly person or yourself," Chase said.

"Chase!" Gitana said as she watched Donna's eyes fill with tears.

"No, she's right. I was being an irresponsible driver and a disobedient citizen," Donna said.

Then Chase felt bad. "I know you're truly sorry and you won't do it again." She patted Donna's shoulders.

"Who made you the traffic goddess?" Gitana said.

"I got a safe driver certificate from the insurance company and I know about that ticket you got in the safety corridor."

"How'd you find out about that?" Gitana said.

"Little eyes, ears and mouths."

"How come you didn't say anything?" Gitana asked.

Chase pulled a beer out of the fridge. "Because I thought better of it. Bud and I had a little talk. We decided that it was her job to keep a sharp eye on the speedometer and to indicate any infractions at the time of occurrence. We decided to let you slide."

Gitana pinched her. "That was sneaky."

"So was not telling me about the ticket." She sipped her beer and sat next to Donna, who still had her head in her hands on the kitchen island. She patted her back. "I think we've all learned valuable lessons here today."

"Gag me," Gitana said, digging out the pizza dough from the freezer.

Donna sat up. "I'm sorry I let you down today." Her eyes were bleary.

"You didn't let me down. You made me live up to my obligations without having my hand held. That's a big thing." She kissed Donna's cheek. "Now, help me get all those books out of the car. It'll cheer you up."

"Oh, yeah, sure," Gitana said. She shook her head and grated the parmesan cheese.

Later that night as Gitana and Donna sat in the den laughing uproariously at *The Beverly Hills Chihuahua* in a somewhat inebriated state, Chase and Bud sat cuddled in bed, going over *OED* definitions with Chase adding details about the references to books Bud had yet to read. As there were stress-reducing drunkards downstairs there were book-stoned occupants upstairs.

"Today was really hard on them," Bud said, looking up from the book. "I'm not certain we shouldn't be offended."

"I think we might have to cut them some slack. I have been known to mess things up," Chase said.

"You don't do it so much anymore," Bud conceded.

"Thanks, but nonetheless I can understand their apprehension. What they fail to notice is that I have you now and you help keep things straight."

"I really feel that we are a good team, the yin and yang of it. We should look that up."

"Let's."

"We have to make that donation tomorrow," Bud said, looking suddenly worried.

"Are you concerned about God's low opinion of us?" Chase said as she reached for the "Y" volume of the *OED*. They were surrounded by all twenty volumes.

"Jacinda says it's best not to mess around with the big guy."

"I'll do it first thing in the morning."

"I don't think they're going to feel good in the morning," Bud replied, taking the book from Chase as the laughter downstairs grew louder.

"No, they're not."

Chapter Sixteen—Desire
Can one desire too much of a good thing?—Cervantes

"I don't know if this is such a great idea," Chase said, as Lou led her into her store, Erotique. She did a double take at the leather outfit on the mannequin located at the entrance to the showroom.

"Her name is Monique," Lou said, guiding Chase further into the den of sex.

"Nice outfit, I've never seen one quite like it." Chase looked around, horrified.

"You're going to be all right," Lou said as she flipped on more lights. Chase had arrived just as the store was opening.

"Well, I mean, maybe I've changed my mind." She glanced at the dildo display and tried to imagine Gitana's response to something like that.

"Chase, when was the last time you two made love?" Lou

straightened up one of the dildos, an overly large, purple one.

"Um, let me think. It seems like it was just the other day," Chase fumbled.

"You can't remember."

"We've been kind of busy and Bud is around a lot—that is a legitimate complication and I guess I haven't been feeling very lesbian lately." Chase studied the lube display. Had vaginal dryness set in already? she wondered.

"You're not a bad lesbian. You just need to set aside special time just for the two of you. Now, look over here."

Just then the shop bell rang and a customer came in. Chase prayed it wasn't anyone she knew or who would know her. That was the problem with book signings—people were starting to recognize her. She looked across the shop to see Marsha from her SUP group—"I-might-be-a-lesbian" Marsha.

"What are you doing here?" Chase said.

"What are you doing here?"

Chase groped. "Research."

"Let's be honest. You want to pep up your love life," Lou said, looking first at Chase and then at Marsha, "and you, I've seen you at the Community Center with Lacey so I'd say you were bi-curious."

"Oh, God, this is so embarrassing," Marsha said, heading for the door.

"Get back here. Lou is going to help us," Chase said.

"I think we should start with the bedroom ensemble—the romance room."

Chase blanched and Marsha's face displayed terror.

Lou led them back to a small room that was set up as a display. It was an honest-to-goodness bedroom complete with a queen-sized bed and two nightstands. One side of the bed had the coverlet pulled back so the red satin sheets were exposed.

"Now, both of you get in. I'm certain neither of you have satin sheets and there is nothing like them against bare skin. They are fabulous."

"I am not taking my clothes off," Chase and Marsha said in unison.

"You've got shorts on, that will suffice."

They both looked down at their legs like they were realizing for the first time they were indeed wearing shorts, the fine June weather having warranted such attire.

"Freshly shaved is best. Hop in." Lou pushed them toward the bed. She was a persuasive saleswoman; both of them did as she instructed.

"Okay, now hold out your wrists." They complied as she rubbed scented oil on them and then she lit fragrant candles and turned down the lights. They sat rigid. "You two look like virgins not excited about the consummation."

Marsha stared at Chase. "I'm supposed to feel sexy and relaxed, right?"

"The sheets are nice," Chase offered.

Lou hit the CD player and soft music played. "Relax, just breathe and think about your girlfriends."

"I don't have one," Marsha blurted.

"Not as yet," Lou said as she sat on the edge of the bed. Chase was feeling more relaxed and she was definitely having lesbian thoughts.

"I think this might work. It's a little packaged, but all romance is except this is more sensual," Chase said, smelling the oil on her wrist. "Can I put this all over her body?"

"That's what it's for."

"I like the candles," Marsha assented.

"They are sandalwood, it's less intrusive than some of our other scents—a good beginner scent."

"Okay, we'll take it," Chase said.

"But I don't have anyone to share it with," Marsha said.

"With this stuff when you do you'll be a hit." Chase was full of lesbian thoughts now. They'd need a babysitter.

"That's the spirit," Lou said. She went in the back to get two of the All-Inclusive Wonder Night Kits.

As Lou rang up the sale, Chase inquired about yoga. "You're going tonight, right. I can't do it without you."

"Of course. Last week Peter had a summer cold and I didn't want him giving it to the rest of the class."

"Great. See you tonight."

Outside the shop, Marsha said, "Can we go have coffee?"

"Sure." Chase thought a latte and a biscotti sounded good. They went to the Cuppa Joe's on the corner. She had no idea that she'd be paying for this privilege by listening to Marsha's entire life history, not to mention that the biscotti was not its usual good self. It seemed to have overextended its normal life span.

"I mean, I don't know what I was thinking when I got married. It just seemed like the thing to do. Looking back on it now, I think I liked his family so I overlooked his faults. And he was so bad in bed. I didn't have much experience but it's not like the Middle Ages anymore. One knows things and then, of course, you hear things. I mean, he was a ram-bam-not-even-a-thank-you man. He'd just hop on and thrust away, make a deposit and roll over and fall asleep. Do women do that?"

Chase wished her latte would cool off enough so she could guzzle it and run. Other people's sex lives did not interest her and hearing about them was even worse. "Do what?" She didn't know if Marsha was referring to the ramming part or the falling asleep part.

"Fall asleep after sex." Marsha looked at her intently.

"I suppose it depends on what time it is," Chase replied. If she and Gitana made love in the morning, or when they used to before Bud hopped in bed with them at the crack of dawn, they didn't fall asleep, but if they made love before bed, they did. The "used to" line stuck in her mind like a goathead spur in her heel—instant and sharp. She and Gitana did need to work on their sex life. Did having children always smother a libido? She'd ask Lou. Lou, it appeared, knew everything about libidos.

"But women are better than men in bed," Marsha said, snapping off a chunk of biscotti with a decisive movement like she'd already made up her mind.

"From what I've heard...I've never actually slept with a man." Chase chugged her latte.

"You've never slept with a man!" Marsha said it a little too loudly and Cuppa Joe's became quiet for a moment and people stared.

Chase intently studied her coffee cup. "Uh, no."

Marsha noticed her faux pas and then, in a suddenly assertive moment, said equally loudly, "Good for you. You'll make a great nun."

Chase smiled. "I'm not sure Lily would approve, but it was a good social lie."

"I'm sorry. I didn't mean to do that. I've just never known anyone who hasn't…except nuns."

Chase studied her. "Marsha, is there someone who you'd like to sleep with?"

"You, if you weren't married, but as a second choice, I'd have to say Lou," Marsha replied candidly.

"So why don't you do it?"

"You mean jump into Sappho's pool, just like that?" Marsha said.

"You don't appear to be overly impressed with men and you seem to be more woman-oriented so I don't see how it could hurt. I'm not certain about Lou, though. She's had a bit of a rough ride and I don't think a roll in the hay is what she's looking for, but there are plenty of others."

"Oh, I'm looking for long-term," Marsha said emphatically.

"I see."

"So I am going to ask Lou out. We can have a drawn-out dating period before we have sex."

"You might want to ask Lou about that," Chase said cautiously.

"Oh, I will."

"Like tomorrow or the next day, perhaps," Chase said, alarmed at the speed at which Marsha was heading for Sappho's pond and that fateful jump.

"Well, of course. I can't go walking right back in there and say now that I've got this set-up, do you want to try it out with me and by the way I've never done this before. I'll send her flowers first."

That night at yoga class they were practicing the *ubhaya padangusthasana* pose, which Chase referred to as the trying-to-pull-your-toes-while-lying-chin-in-on-your-back. She would never understand why yoga had such a big word fetish. Why couldn't they just call it something like, "just-try-and-get-those-toes-shoved-in-your-mouth-while-lying-on-your-back   pose?" She frowned. Perhaps that wasn't any better. She had no idea when she signed up for yoga class that she'd be learning a foreign language at the same time. Bud did not seem to have any trouble with the language barrier or the poses and neither did Peter, so both she and Lou looked to them for guidance.

As she felt her hamstrings stretching to a place they'd never been before, she said, "Lou, do you like flowers?" This seemed like a good intro line to the Marsha dilemma. Chase was suffering a pang of conscience about letting Marsha loose on Lou. That hadn't been her intention. She'd just thought at the time that Marsha might as well stop dilly-dallying about her sexuality and make a decision. She was hoping Lou thought flowers were stupid and Marsha's plan would fail.

"I love flowers. People don't seem to bother with them anymore. I'm a true romantic at heart. I can't remember the last time someone sent me flowers."

"Oh. I can bring you some. My flower garden is just starting to bloom." June was the perfect time for fresh flowers. The first buds were stunning, as if the plant was showing its stuff after striving so hard. She was teaching Bud all the names of the flowers as part of her at-home nature studies. Chase wanted her up and running for school in the fall so she'd bumped up study hour to twice a day. Bud didn't seem to mind. Chase had a sneaking suspicion that Bud intuited that knowing more would ease up her study burden in the fall.

"That would be great."

Chase tried another tactic. "So what did you think of Marsha?'"

Bud nudged her. They were starting a new pose. "*Natarajasana.*"

"Which one is that?" Chase whispered.

"The Heil-Hitler-while-trying-to-stick-your-foot-up-your-butt one," Bud responded.

"Ugh," Chase said, assuming the pose. Lou was already in position and looked pretty good.

"I thought she was nice. I hope she finds someone. Is she gay? I couldn't really tell."

"Not at the moment. She wants to be and she's lesbian shopping."

"Well, I'm sure the sheet set will be a pleasant surprise."

"To everyone but you, and it's you she has her eye on."

Lou's back foot hit the ground with a thud. Peter looked over at her, alarmed. "It's all right, honey. Mommy just lost her balance."

"I shouldn't have blurted it out like that, but I didn't know what else to do. She's going to send you flowers and wants to have a long-term relationship."

There was another thud. Paul, the instructor looked up. "Lou, you can hold on to the side bar if you want. There is no shame in yoga."

"Uh, no. I'm all right."

Bud gave Chase a reproachful glance.

"Sorry."

They didn't resume their conversation until after class as Bud and Peter were picking up the cockroaches from under the Dixie cups and giving the relocation bag to Paul, who smiled at them benevolently.

"I don't think dating Marsha is a good idea," Lou said.

"Maybe after she's run through a few unsatisfactory girlfriends and gotten enough girl-guide lesbian badges it would be all right, but I really think cardinal Lesbian Rule Number One applies here," Chase said.

"Don't date straight women." Lou nodded sagely.

"Or baby dykes unless you're hard of heart and can withstand the growing pains."

"I'm soft-hearted, and I have all the growing pains I need with that little one," Lou said, as they watched Peter give Bud's hair a tug and she belted him in the arm. "She's got a pretty good left."

"Great. I can see it now. I'll be going to school to talk about Bud's aggressive approach to diplomacy."

They watched as Bud and Peter smiled at each other and came toward them holding hands. "Do you think that was some sort of early childhood courting dance?" Lou said.

"I hope so. If she turns out gay I'm going to be in big trouble."

"Why?"

"Because everyone will think I brainwashed her into being a lesbian," Chase said.

Lou seemed to ponder this. "Well, most of us gay people are begotten of straight parents, so according to the stats it would seem Bud has a pretty high chance of being straight coming from two gay parents."

"Of course, I won't let her date until she's at least twenty-five and out of college," Chase said emphatically.

Lou smiled enigmatically.

Chapter Seventeen—Love
My Lesbia, let us live and love.—Catullus

While Gitana was taking a bath, Chase fixed up the bedroom. Bud was spending the night with Stella, ostensibly to help her with the big gala dinner party the following evening. Bud had already spent the night at Jacinda's but not at Stella's. Bud had instituted these sleepovers as an apron string-cutting device saying, "I'm not a baby anymore. I have to make my way in the world."

To which Chase had responded, "You're four."

"Going on five and I'm mature for my age. These are my highly responsible relatives who have raised children and know all about us. I think it will be all right."

Not wanting to discredit these relatives, Chase was stuck for an answer. Gitana had been the deciding vote. "Of course, she can spend the night with Jacinda and Stella. They're her grandparents and they'd love to have her. You can't smother her. We don't want her to get weird."

Trying to make the best of the situation and to take her mind off empty nest syndrome, Chase was going to break out the All-Inclusive Wonder Night Kit. As she set up the incense holder with the sandalwood scent she felt a bit like Wile E. Coyote with his kit from Acme. She put the satin sheets on the bed and set the oil on the nightstand. She'd downloaded, or rather Bud had downloaded, the soft music on her iPod, which stood ready in its dock on the dresser. Then she lit the candles. She stood back and surveyed the room.

"Honey, what are you doing in there?" Gitana inquired. "And what's that smell?"

She heard the splash of the water as Gitana got out of the tub. Chase peeked around the door. "Don't put your clothes on yet," she instructed.

"Why?"

"You'll see. I have a surprise for you," Chase said.

"You didn't buy me clothes, did you?"

"Of course not, especially since Myra's got me a lifetime supply of gift cards for the Gap—not one of your favorite stores."

"Too stodgy," Gitana said.

Chase turned on the music as Gitana entered the transformed bedroom. She wrinkled her brow. "What's all this?"

"It's the All-Inclusive Wonder Night Kit," Chase said, beaming.

"Wonder night?"

"I personally think it should be called the Wonderful Night Kit. Come here, sit on the sheets. Did you shave your legs? It's best that way."

Gitana sat down and ran her hands along the sheets. Chase studied the scented oil and suddenly ruminated on the effect of oil on satin sheets. Maybe she should just put a little under Gitana's nose and call it good. The incense was nice, though.

"These are smooth, but what is this all about?"

Chase went to fiddle with the iPod so she wouldn't have to look at Gitana. She heard the soft swishing of the sheets and then Gitana was behind her, putting her arms around Chase's hips.

"Have you been missing something lately?" she said as she nestled her face into Chase's neck.

Chase flushed and her lesbian nether regions amped up as Gitana pulled her hips into her and then ran her hands up the inside of Chase's thighs.

"Maybe a little. It seems I've been neglecting my Sapphic duties." She turned around and said, "I've been missing you in my arms while we do amorous things."

"Well, let's see what we can do about that," Gitana said, taking her hand and leading her to the bed. She slipped off Chase's T-shirt and boxer shorts, lingering in the down under until Chase quivered. "I think your Sapphic tendencies are returning."

As they slipped between the sheets and into each others' arms, Chase thought that Lou did know a lot about the erotic side of things. She wondered if the shop had a library of sorts—certainly this kind of stuff could be even further enhanced.

"You didn't have to go to all this trouble, but it is awfully nice," Gitana said, as she ran her index finger around Chase's nipple and then down her stomach.

"There's scented oil, but I can't figure out how you can use it and not fuck up the sheets," Chase said. She was about to elucidate on the virtues of the rest of the kit when Gitana slipped her tongue between Chase's legs and she quite forgot about the kit altogether. When Gitana eased her fingers inside and came up to kiss Chase and guide her fingers inside her, Chase forgot the rest of the world. They moved in sync until, as if planned, their bodies convulsed. Chase moaned rather loudly and then she remembered Bud. "Bud will hear."

"Bud's on a sleepover," Gitana said as she gently pushed Chase's head between her legs.

Chase ran the tip of her tongue up the inside of Gitana's thigh. "I think I could learn to like sleepovers." She plunged her tongue between Gitana's legs and tasted the sweetness.

Gitana gasped as she said, "Why do you think they were invented?"

They didn't talk anymore after that. It was all body talk and there was a lot of it. Their bodies must have seen this as two long lost friends being reunited. As a point of reference for Marsha,

Chase thought, they did fall asleep after making love that night but did not in the morning. They decided the scented oil made the dogs smell nice.

In the morning they ate a huge breakfast of waffles, scrambled eggs, hash browns and yogurt with blueberries.

"I'm famished," Gitana said, putting another waffle on her plate.

"I think it was all the p.m. aerobics," Chase said, helping herself to more hash browns.

"You can tell Lou her All-Inclusive Wonder Night Kit makes the perfect prelude to an evening of amazing sex," Gitana said, running her hand up the inside of Chase's thigh.

"Maybe we could take a quick shower together before we pick up Bud?" Chase suggested.

"Or we could get Donna to pick up Bud. She's bringing up my fancy dress and the agenda for the next three days of our lives, which are not going to be fun," Gitana said.

"At least you get to miss the Santa Fe sightseeing tour with Lacey and the Literary Furies."

Gitana put her hand on her heart. "I am so disappointed."

"In lieu of that I think we both deserve a bit of fun and frolic," Chase said. She moaned a little as Gitana pressed her hand against her lesbian equipment, which responded quickly. "I'll call Donna."

Gitana kissed Chase's neck while she talked to Donna.

"Chase, you really need to be on your best behavior. Promise me no off-the-cuff odd remarks, no neurotic moments, no disappearing, no being impatient, no arguing with Lacey or anyone else, for that matter, about the state of the Lesbian Nation," Donna said.

"So you're pretty much asking me to completely revamp my entire personality in the next..." she glanced at the clock, "eleven hours."

"Would you? Just for me. Myra will kill me if this falls through and then I'll have to go back to New York and be retrained and you know I don't like New York, it's too fast for me. I'm just a small-town girl from a backward state and I can't handle all that noise and rushing about. Besides, I got a really bad attack of gastritis while I was there—all that strange food and no red or green chili."

"Donna, stop! You're beginning to sound like the old me. I will be on my best behavior and Gitana is helping me realize my potential as a new and improved person. So we'll see you in a couple hours."

"Don't forget to finish the blurb on your lesbian novel and a sample chapter, preferably one with a hot sex scene in it."

"I won't." Chase clicked off and put Gitana's hand inside the waistband of her boxer shorts. "I've never done it in a chair."

"Yes, you have. I tied you up once—it was your office chair in the writing studio."

"The good old days," Chase said as she moved against Gitana's hand.

"Are back again," Gitana added.

"Yes, they are."

Later in the writing studio Chase was arguing with her muses. The Muse of the Divine Vulva was threatening to throttle the Muse of Commercial Endeavor. The Divine Vulva was usually pretty laid-back and spent a good portion of her time in a beach chair, eating shrimp cocktails, drinking piña coladas and singing that stupid song about piña coladas. Chase still couldn't figure this out because she didn't eat shrimp, having seen them in their natural habitat at the estuary in Rocky Point, and she positively despised fruity drinks, so why her muse was such an avid fan of both of them didn't make any sense.

Divine Vulva was out of her beach chair and fuming. "This is none of your business. I'm helping her decide on the sample chapter and it's going to be hot, hot, hot."

"I know this is for the Lesbian Nation. However, that does not exclude me from the discussion. I think she should sample a chapter that displays the depth of her writing skills—like the library scene where the protagonist is talking about Mary Daly and the politics of language," Commercial Endeavor retorted, picking up the stapler, her weapon of choice.

"Put that down. This is a civil discussion," Chase said, making a grab for the stapler. She missed.

"I will only use it for purposes of self-defense," Commercial Endeavor said sanctimoniously.

Divine Vulva glowered but took a step backward. "That chapter is stupid. It's nothing but talk and more talk."

"Hey," Chase said.

"That chapter is necessary. The mission statement of the commune is about self-enlightenment and that scene demonstrates that very theme," Commercial Endeavor stated.

"Oh, get over it. The commune is about lesbians being funny and having sex," Divine Vulva said.

Chase was offended. "No, it's not. It's about growth, redemption…"

"And sex," Divine Vulva cut in.

This would have gone on forever had Donna not arrived and put a stop to it. Divine Vulva flounced down in her beach chair and snatched up her piña colada. She gave Commercial Endeavor the finger but she had resumed reading *Publisher's Weekly.* Chase sat with her head in her hands.

"What's wrong? Are you feeling all right? Do you have a fever? Oh, no, you can't be sick. It'll ruin everything." Donna pulled Chase's head back and felt her forehead. "You don't have a fever. It's not mental, is it? Have you taken your medication?"

"Donna, relax. I'm fine. I just can't figure out what to use for the sample chapter. One side of me thinks I should read something hot, hot, hot"—she glanced in the direction of Divine Vulva, who stuck her tongue out at Commercial Endeavor, who disdained to look. "But the other side thinks I should choose something with more substance." At this Commercial Endeavor nodded approvingly and Divine Vulva slurped her drink loudly.

Donna sat on the couch and looked thoughtful. "Why don't you do both?"

"I don't think there is a scene that has both."

Donna, who'd read everything Chase had ever written, including rough drafts which normally Chase never trusted to anyone, snapped her fingers. "I know. How about that scene in the garden where Elsa reads Anne Cameron's *Earth Witch?*

Now, that scene is hot and educational. Anyone that reads erotic, feminist poetry and makes love to you at the same time could live in my bed forever. I love that scene and if I ever wanted to be a character it would be Terry at that moment."

"You are fucking brilliant. What would I do without you? Now where is that scene?" Chase rifled through the manuscript.

"It starts on page two hundred and thirty."

Chase raised an eye. "How in the hell do you know that?" she said as she found the page.

"The Muslims often memorize the Koran. I make it a point to memorize your fiction."

"Wow."

"Okay, let me make you a copy off the hard drive and I'll enlarge the font size so that it'll be easier to read."

Chase suddenly felt uncertain. "I don't know if I can do this."

Donna came over and rubbed her shoulders. "I'm packing the audience with your friends. Every time you feel the least bit nervous just find the face of someone who knows and loves you. Remember your first book reading at the Lesbian Lights Bookstore? Did I not hook you up?"

"Yes." Chase still felt forlorn. "You know I don't do well under pressure and sitting on a panel is not going to be a low-key event and it's going to be web-streamed. This is like my worst fucking nightmare," Chase croaked. She was working herself up into a complete panic attack.

Donna pulled a Dos Equis from the dorm fridge, opened it quickly, shoved in a lime and pulled a pack of Mentos and a vial of lavender oil from her briefcase. She handed it all to Chase. She rubbed Chase's temples with the lavender oil while Chase sucked on a Mento and chugged the beer.

"Better?"

"I think so. Thank you."

"Don't worry. You didn't give me a chance to show you my new secret weapon." Donna pulled out a tiny electronic device and handed it to Chase.

"What is it?"

"The world's smallest Bluetooth. Put it in your ear and let

your hair out of the ponytail. I want to make sure it doesn't show. Although, I don't really think anyone would really notice or care. Everyone is so hooked up these days."

Chase did as instructed.

Donna surveyed her. "Fabulous."

"But what's it for?"

"I'll be backstage listening and if you get stuck I'll be on my phone and I can help you. All you have to do to cover the delay is look meditative for a moment and, *voila!*, we are good."

"We can do that? Isn't it kind of dishonest?"

"What's dishonest about it? I'm your right-hand woman. I look after you. Politicians have aids and speechwriters and all sorts of assistants. Their staff would never let their person get into a jam. It's downright irresponsible if they do," Donna said vehemently.

Chase nodded.

"Okay, let's try it out. I'll go in the bathroom and you listen. I'll ask you a question and you wait for me to tell you the response—that way we can gauge the time delay."

"Ask me a hard one."

From the recesses of the bathroom, Donna yelled, "Ms. Banter, can you explain to me the polemics in Rita Mae Brown's novel *Six of One*?"

"Are you fucking high? How the hell would I know that? Besides I was a baby dyke when I read it and all I really remember was the scene where the rich lesbian Celeste rips off the shirt of her lover, Ramelle, in a passionate moment and buys her a whole bunch of new ones the next day that she spreads out on the bed." Chase popped another Mento.

"See, that's a good example. The shirt-ripping scene could be viewed as an instance of violence and indicative of a rape although it was consensual sex. There's also the highly controversial part where Ramelle sleeps with Celeste's brother, Curtis, and bears his child. That's not exactly proper lesbian behavior and then there's always the southern manners thing."

"Oh, my god," Chase said.

"You're doing fine. I can hear you and if you don't say things like 'are you fucking high?' we'll be all right. Besides my knowledge of lesbian fiction is way above average and I can vie with the best of them. And there's always the passing the buck trick. If you can't or I can't answer a question, we'll pass it along with the usual statement that 'I think this is a better question for my esteemed panelist so and so.'"

"How will I know which one to pass it to?"

"I'll tell you."

Chase had been so busy she hadn't noticed Gitana standing in the doorway wearing a low-backed black velvet dress with a somewhat plunging neckline. "Chase, who are you talking to?"

Chase swiveled around in her office chair. "I'm talking to Donna. You aren't wearing that tonight?"

"Why not?"

"It's practically indecent."

"I picked out that dress. It's not indecent. It's sexy and stylish," Donna said, through the Bluetooth.

"You're responsible for that?"

"Where exactly is Donna?"

"In the bathroom." Chase was now walking around Gitana, surveying the dress up close.

"What bathroom? Are you two channeling each other now?"

"No, she's going to save my ass with technology," Chase said, running her hand up Gitana's naked back, suddenly feeling very lesbian and remembering the passionate shirt-ripping scene. She didn't want to rip the dress off Gitana, but she did want to remove it very slowly. Gitana blushed.

Donna came out of the bathroom holding her phone. She pulled back Chase's hair and demonstrated how everything worked while Chase admired Gitana's plunging neckline.

"That's brilliant and it might actually produce a positive psychological reaction that might enable you to answer all the questions on your own just because you know you have Donna as a backup," Gitana said brightly.

Chase and Donna looked dubious.

"Oh, ye of little faith," Gitana said.

"Now about that dress...." Chase said, shoving her lust aside.

"She looks fabulous and how often do we get to have a fancy dress party?" Donna asked, studying Gitana and nodding approvingly.

"I think it's politically incorrect," Chase said.

They both look at her quizzically. "Why?" Donna inquired.

"Because we are exploiting her feminine attributes, which can be construed as sexist, and if I am dressed in a tuxedo," Chase still couldn't believe Lacey had talked her into that as well, "and she is in a ball gown, we are portraying a lesbian stereotype of butch and femme."

When Gitana glanced at Donna for help Chase knew that her logic was sound. Donna bit her lower lip—a thinking posture. "Or the dress and the suit serve as an homage to the glorious past when lesbians had to be courageous, and dress-up was part of the scene—that sense of having an identity."

Chase furrowed her brow. Donna did have a point. People's points were getting on her nerves.

Gitana stepped in. "Chase, please. I like this dress and the party is all women, except for Bo, who doesn't like boobs."

"Only if I get to take the dress off slowly later on in the privacy of our bedroom," Chase said.

"It's a deal," Gitana said.

Chapter Eighteen—Revenge
Souls made of fire, and children of the sun,
With whom revenge is virtue.—*Young*

Chase was busy pulling more Chilean white wine out of Stella's wine fridge when she turned around to find P.H. Kinjera standing behind her and making no bones about the fact that she'd been staring at her ass. Chase had spent as much time as was politely necessary with the new guests and was now assisting in food and drink procurement. She'd stood by as Lacey did all the introductions and Stella doled out New Mexican appetizers— taquitos, bean and cheese rolls ups, Jacinda's homemade salsa with authentic chips and stuffed green chilies with cream cheese. The rest of the dinner, which was more native cuisine, was going to blow their bowels to seventh heaven. Chase had mentioned this fact and was pooh-hawed. "These are newbies to the cultural diversity of New Mexico and it would be a social crime not to immerse them in the culture," Stella had informed her.

"So here you are. I wondered where our lovely romantic writer had gone," P.H. said as Chase straightened up and tried to politely inch away. She pretended to look for a corkscrew.

"Romantic comedy actually—there is a difference," Chase said as she opened another drawer.

"And what would that be?" P.H. inched closer, leaning against the counter and exuding trouble.

This wasn't the first time Chase had been cornered in a kitchen. Stella's kitchen had an advantage—it was large. It was those tiny studio apartment kitchens you had to beware of and getting cornered was yet another reason that Chase avoided parties. She was like those people who weren't fond of cats yet attracted cats by the virtue of that fact. Chase had read somewhere that cats were drawn to these kinds of people because they saw them as no threat and could be counted on to mostly let them be with only a perfunctory pat just to look polite. Chase didn't want to get too friendly with anyone, yet she seemed to attract people who insisted on getting friendly, usually too friendly.

Chase continued rummaging, knowing full well that the corkscrew was sitting on the counter next to P.H. She was using the ruse to get as far from P.H. as was possible. "Well, my work is more about exploring the foibles of lesbian life and less about melodrama—not that there is anything wrong with melodrama."

"Melodramatic lesbian fiction seems to be more about the trials of being lesbian, loss of partners, trouble with parents, coming out, past relationships that have not been resolved and then some serious sex scenes."

"That pretty much sums it up," Chase said.

"And your fiction seems to be interested in redemption through the realization of our faults. You teach through humor."

Chase had managed to put the kitchen island between them. "So you've read some of my stuff?"

"All eleven of them. The jacket cover photo proved very inspirational. I wanted to know the writer through her works and especially before I met such a beautiful weaver of words."

Chase blushed slightly and hated herself for it. P.H. was

definitely the Lothario Chase had pegged her for. She was a slightly built woman with a pretty nose, small mouth and almond-colored eyes. Her hair was black and spiked and if she wore a kimono she would have made a perfect courtesan.

"Don't you find, however, that lesbian fiction on the whole, focuses too much on monogamous relationships, the getting of one and the keeping of one? Your fourth novel, *Whatever She Wants*, did explore the idea of non-monogamous relationships, but in the end you too succumbed." She had picked up the "lost" corkscrew and was coming toward Chase. She playfully wagged it at Chase, who attempted to grab it but was rebuked. "Not so fast." She came closer. "Don't you ever get tired of always fucking the same woman over and over again? What if one could taste the delights of others but still maintain the original relationship and not harm it in any way?"

"I'd say you were dreaming. The mind and the human heart do not work that way."

P.H. handed Chase the corkscrew and she took it, hoping this would put an end to the antics, but instead just as Chase was inching away P.H. put her arms on either side of Chase, effectively pinning her to the kitchen island. "Ah, but I think with a little practice it could be. Partner number one finds a lover and succumbs, meanwhile partner number two is allowed to do the same thing, all with the understanding that the secondary lovers remain in that position for as long as all parties agree."

"Just keep it loose and easy," Chase said.

"Exactly."

"You act like having sex outside a relationship is the equivalent of joining a book club and meeting a few kindred spirits." Chase could feel her face getting hot as P.H. leaned in closer.

"It could be. Have you ever tried it?"

"Once when I was very young and it didn't get a good reception." She hated having to admit to this, but she didn't want P.H. to think that she was a possible candidate because she had never tried having more than one girlfriend at a time and thus had no viable experience to build her case on. "Besides, it wasn't a committed relationship. We were baby dykes playing around." She glanced up at the clock on the wall just over P.H.'s head.

Where the fuck was Gitana? She had had to work late but would arrive in time for dinner.

"I think you could do it and I'd like to be your first experiment." It appeared she was going to lean in and kiss Chase but for the timely arrival of Gitana.

"There you are," Gitana said. "Stella told me you were getting the wine." She glanced at P.H., who took a step back. "I don't believe we've met. I'm Chase's life partner, Gitana Ortega." She said this pointedly.

"A pleasure to meet you. P.H. Kinjera. I am a big admirer of your partner."

"I can see that," Gitana said sweetly. "So am I." She took Chase's arm. "Your mother sent me to find you. She wants the wine in this century."

"Of course," Chase said, grabbing the wine and the corkscrew. Gitana put her arm around Chase's waist and then moved her right hand lower, giving Chase's bum a squeeze as she glanced over her shoulder at P.H.

"Was that proprietary?" Chase said.

"Damn right. She's lucky I didn't deck her," Gitana said as they passed into the living room. "Are you all right?"

"I think I need a stiff drink."

Gitana laughed.

Donna came flying up. "She propositioned you, didn't she?"

"You knew she was a letch and you didn't tell me?" Chase said, alarmed at this sudden lapse in her P.A.'s behavior.

"Well, I'd heard things so I spent almost a half an hour extolling the virtues of your relationship—you'd think she would have gotten the point." Donna appeared to be just as upset as Chase. "Oh, my goodness, this is horrid."

Gitana put her hand on Donna's arm. "I'm not exactly excited about it, but I think we got the point across."

"Damn her! Do you know how many perfectly wonderful relationships she's managed to screw up by offering a little on the side, and the worst part is that she makes it sound like it's part of normal human behavior."

"How do you know all this?" Chase asked.

"Anyone who knows anything about the current lesbian intelligentsia knows about the mind fucks that go on there."

"So this whole panel-thing-touring-group of 'let's get our lezzie stuff out there' is all about rock star fucking?" Chase was mortified.

Donna nodded, not meeting Chase's gaze.

"There you are," Stella said, taking the wine. Seeing it was unopened she looked quizzically at Chase, who handed her the corkscrew. "Why didn't you open it in the kitchen?"

"I was accosted by a Lothario and had to make a hasty exit."

"P.H.?" Stella said. She smiled sagely.

"How did you know?" Chase inquired.

"She propositioned me earlier. She says she loves older women and being straight is not a problem in her world. Of course, if I were going to fall madly in love with a woman it would have to be Peggy."

Gitana was not concerned by this and said, "So how did you get away from her?"

Chase stared at her mother and seriously contemplated what she hoped had been a flippant remark.

"I told her I had a bladder infection," Stella said, waving at Peggy who'd just come in.

"I'd stick close to Ellen McNeil if I were you. She's dedicated to true love and longevity."

"We'll keep an eye on her," Gitana said, patting Donna on the shoulder. "Stop worrying and please spend some serious time with Lacey, who's been promising the world to everyone and I'm not certain she has any real idea of the consequences of what she's doing."

"Like what?" Donna said.

"Like promising Delia she could make the opening speech."

"Oh, no!" Donna said, rushing off, to find Lacey and put an end to the madness. She had her cell phone plastered to her ear. Evidently, she was going to locate Lacey one way or the other.

"Can't we just go and see Stella's new library and hide out until dinner?" Chase said, snagging a Corona off a tray as a rent-a-waiter went by.

"What about Isabel and Lily? I thought they were coming. And we're supposed to keep P.H. away from Ellen."

"Lily and Isabel will be fine. Alma is here and you know how much she and Lily enjoy each other's company. Isabel and my mother can talk books. We'll just check on Ellen about bedtime and make sure she goes to her own." Chase had invited Sandra and Marsha from the SUP group as well, thinking this would be a great group opportunity, but they'd been called away for the funeral of Sandra's great aunt. Lily had given them both serious instructions on how to properly behave at the funeral and the group had donned black and performed a mock wake to facilitate the learning process. Chase, not one for funerals, had found it most instructive as she'd just killed off the victim in her mystery novel.

"Okay, but let's just kind of mill around the crowd, wave a few times and then ease out of the room," Gitana suggested.

As they reached the edge of the living room, Chase said, "Very good. Where'd you learn to do that routine?"

Gitana smiled slyly. "From attending church social functions, quinceaneras, weddings, funerals and every other kind of disagreeable social gathering. You should see Graciela do it. She's incredible. She can enter and exit a room and give the appearance of always having been there."

They entered the library, which Stella had just redone to go with the rest of her new décor. It was beautiful and looked like it came right out of an English country house. It was dark paneled and had floor-to-ceiling bookcases. Stella had combined two rooms so that the library was spacious. It had a gas fireplace with an ornately carved mantel and a large Victorian-style desk. By the stack of books there were two long reading tables. Of these Chase was envious. She always found it extremely difficult to do reference work on a desk crowded with computer equipment. Gitana ran her hand along the reading table.

"You need one of these," she stated. She looked around, "Actually, you need a proper library." She hoisted herself up on the table.

"And just where would we put this library? The studio certainly isn't big enough." She gazed down at Gitana, who looked absolutely gorgeous. She had a clear view of her lovely breasts. Chase suddenly wished they were at home—not solely because she wanted to get away from these people, but because she had an incredible longing to be in bed, making love to her beautiful partner. It was more intense at this moment than in the earlier days of their love and it almost frightened her. Before Gitana could respond, Chase kissed her softly at first and then more urgently. Their tongues intertwined and then something happened to them simultaneously. Chase pulled up Gitana's lovely dress and Gitana pulled her into her, unbuttoning Chase's dress shirt and reaching for her breast and kissing it softly. Chase eased Gitana back onto the library table while Gitana unzipped her pants and reached inside. Chase let out a soft moan of delight. Gitana guided Chase's hand between her legs and they moved against one another slowly at first and then hard and fast, exploding into each other together.

They lay breathing hard, their bodies wound around each other in a state of moderate undress when the library door opened and they heard Stella's voice.

"I've just had it redone and it positively oozes authenticity," Stella said, as she switched on the overhead lighting. Standing next to her were Alma, Lily, Isabel, P.H. and Ellen McNeil, who looked more stricken than Chase.

"What on earth are you two doing?" Stella said indignantly. "On my library table!"

"I would say that it was more than apparent," P.H. said, her neat white teeth gleaming as she smiled.

Alma kindly looked away and began examining the books, as did Ellen. Isabel smirked as Chase tidied herself and Gitana slid off the table. "I think I'll go get a beer. Chase, would you like one?" and she sidled out of the room as if nothing were wrong. Chase nodded belatedly.

Stella glared at both of them.

"Young lady," Lily said as she stood next to Stella. "This is very high on the SUP scale, about a ninety-seven, I'd say, of socially unacceptable behavior at a dinner party—not to mention in your mother's library. I suggest you apologize and curb your lust for a more appropriate time. I am aware that you feel that you are, so to speak, 'losing your lezzie,' but this is not the time or the place to exercise your libido."

Chase stood mortified.

"Losing your lezzie, eh," P.H. said smugly.

Now that was socially unacceptable on Lily's part, Chase thought.

"Perhaps we should start dinner. Lacey and Jasmine have arrived." Stella glared at Chase with a look that meant "I will deal with you later."

In the living room, Gitana handed Chase a Dos Equis and smiled weakly. "Sorry about that," she said.

"No, it was entirely my fault," Chase said. She took a pull on her beer and felt better.

"By the way, I don't think you're losing your lezzie at all," Gitana said.

"Thanks."

Lacey and Jasmine came over. "I'm so sorry we're late. I had to check things out with the film crew. It appeared they wanted a better backdrop for the panel. They said the community bulletin board was too busy looking so we had to pull it down and repaint the wall a light shade of gray."

"You had to paint a wall." Chase was incredulous.

"Believe me it was the fastest paint job ever," Jasmine said. She pulled a strand of Lacey's hair to get a paint globule off.

"How is everyone doing, anyway?" Lacey inquired, looking at Ellen and P.H. talking to Stella, who appeared gracious. Delia and Graciela were chatting with Alma and Lily, and Isabel and Peggy were laughing in the corner.

"Well, P.H. attempted to seduce me in the kitchen, and Gitana and I got caught fucking in the library," Chase said.

"We always miss all the good stuff," Jasmine whined.

Lacey looked mortified, which was what Chase intended. "I bet Lily would find that socially unacceptable."

"She did, as she was one of the people standing in the doorway," Chase retorted. "But let's not tell Donna. She's already having a rather stressful evening," she said, glancing at Donna, who was discreetly talking on the phone in the hallway.

"Well, I certainly hope dinner goes off better," Lacey said as Stella informed everyone that it was ready.

Dinner did not go off well. P.H. was lurid, Ellen was naïve and Donna was fretful. Graciela and Delia listened with delight as Lily recounted her former life as a person with socially unacceptable proclivities. It was better than a reformed alcoholic or a criminal turned Christian. "Then, you see, it really wasn't nice to shred her thesis paper and stick it in the coconut cream pie, but my sister's whole superior attitude about getting her doctorate was disgusting."

"She didn't have another copy?" Delia asked incredulously.

"I don't have copies of my work, just a notebook," Chase said.

Gitana leaned over and took her hand. "I promise never to shred your manuscript and serve it for dessert."

"Dear child, this was in the pre-tech era and typewriters were the only method of providing a printed document. It was not possible to do multiple copies unless you used a copy machine, which was expensive."

Stella entered the conversation. "And smelled of noxious blue ink."

"Dittos, they called them," Peggy piped in.

Chase glanced over at P.H. and at Ellen who was hanging on P.H.'s every word. She'd have Ellen in bed in a matter of hours and then break her heart in the same amount of time. Chase hoped it would be after the panel discussion. Chase wished a yeast infection on P.H. and then realized that was another socially unacceptable faux pas. Then she decided she didn't care. It would serve her right—the evil lesbian.

"Don't you remember all the White Out you had to use to get rid of typing errors," Stella said.

"Or you had to retype the whole page," Alma added.

The rent-a-staff waiter brought out the gazpacho and Indian fry bread. Chase stuck with the fry bread as the peppers in the gazpacho were sure to turn her stomach into a minefield of gastric warfare.

Isabel leaned over and whispered to Chase, "I'm a born and bred New Mexican, but I can't eat this stuff without having a blowout."

"Stick with the fry bread, the cheese platter and the blackened trout," Chase advised. She hoped that her mother's idea of local cuisine would also give P.H. the shits to go along with the yeast infection.

The minute that dinner was completed and despite the pleas of Donna, Chase grabbed Gitana, bid her mother goodbye to which she paid little or no attention as she was talking to Isabel, who did acknowledge her departure.

"Had enough?" Isabel said coyly. "Don't worry, I'll take notes."

Once in the car, Chase sighed deeply and put her head on the steering wheel. Gitana took her hand. "It'll be over before you know it."

"It's even more horrible than I thought. I can't believe Lacey talked me into it." Chase moaned.

There was a tap tap on the window and they both jumped. Chase peered out. "Speak of the devil." She let the window down. "I'm not really in the mood to see you right now," Chase said in what she thought was a diplomatic fashion.

Lacey pouted. "What's wrong? I thought you did great, well, with the exception of the library thing."

"I don't like my peers."

"Ellen is nice," Lacey ventured.

"She's going to be a meat sandwich for that pariah you call a linguist. She's more like a cunnilinguist."

Lacey sighed. "I am trying to disengage that particular time bomb."

There was some shuffling around and giggling on the front lawn. "Shit!" Lacey said, and with a move that would have made a Navy SEAL proud she jumped in the backseat. "Let's go for a drive around the block."

"Lacey, we're going home. I'm not up to having any more discussions or whatever you're up to."

"Just one turn around the block, quick." She ducked down in the seat.

"Lacey, it's dark and we have tinted windows," Gitana said, in her best soothing-a-small-child voice. "Now, why don't you tell us what's wrong?"

"Can't we just drive for a minute?"

"All right," Chase said. "One turn around the block and I mean it." She started the car and pulled out of the drive. "Okay, start talking."

"I've got a huge problem, well, two huge problems and one of them is your fault."

"What the hell did I do? I don't want to do this thing and now that I reconsider I don't have to."

"You wouldn't!" Lacey hissed.

Gitana, ever the mediator, said, "Just tell us the problems and we'll group-solve."

"Everyone except Jasmine and Chase wants to open the conference. Ellen, I can probably talk out of it although she does have her point about being the beginning of developing gayness with her stories. Delia feels that as a delegate of New Mexico she should open the conference which is a good point and P.H. is simply being an egotistical cunt."

"What's the other problem?" Gitana inquired as if the first one weren't big enough.

"The seating arrangements. P.H. insists on being seated next to Chase."

"Hmm," Gitana said. "What does Donna say about all this?"

"She told me that I'd better fix this whole thing and make it look good for Chase so that Myra won't make her return to New York for a further torture session and if I don't she'll personally remove my clitoris with a meat cleaver."

"I don't consider that a good choice of cutlery for such a procedure," Chase said, trying to imagine it.

"Donna used to be so mild-mannered," Gitana mused.

"What am I going to do?" Lacey moaned.

Chase, out of compassion, made another turn around the block.

"Honey, how long in terms of hours did Addison's strep throat take to incubate?"

Chase, ever the cataloger along with Addison who was simply fascinated by viruses, had been taking notes. "Addison is fairly certain after her first exposure, when she'd shaken hands with the opposing team's debate leader, about seven hours and thirteen minutes with full blown symptoms in twelve."

Gitana glanced at the illuminated clock on the dash. "Perfect." She plucked her phone from her bag and dialed.

During the course of the conversation, Chase caught the gist and smiled with gleeful savagery. She glanced over at Gitana, who smiled sweetly.

"Where are we going?" Lacey said as if she feared she was being abducted.

"We're going to get Addison," Chase said as she turned onto Juan Tabo and made for the freeway.

"Because why?" Lacey said.

"Because she wants to meet P.H. Kinjera and get her autograph. You wouldn't happen to have one of her books?" Chase said.

"I do in my purse, which is back at the house because I wasn't aware I was going on a trip."

"This is going to solve your problem," Gitana said.

Lacey perked up. "It is? But how?"

"Addison is going to give P.H. a case of strep throat," Chase said, getting off the freeway.

Lacey appeared to be thinking—at least Chase gave her the benefit of the doubt that when she was quiet she was thinking. "Isn't that kind of mean?"

"I wouldn't call it mean. I'd call it unethical and vindictive," Chase replied as she turned into Tanoan and pulled up in Addison's drive.

"But she could get everyone sick," Lacey said as Chase honked the horn.

"We'll take precautions. We'll have her meet P.H. on the back patio because although Addison is precocious, she is also extremely shy," Gitana said.

Addison exited the house wearing gloves, a top-to-toe plastic suit made out of what appeared to be raincoat material with matching Wellington boots and a face mask. She had her enormous backpack, which she swung in the backseat next to Lacey. "Don't worry. I am completely isolated. You won't get it."

"Thanks for doing this," Chase said.

"Anything to help a friend. Besides this is a great science project," Addison said, her voice muffled by the mask.

"And what a hands-on experience. Did you bring the other thing?" Chase asked.

Addison dug around in her backpack and pulled out a used pickle jar full of a yellow viscous substance. "It's right here."

Lacey leaned away in horror. "What the hell is that?"

"It's sputum. I've been saving it until I'm better so I can look at it under a microscope. I've got one ordered, but it hasn't arrived yet. I'm keeping my specimens in the fridge until then. This is only one sample. I have more," she said as if she thought they might be concerned that she was sacrificing her project for them.

"Did you know that the flu virus viewed through a microscope resembles a spiral ham stuck with cloves?" Chase added. She exited the freeway and headed for Four Hills.

"We've been studying viruses together," Addison said.

"Great," Lacey said, inching farther away from her.

"I thought I'd dip the pen into the sample just prior to the interview so the virus will be at its peak performance level," Addison said.

"Perfect. Chase, who is so popular with P.H., can go in and get her and then we can execute our plan," Gitana said.

"You're starting to sound as bad as them," Lacey said.

"If you mess with me and mine there will be retribution," Gitana said.

"That sounds like Old Testament doctrine," Chase said as she pulled into the driveway of Stella's house.

"Now, Lacey, try and look natural and relaxed when you go in, like everything is supra-normal and you just went out to get some air. Get the book and bring it out to the alcove patio. Addison will de-suit herself and contaminate the pen," Gitana said.

"We could still get it," Lacey said.

"We won't. In the open air and without close contact for such a short period of time the virus does not have a conducive environment for contamination. P.H. touching the pen on the other hand..." Chase replied.

"Studying viruses is weird," Lacey said, getting out of the car.

"But it certainly comes in handy. Now, act natural and hurry up," Chase said.

Gitana and Addison crept around the side of the house. They would use the side patio that had more privacy and was usually vacant because it was hidden. Chase left them at the corner of the house and slipped inside.

Chase found P.H. having an animated conversation with Lily. "I still consider your combining of, pardon my language, fuck and cunt to create "funting" as a way to describe lesbian sex disarming and rude," Lily said, pursing her lips at P.H. like she wanted to rid her mouth of a foul taste.

"If I may borrow P.H. for a moment. I have a fan who would really like you to autograph her copy of your latest book," Chase said, smiling at P.H. and giving her her best come-hither look. She hoped she didn't get jumped on the way to the patio. She'd have to move fast.

"Please do," Lily said.

"And where is this fan of yours?" P.H. inquired as Chase led her toward the patio.

"She's outside. Addison is very shy," Chase said.

Once outside, they met Gitana and Addison. "Ms. Kinjera, I'm so glad to meet you. I've been a fan of yours since your first book, *The Funting Factor.* I think it's very important that women create a language of their own." Addison thrust out the copy of P.H.'s latest book *If Not Now Then When.*

"How old are you?" P.H. said, peering down at Addison who was impeccably dressed in what Chase would have called literary fashion—cream-colored trousers, a hunter green oxford shirt with a pale green ascot and a tweed blazer. She looked like a midget English professor.

"Eleven," Addison said, handing her the pen.

P.H. looked perplexed but opened up the book. "What would you like the inscription to be?"

"'To Addison, with love and affection' will be fine."

"That's a little personal, don't you think?" P.H. said.

Addison touched P.H.'s leg. "I hope that we'll get to be great friends," she said.

P.H. jumped back and hurriedly signed the book. "Maybe when you're a little older," she said, handing Addison her book. "Look, it was nice meeting you, but I really need to get back inside." She bailed quickly, which was fortuitous as they all burst out laughing.

"Okay, where did you get the little suit?" Chase said.

"From the drama department. We're doing a play one of the kids wrote, it's pretty stupid, kind of a combination of *Mrs. Dalloway* meets Harriet Vane from the Dorothy Sayers book *Strong Poison*."

"That doesn't sound half bad," Chase said.

"It's overly dramatic without interludes of rest so the audience has no time to regain its emotions."

"What part do you play?" Gitana asked.

"I'm Harriet Vane."

"That's a pretty big part," Chase said.

"I'm the only other person besides the so-called playwright who has ever read a Dorothy Sayers novel."

"I thought the hand on the leg was pretty good too," Chase said.

"That was for you," Addison said.

"How'd you know?" Chase said.

"I didn't, but I saw her make a move for your bum as you came through the door. I can guess the rest—the old kitchen island move."

"Yes."

"Okay, we better get you home before your mom sees you," Chase said.

Addison dressed and they were off.

As Chase got back on the freeway she said, "I hope it works."

"It will. The dose I gave her was from the immediate onset. She'll be sick by morning."

"We better keep her away from Ellen. We can't have two of them getting sick," Gitana said.

"Don't worry, Lacey is busy getting Ellen snockered. She'll put her to bed before P.H. gets her claws into her," Chase said.

"We're bad," Gitana said.

"What happened to Old Testament judgment?" Chase said, pulling into Tanoan.

"Ellen didn't do anything," Gitana said.

"We're protecting Ellen from a lecherous viper as well as a contagious disease. Getting her drunk and passed out is the only way I can think of keeping her safe. She'll thank us when she doesn't have strep in the morning. Stella will fix her up with her world famous hangover elixir. Don't worry," Chase said, squeezing Gitana's hand.

They pulled into Addison's drive. "You were fabulous," Chase said.

"I wish I could be there tomorrow," Addison said, through her mask. "But that wouldn't be socially responsible."

"I wish you could too."

"At least there's the webcam," Addison said brightly. She was looking feverish.

"Are you all right? We didn't make you sicker, did we?" Chase said, alarmed.

"No. I'm fine. I just need to lie down. Call me tomorrow?"

"Of course. I'm going to need a pep talk," Chase said.

Chapter Nineteen—Revolution
Revolutions are not made: they come. A revolution is as
natural a growth as an oak.
It comes out of the past. Its foundations are laid far back.—
Wendell Phillips

By eight thirty the next morning, P.H. Kinjera was isolated in the east wing and Stella's personal physician had diagnosed her malady as strep throat. She was to remain in bed and anyone who came in contact with her was to wear a mask.

"What are we going to do?" Donna said, wringing her hands outside the sick room. "We're short a panelist, Ellen has a horrible hangover and Delia refuses to give up her place as the intro speaker."

"Oh, I think it will all work out," Chase said, leaning against the wall.

Lacey came running up the stairs. "It's all set." She kissed Chase on both cheeks. "You are so marvelous, you and Gitana."

"Yes, my brilliantly conniving partner," Chase said.

"What are you talking about? Myra's going to kill me if this snafus."

"It won't. Isabel is taking P.H.'s place. She's going to plug the library and gay books angle and she's funny and articulate so her being straight will be overlooked if anyone finds out. We're going low-key on that," Lacey said, looking pointedly at both of them.

"I'm not going to out her," Chase said.

"Me neither. I'll pretend to be her girlfriend if need be," Donna said.

Lacey put her forefinger to her lips. "That might not be a bad idea. You don't have to lip lock or anything, but you could look kind of chummy." She addressed Chase, "Do you think Isabel would mind?"

"I don't think so. I have a feeling she'd find the whole thing rather amusing."

"Perfect. The Ellen question also has been decided. Ellen, it seems, is a little under the weather so she's given up her bid to be the intro speaker. Delia has conceded to mention some of Ellen's key points. How is that for managerial skills?"

"You are truly amazing," Donna said, looking at Lacey with newfound awe. "Maybe you could help me with Myra."

"You could pretend to quit and Lacey could take over and give Myra such a time of it that she'd be begging to take you back," Chase said mockingly.

Lacey and Donna looked at her and then at each other. "That's brilliant," Donna said.

"I think we could pull it off. You could say that you've found a replacement and that you need some time to reflect on the direction your life is taking," Lacey said, rubbing her hands together like some evil cartoon genius.

"I was just kidding," Chase said.

"We're not," Donna said, flipping on her heels and heading for the front door.

"We'd better get down to the Community Center and see how the film crew is doing," Lacey said. She suddenly noticed Chase's outfit of khaki shorts and a T-shirt that had a kernel of corn blown up to the size of a dessert plate. "What does that mean?" she said, pointing at the corn.

"I have no idea, but I thought it was funny. It was only a dollar at Thrift Town."

Lacey peered at her. "Where is the suit?"

"What suit?" Chase said as she bounced out the front door and toward Lacey's car.

Lacey grabbed her by the shoulders. "You know damn well what I'm talking about. You are not going to fuck up my project that I have worked so hard on by appearing in a T-shirt with a piece of corn on it. Now, where is the fucking suit?"

Chase had backed away in alarm. "Lacey, relax. Gitana has it and will bring it to the Center where I will change into it. I don't want it to look scruffy by the time this whole," she refrained from saying pathetic, "affair commences."

"Oh, well, that was good thinking. Sorry." Lacey looked sheepish as they got in the car.

Once in the car, Chase took Lacey's hand. "I don't mean this as a criticism..." That wasn't exactly the right word. "I mean, I think you've done a marvelous job on all of this."

Lacey glared at her as she flipped off the driver in front of her for cutting her off as they got on the freeway and then proceeded to have a moment of road rage as she tailgated the offending driver, who quickly sensing the danger got over into the farthest lane available.

Chase's elation at beginning to get her lezzie back was suffering a major setback. Lacey was becoming Donald Trump with better hair. Between her, Donna and P.H., it felt like lesbians were going all corporate and that promotion and a ruthless seeking of attention and selling of product were taking over. Did she want to be part of this new aggressive attitude?

"Now, what were you saying?" Lacey said as she exited the freeway and headed down Lomas to the Community Center.

"Oh, it was nothing."

"You said something about criticism. If you have something to say I want you to say it." Lacey whipped into the parking lot of the Community Center.

"We can talk about it later," Chase said, reaching for the

door handle. The lock went down. Chase tried the knob. Lacey had kicked in the child-proof device.

"Now," Lacey said. She didn't exactly look murderous, but Chase felt her heart quicken.

Chase chose her words carefully, or at least she hoped she had. "I just think that we might all be losing our sense of fun and going kind of corporate. I mean lesbians used to be easy-going, under-the-radar kind of people and now we're sort of stepping out on stage and suffering a bit of emotional backlash because of it. I'm concerned for the psyche of our people."

Lacey was drumming her fingers on the steering wheel and looking very pensive. Chase couldn't remember the last time she saw Lacey this serious except maybe when the iPhone came out with no instruction manual. "I think you're right."

Chase was relieved. Maybe they could get through this, go home and take up life as usual—maybe sell some more books and call the whole thing good.

"But…"

Chase's head snapped back around.

"I don't want 'our people' to go back to happy Lesbian Land. I want corporate, but our own corporate, I want center stage, but I want us to create, build and utilize the stage in our own way and I want us all to have emotionally healthy psyches. These are growing pains. I have bigger plans yet and you're going to help me whether you like it or not. I don't care if you're not a group person or that you march to a different accordion, you're going to be there." Lacey unlocked the doors and got out.

"It's drum."

"What?"

"Marching to a different drum," Chase corrected.

"In your case, it's an accordion."

Chase sat wondering if she'd just unlocked Pandora's box. Lacey opened her door. "Come on, we've got work to do."

"Viva the Revolution," Chase said weakly.

"That's right, baby. When this is all over with I want to show you this piece of property I've got my eye on out by Galisteo."

"You're moving to the country?" Chase was incredulous.

Lacey had never lived more than four blocks from the nearest Starbucks. Galisteo didn't even have a gas station.

"No, the Revolution is."

Chase was still in a state of shock when Isabel sidled up to her. "How are you holding up?"

"Lacey wants to start a revolution or something. I thought this was just a book group thing." She looked around at all the film equipment and people scurrying everywhere.

"I kind of got the gist of it last night. I brought you a book. I think it might help," Isabel said, pulling a copy of Erich Fromm's *Marx's Concept of Man* from her bag.

Chase automatically read the back cover. "What is she thinking of doing, creating the Republic of Lesbekistan?"

"No, I think it's more along the lines of an institute aimed at education, arts, culture, finance and political theory so that lesbians are better equipped for the world at large."

"Worldwide lesbian domination," Chase said.

A camerawoman clapped her on the back. "That's the spirit!"

Isabel smiled wanly at her. "I don't know, but I might take my vacation and help her set up the library if she does get the thing up and running."

"Are you serious?"

"Chase, has it ever occurred to you that lesbians are about nature's best chance to see what a world run by women would really look like? Think about it—a straight woman's body and mind are tied to men, so no matter how incredible a woman may be she is still held hostage by her reproductive organs and her place on the planet in relation to men. Lesbians are not part of that equation. You all just have to stop being the parlor mice. Lacey seems to want to build the house for you."

Chase bit her lip. "I think I just want to go back to Kansas."

"Just remember, Dorothy wasn't the same Dorothy when she got back."

"That's what I'm afraid of," Chase said as she felt a tug at her T-shirt. She looked down to find Bud, who smiled up at her.

"Gitana put the suit back in the dressing area. She hopes you're not panicking, but she's got to run back to the house because P.H. needs some Imodium. I think that dose of hot pepper paste I put in her fry bread may have done it, but I did feel she deserved it. Besides what you did was worse," Bud said.

"You were responsible for that?" Isabel said. "I thought you were upstairs in bed."

"And miss the party? I spied," Bud replied, not looking in the least penitent.

"Inadvertently, it seems we've become a family of poisoners," Chase said.

"The political intrigue begins," Isabel said.

"Speaking of poisoners," Chase said, pointing at Lacey helping Ellen to a chair and pulling a Gatorade and a packet of Lay's potato chips from her enormous purse.

"Does she have an icebox in there?" Bud inquired.

"She could have," Chase said.

"Ellen looks ghastly, but I suppose a sour stomach is better than a broken heart," Isabel mused.

Donna came rushing in and gave Isabel a peck on the cheek and said, "Hi, honey. Everything okay?" She scanned the crowd to see if anyone was watching. Two of the camerawomen noticed them and Donna took Isabel's hand and gave them a proprietary glance. One of them gave Donna the thumbs-up sign. She leaned over and whispered in Isabel's ear, "I hope you don't mind, but we can't have it leak out that you're straight, especially if the Pink Mafia shows up, which with Chase as one of the panelists I'm sure they will."

"The Pink Mafia?" Isabel said, her brows furrowing.

"It's the watchdog organization that sees to it that we don't stray too far from our lesbian roots. They don't like turncoats. They didn't like it when Chase went mainstream and she received an ultimatum to come up with a new lesbian novel," Donna explained.

"What would they do if she hadn't?" Isabel asked, staring at Chase. "Break her fingers or something?"

"Cut out her clitoris I think is more their style," Donna said.

Isabel winced.

"Can I go watch them set up the camera gear? I won't get in the way." Bud looked up at Chase imploringly.

"God, that look kills me," Chase said. "All right, but be careful and try not to be too precocious. It freaks people out."

"I'll dumb down," Bud promised and she trotted off toward the two women.

"Why do you want her to do that?" Isabel asked.

"Because I don't want the Mensa people getting a hold of her."

"Why not?"

"We're not group people. I better go change. I see Lacey coming my way," Chase said.

"Honey," Isabel said, referring to Donna, "Why don't the two of us go over my notes and you can see if they come across as authentically," Isabel lowered her voice and said, "gay."

Chase rolled her eyes. "This is just fucking absurd. Why can't everyone just be themselves? We got rid of a lecher and brought in a librarian. That seems like a really good trade-off to me."

"Shush. The walls have ears and we don't want to blow it now. Maybe when we all get to heaven and everyone gets along and we have civil rights and we don't have to wait for straight people to decide whether we can get married or not, then everyone can just be themselves," Donna said.

"I never did understand that part. How does you all getting married have anything to do with straight couples? Will there be a shortage of wedding cakes and preachers?" Isabel said.

"I think they're afraid we'll do it better," Donna said.

Chase shook her head and made for the dressing room. This getting-her-lezzie thing back was starting to grate on her nerves. She hadn't realized before that sharing your life and your sheets with another woman was so complicated. Her suit was hanging on the hook by the door, the door with the gold star on it to indicate that the panelists were indeed important. It didn't appear to matter that it was the restroom at large as well. Someone was retching up what seemed like her large intestine in the handicap stall. Chase, not one for nursing others, felt enough compassion for her fellow creature to check on her, especially since she had a pretty good idea who it was. "Ellen, is that you?"

A nasty retch and then a feeble voice said, "Yes."

"Having a hard time? Is there anything I can do?" Chase had no idea what she could do except be empathetic.

"Make last night and those six shots of Patrón go away." Another retch.

"Yeah, that tequila is a little too smooth for its own good," Chase commiserated. "Have you kept anything down?"

"Not yet, but I'm hoping to in the next year or two," Ellen said, flushing the toilet and exiting the stall.

Chase pulled over one of the straightback chairs that had been thoughtfully provided for the gold star people. Ellen sat down gratefully. Chase got her some wet paper towels to put on her forehead.

Graciela and Gitana came in. "Chase, you're not dressed. Lacey wants to check you out to make sure you don't pull any funny business," Gitana said.

"She doesn't look good," Graciela said, peering down at Ellen.

"She's not," Chase concurred.

"Chase, you get dressed, and Graciela, queen of the hangover, you need to come up with something quick or we're going to be looking for a new panelist."

Graciela appeared to contemplate. "Stick out your tongue," she instructed Ellen. "Ew, that doesn't look good. Thrown up everything?"

Ellen nodded.

"What does her tongue tell you?" Chase asked as she pulled off her corn T-shirt and donned the dress shirt.

"Nothing. I just like to get people to do it," Graciela said.

"Graciela, this isn't helping," Gitana said as she handed Chase her pants and belt.

"Stop worrying. I'll be right back with the sure-fire remedy. You were drinking tequila?"

"Yes."

"What kind?"

"Patrón, the white kind," Ellen said, putting the cold towels that Gitana had handed her on her forehead.

"Okay, just hang on. I'm just going to run up the street to that corner market. I'll be back in ten minutes."

Chase had finished dressing. "You look really nice," Ellen said weakly.

Gitana kissed Chase's cheek. "You do."

"I still have to get changed," Ellen said, indicating a pastel blue sundress hanging up behind her.

"I'll help you." Gitana surveyed her. "You need some color in your face. Chase, go see if Lacey or someone has some bronzer or something."

"What's that?" Chase asked.

"Makeup. Just go find someone with makeup," Gitana said.

Chase dashed from the bathroom. Volunteers were setting up the folding chairs. Chase found Lacey and Bud helping with the camera angles. Bud was seated on a phone book to add height as she sat on the platform in the middle panelist's position. Lacey and one of the camerawomen were taking turns looking through the viewfinder. Bud waved at her.

"Lacey, I need some makeup," Chase said.

Lacey pulled back from the camera. "You look fine the way you are. We want you to look as natural as possible."

"Oh, yeah, that's why I've got this monkey suit on. No, it's not for me. Ellen is looking a little sickly so Gitana thought we could spice up her color a bit. She said something about bronzer."

"I've pretty much given that stuff up. I really feel that being a lipstick lesbian just doesn't hold true to my sense of self. Men do not feel the need to alter or fabricate their facial features and I subscribe to the same notion of personhood as an 'as is' existence."

"Oh, for fuck's sake never mind." Chase scanned the room for a lipstick lesbian. There didn't appear to be any. This is a tough crowd, she thought. Then she spied Isabel, who did appear to have to have some makeup on.

"Isabel, do you have a makeup bag?"

"Yes."

"Come with me. We need you in the bathroom." Chase took her elbow and led her through the crowd.

"Should I take mine off? I just have a little mascara on," Isabel said as they entered the gold star room.

"No. We need to put some on Ellen, who looks white as a sheet."

"Oh, I've got bronzer. It'll give her that healthy glow of an outdoorsy type. I put some on before I go in REI so I don't look like I spend all my time indoors."

"But you do," Chase said, thinking 'Is everyone trying to be something they're not?'

"I know, but I really like their shoes for wandering around at work."

"Book hiking."

"Precisely." Isabel took one look at Ellen, who was now dressed. "She does need some color." She rooted around in her bag until she found the tube of bronzer. She handed it to Gitana, who was putting Ellen's beautiful long dark hair up in a stylish sort of careless bun.

"Some color in your face..." Gitana said.

"And something to keep me from throwing up and I'll be all set," Ellen said glumly.

"I've got just the ticket," Graciela said as she came through the door carrying a brown paper bag. She put the bag on the counter and pulled out a four-pack of Red Bull and a forty-ounce Budweiser Chelada, a bottle of Aleve and a pack of peppermint Mentos. Chase's eyes lit up. "Hands off, buddy. These are for the sick lady."

"What are you going to do?" Gitana asked.

"Well, she's going to drink one Red Bull, which is full of B vitamins, take an Aleve for her pounding head, then she's going to get down at least a third of the can of Chelada, hair of dog—it's going to fool her body into thinking everything is all right—and the Mentos have peppermint in them, which helps with a tummy ache, not to mention covering up the alcohol smell. It'll work, trust me."

"Are you sure?" Ellen said.

"It doesn't look like you have a lot of options, honey," Graciela said, opening the Red Bull and then giving her two Aleve tablets. "Chug the Red Bull, because timing is everything."

Ellen obeyed. When she was finished, Graciela handed her the Chelada. "Okay, now slowly sip this," she said.

Gitana finished her hair and Isabel applied the bronzer. "You look much better," Gitana said as she and Isabel surveyed their work.

If only Lacey could see this homespun girlie moment in the bathroom, Chase thought smugly.

Ellen finished the Chelada. She looked up in wonder at Graciela, who handed her a Mentos and reluctantly gave one to Chase. "I feel a lot better."

There was an urgent tapping on the door and Donna stuck her head in. "It's show time, everyone." She looked them over as they left the room. "You all look very nice. Chase, where are your shoes?"

They all looked down at her feet. She'd been standing in her bare feet after she'd taken off her Teva sandals to put her pants on. Chase pursed her lips. "You didn't bring them?" she asked Gitana.

"I thought you had them," Gitana said. "They weren't with your suit."

Chase thought for a moment. "I don't have any shoes to go with this suit. Lacey and I never got any. How do my toenails look?"

They all peered at them. "Pretty good," Graciela said.

"It could be a signature thing...like you meant to do it," Isabel said.

Donna looked skeptical. "But how do we keep Lacey from seeing it?"

"I'll take care of that or rather I'll help Delia take care of that. Wait until you hear her opening speech," Graciela said.

"I can only imagine. She's right. My feet will be the last thing on Lacey's mind."

"Just walk on my inside," Isabel said, "until we get up to the platform. Then if she does notice it'll be too late to do anything about it."

"Brilliant."

People were taking their seats and Jasmine and Delia were already seated at the panel table on the dais. Jasmine looked very nice in an obviously expensive, sage green, V-necked cashmere sweater that accentuated her well-formed breasts—Lacey's idea,

Chase was sure—with a nice pair of camel-colored trousers.

"How come Jasmine didn't have to wear a suit?" Chase whispered savagely at Donna.

"Lacey didn't want everyone to look too butch," Donna replied.

"Oh, so now I look butch."

"No. You look professional and the suit looks nice except for the lack of footwear," Donna said.

"Look at Delia's outfit," Isabel said.

Delia was wearing a red skirt that seemed to have multiple layers that gave her the appearance of a char woman in a Dickens' novel and then a leather halter top that looked straight out of *The Rocky Horror Picture Show.* She looked like a char-tart who was going to do some laundry while bent over and fucking a customer.

"Wow," Gitana said.

"How the hell did she get away with that?" Chase said.

"Delia is as strong-willed as Lacey." Donna dug around in her bag. "Oh, no, hold on. I almost forgot to give you this."

"You shouldn't have," Chase said as she stepped up on the makeshift stage.

"No, it's the ear bug silly, in case you get stuck," Donna said, handing it discreetly to Chase.

"Fuck, I forgot." She kissed Donna on both cheeks. "You're the best P.A. ever."

"Hey, what about me?" Gitana said, puckering up. "A kiss for luck."

Chase kissed her. "Say a couple Hail Mary's for me, Bud too."

"Bud already took care of her end. She made your coffee with holy water."

Isabel and Chase looked at each other as they took their seats. "I don't know about that," Isabel said.

"Me either," Chase said, wondering if the Holy Ghost was making his way through her kidneys as they spoke.

"Ladies and more ladies," Lacey said. "Oh, and our one honorary lesbian, Bo Brighton."

Bo stood up and took a bow.

"We are gathered here, not to perform a wedding because we are denied that by law, but we are here as part of the intellectual, emotional, spiritual and sexual awakening of a new generation of lesbians."

Ellen leaned over to Chase and said, "I thought this was a book group."

"I guess we're living large," Chase replied.

Lacey continued, "Today we have brought forth some of the greatest thinkers and writers of our time to answer questions about how they are helping to form this new lesbian nation through their works of fiction."

"See, I told you. You better read that book on Marx that I gave you," Isabel whispered.

Chase glanced over at Jasmine to see how she was taking it. Jasmine was staring up in awe of Lacey. Delia was preening and cracking her knuckles, two completely opposing gestures that Chase found disconcerting.

"Now, I'd like to turn the floor over to Delia Montoya, our first speaker for the day. She writes erotic fiction..." This was greeted with great applause.

That figures, Chase thought. It's always about the vagina.

"And she runs an e-book site that is listed on your program. Please support your local writers and buy a book," Lacey finished.

Delia stood up. "Not only do we need it in the sheets—we need it in the streets."

This was also greeted with great applause. Wow, Chase thought. She had expected something along the lines of Lacey's introductory sentence: "We are gathered here today to join this absurd idea to an equally absurd idea that lesbians will shortly be running the planet and shipping the straight people off to another nice planet filled with suburban housing developments and family sitcoms." And here Chase had thought she was just writing a silly little novel on the foibles of a lesbian commune when in actuality she was part of a revolution—her mind played images of *Doctor Zhivago*. She hoped she didn't end up being the persecuted doctor or his poor lover Lara. With Lacey, it seemed, anything was possible. Somehow she didn't think Lacey was going to let her get away with her usual excuse of "I'm just not a group person."

"It's time as a nation that we stand up for ourselves, our senses of self, not hiding, not making a hullabaloo about coming out or the toaster oven. Because we don't become lesbians. We are born lesbians."

Ellen's face gained some natural color as she realized Delia was dissing her novels.

Before Ellen got a chance to say anything, one of the audience members stood up and pointed a hostile finger at Delia. "What about those of us who work at appliance stores? The toaster oven is just the beginning of lesbian appliance purchases, the U-Haul, the move-in, the dishwasher and washer and dryer—that is an important part of our heritage." The burly woman sat down and her partner, a petite woman dressed in a frilly white dress, nodded her agreement.

"I like coming-out stories," a baby dyke chimed in. "And the toaster oven thing is the equivalent of the Neighborhood Meet and Greet."

Isabel gave Ellen a gentle nudge and whispered, "I think this would be a good place for you to start in."

"And maybe get Tinkerbell to shut her trap before we end up with a fistfight over lesbian rites and rituals," Chase added.

Ellen rang the tiny bell that each panelist had been given to indicate that they desired the floor. Delia looked over, perturbed. "Yes?" she inquired, giving Ellen the stink eye.

"I agree with the audience member that coming-out stories are important," Ellen said.

"You would. You write them," Delia said.

Isabel sighed. "I think you're going to need to be a little more forceful."

"You might have to jump in here," Chase suggested. "Like how many times those kinds of books are checked out or something."

"I don't have those kind of statistics," Isabel whispered.

"Make something up, just say 'a lot,'" Chase said.

Ellen's face got red. "That's because I think they help people come to terms with difficult situations so that coming-out lesbians don't feel so alone and disconnected."

"They aren't alone. They have us," Delia snapped back.

"Not if you live in the middle of nowhere," someone chimed in.

"Move to a big city then," Delia retorted.

Isabel rang her bell but didn't wait for Delia. "As a librarian, I have intimate knowledge of the kind of books that people check out. A lot of coming-out books—including Ellen's—are very popular."

"Good one," Chase said and clapped her hands, which seemed to enthuse some of the coming-out people who also clapped.

Donna piped in on Chase's ear bug. "That was good. We've got to get Delia to shut up and sit down. Get Jasmine going, Lacey thinks it will help."

Chase felt kind of silly but rang her bell. "And I think that writers like Jasmine Ellis are also good examples of positive role models for well-established lesbians who are already comfortable with their sexuality—her books are the next logical stepping stone for lesbian readers, even those who don't want to live in big cities."

"Thank you," Jasmine said. "As a relatively new member of the lesbian community, I commend my fellow panelists for their previous work and commiserate with them. We have won hard victories in getting our works published so that lesbian lives are more visible."

"Wow, that was impressive," Ellen whispered.

Jasmine continued. "So turn off your television, buy a book and read it to your lover while you're between the sheets." Jasmine blushed at the subsequent applause, the most fervent being from Lacey.

"Which is where erotica comes in," Delia said, taking the floor again.

"Ugh," Chase said.

"It's not like I can bring the library into it this time. We don't stock it," Isabel said.

"Oh, I think Delia is going to get hers in just a minute," Chase said, cocking her head in the direction of a woman dressed like she'd just come from the capital building.

"Haven't we seen her before?" Isabel asked.

"She's the lesbian mother of twin girls. We saw her at the PTO meeting that we all got thrown out of," Chase said.

"I don't think the lesbian community is the right place for erotica, which is really just a pretext for pornography," the woman said.

"What!" Delia said.

"I've read Jasmine's and Chase Banter's novels and they deal with the sex issue in a tasteful fashion. It's there, but it certainly doesn't need to be explained in all its details. We all know what goes where."

"Well, I bet you haven't read mine," Delia taunted.

"As a matter of fact, I have. I don't make decisions lightly or without the facts. Your stories and your website is simply women-oriented pornography," the woman said.

Some of the women in the audience clapped.

Jasmine leaned over. "Delia is really getting tiresome. This is a forum, not a battleground."

"I think her underpants are all twisted up in that char-tart outfit of hers," Chase said.

There was a strong voice from the back of the room. "I think the erotica issue is a personal choice—a moot point that no amount of arguing will ever resolve. Let's get back to the importance of lesbian writing and its need for financial support. We nearly lost one of our writers to the mainstream because of the lack of support by the reading public. I'm speaking of Chase Banter."

"Oh, shit!" Chase said.

"What?" Jasmine said.

"It's the Pink Mafia," Chase said, glancing at the back row of seats, which was filled with female versions of the Sopranos—suits, dark glasses and short hairdos.

"We are going to pass out order forms with the latest lesbian titles as well as some old favorites. Most of you are probably not aware of the fact that lesbian publishers need your financial support—which means purchasing books directly from them as opposed to the larger distributors. This keeps the money in the family so to speak. The writers get more money and the publishers remain viable. Upon the purchase of a book and receipt of your e-mail address we will put you on the mailing list so you can keep abreast of upcoming releases. My associates will now pass out the forms and pens so you can make your choices during the forum."

"Can they do that?" Isabel said.

"They got me to write another lesbian novel when I had no intention of doing so," Chase said. They definitely need some public relations help, Chase thought. Could that speech be anymore stilted?

The question-and-answer session went a lot smoother once the saner people of the audience got a chance to speak up, which all the panelists found a relief excepting Delia who sat pouting and emanating hostile vibes. Graciela brought her a Red Bull and patted her shoulder as if to say, they just don't understand your genius. Every once in a while Donna would beep in and tell Chase she was doing fine and also that she looked very photogenic for the camera. Okay, so maybe the suit was a good idea—it might give her some much sought-after credibility, especially with Lily who had insisted that she get a copy of the interviews so the SUP group could analyze them. "Do I have to be there?" Chase had asked.

"Of course. This concerns you most," Lily had replied.

As the panel drew to a close Chase felt an overwhelming sense of relief pass over her. It was done, the thing was done. People handed in their order sheets to the Pink Mafia. The head honcho lady, who Donna had discovered was named Max, of all things, came up to Chase and shook her hand. She had a grip like a truck driver.

"I wanted to thank you for picking up the torch and guiding our people."

Not knowing what else to say Chase replied, "Uh, it was no problem."

"I think you may have struggled with your inner lesbian, in fact, I've seen it before. I see with some gentle prodding you've come back. On the part of the Pink Mafia I'd like to present you with this plaque."

"A plaque?"

Gitana and Bud had nestled up close to her by this time.

"Oh, honey, look it's the official Order of the Vulva."

"Yeah, that's great. Thank you so much."

"Just keep up the good work." Max trundled off.

"Vulva?" Bud said.

"How did you know that?" Chase said, staring down at the plaque in confusion.

"Donna told me," Gitana said.

"Thank goodness or I would have been at a total loss."

"She figured as much. I think you better give her a raise," Gitana said, taking Chase's hand.

"Let's get out of here. I've done my civic duty. I want to go home, sit on the deck and have a nice cold beer," Chase said, thinking that with only two weeks left in August the summer was quickly coming to a close and days sitting outside would be finite. Another thought gripped her heart—that of Bud going to school in a mere week.

Bud reached up for the plaque.

"You want it?"

Bud nodded.

"Okay. I now officially award it to you."

Chapter Twenty—Aspiration
What shall I do to be forever known,
And make the age to come my own?—Cowley

"Do you really think you're going to be able to handle this?"

Chase looked over at her only child, a mere babe in arms, and tried not to cry. "I don't know."

"We're not off to a good start here," Bud said as she gazed out the car window at all the other parents and children saying their goodbyes as the first day of the fall term began—even though, as Chase had repeatedly stated, the third week in August was not fall. She couldn't believe that summer had zipped by without her knowledge. June had seen the flowering of the jewel garden. July was hot, the tomatoes had ripened. In August Addison had strep and she and Bud had gotten to "C" in the *OED*. Chase had survived the panel and now school had started.

Chase gripped the wheel of the Mini Cooper with white knuckles.

"They're not going to let us sit here all day and you don't want me to be late for my first day of school. It'll make a bad impression and you know how hard Donna has worked to get me in here and all the time you made me study when I should have been enjoying the last summer before my intellectual incarceration," Bud said.

"Oh, great. Thanks a lot. You're making this so much easier by guilt-tripping me." Chase stared out dolefully at the small children and their parents, several of whom appeared to be suffering the same anxiety she was. "I'm not alone, look at that display of empty-nest syndrome," Chase said as she pointed to a particularly messy scene of tears and clutching.

"If you do that to me, I will never speak to you again ever," Bud said, a new authority in her voice. She put her hand on the door handle. "I'm going to get out now and you may hand me my backpack. Then we will shake hands and I will go up the stairs, turn around, wave and then go inside. Do you understand?"

"I don't even get a hug?"

"You know as well as I that public displays of affection are not part of our family credo." Bud looked at her sternly. "So don't even try it."

Chase took a deep breath and summoned up the small reserve of stoicism that she housed for occasions such as this. "Let's get this party started."

"That's better." Bud exited the car.

Chase pulled her backpack from the car and came around. She bit her lip, which was quivering as she handed the backpack to Bud.

"It's going to be fine. You will pick me up in six and a half hours. I think we can be apart that long." Bud stuck out her hand. "Now wish me well."

"Are you sure you have everything?" Chase asked as she shook Bud's hand.

"Of course I have everything. You made me check it ten times last night and you had Donna verify it," Bud said crossly.

"That's right."

Just then a dark-haired woman impeccably dressed in a rust

cashmere sweater and earth brown trousers, a perfect example of fall colors as Stella would say, came up to them.

"Aren't you Chase Banter, the writer, the lesbian writer?" Before Chase could answer, the woman said, "I saw you on the web at that panelist site. I thought you were spectacular. My name is Evelyn Carter." She stuck out her hand.

Chase suddenly felt woefully underdressed in her usual attire of khaki shorts and a T-shirt that she got at Thrift Town for a dollar-fifty that had "Have you had your shellfish today?" emblazoned on the front of it. Bud was dressed nicely in her tan trousers and blue blazer with white trainers. She'd been so concerned with getting Bud ready, she realized, that she'd paid little attention to her own accoutrements. Well, she thought, I certainly don't resemble the woman in the video anymore.

"And this must be Bud," Evelyn said, patting Bud on the head.

Bud glared at her impolitely but was distracted by Evelyn's little girl, who whispered something in Bud's ear that made her giggle. Chase was trying to keep track of what Evelyn was saying about lesbian parenting and how they, the PLUs ("You know, People Like Us"), have to stick together and her calling over of three of the other mothers ("Friends of mine that are also gay parents, you simply must meet them") that she lost Bud in the process. She looked down one minute at Bud chatting amiably with Evelyn's daughter and the next minute the two of them were holding hands and running up the stairs to the school.

"Bud, wait!" Chase called out.

Bud looked back and waved.

Evelyn took Chase's arm and said, "Oh, they'll be fine. Collins is a very capable child. Now, I want you to meet Mary Elizabeth Phillips and her partner Anne Clemens. They have two boys in the second grade."

Chase smiled at the two women, who appeared to have the same haircut, shoulder-length hair pulled back in a ponytail, and the same variation of the same outfit, Capri pants and polo shirts.

"And this is Essie Marshall. She's a single parent, but looking," Evelyn said brightly.

Chase shook Essie's hand and tried to smile sympathetically as she could tell Essie didn't like her moniker of single-parent-but-looking. "What grade is your child in?" Chase thought this had to be a socially acceptable question in suburban mother-land.

At this Essie brightened. "My little girl, Summer, is just starting this year. Maybe she could meet your daughter. Evelyn says they're in the same grade. Summer is kind of shy."

"Oh, look, Collins has already got her. I told her to keep an eye out for Summer," Evelyn said, pointing. "Don't you two worry. Collins will take care of Bud and Summer. She's very congenial and well-mannered."

As she said this, Chase saw Collins step on the spanking white new trainers of a small boy who had pulled on Summer's long braid. Oh, yes, Chase thought, Collins would be a very useful ally.

"Does Collins like ice cream?" Chase asked, trying to sound nonchalant.

"Absolutely loves the stuff. Her favorite place to go is the Cold Stone Creamery in the Uptown and her favorite flavor is blueberry cream cheese."

"I'll remember that. Perhaps we can all go for ice cream one day soon," Chase said. She could hardly believe she was saying it, but in the protection of their young, mothers were known to go to extreme measures.

"You know, that brings me to my next topic. Now I was hoping we could get some of the gay mothers or fathers, whichever, and have a coffee klatch," Evelyn said.

Mary Elizabeth and Anne were very enthusiastic about this idea. Essie didn't look so sure.

Chase was clueless. "What's a coffee klatch?" She wasn't even certain what the word "klatch" meant.

"We all get together, at a convenient time for everyone, of course, and talk about our issues and, well, drink coffee," Evelyn said. "Now I know Mary E. and Anne, being interior designers, have a very flexible schedule, and Essie, well, now what would we call what you do?"

"I'm an e-trader," she said, and then noting the look of

noncomprehension on everyone's face said, "I create virtual portfolios for people who then decide whether it works for them and they purchase the plan if they like it."

"And I must say it certainly pays well. You should see her house," Evelyn said. "Chase, as we all know, sets her own schedule, I'm sure, so I don't see why Friday mornings wouldn't be a perfect time for the klatch to meet. We drop the kids off and head to Starbucks and yak away. Agreed?"

Before anyone had a chance to respond, the traffic guard, a portly but very serious woman dressed in brown and orange came over. "Ladies, you need to get a move on. This is a drop-off zone only and as you can see it's getting congested."

"Ta ta, everyone," Evelyn said.

As Mary E. and Anne left, Essie touched Chase's arm. "I'll go if you do," she said quietly.

"Ditto. See you tomorrow," Chase said.

She made it three blocks from the school before she parked the car and ran back. She snuck in one of the side doors and made for Bud's classroom, which she knew by heart as she and Bud had tramped all over the school on numerous reconnoitering missions so that Bud would not get lost or head into enemy territory, which was most certainly any grade above hers. They had also rehearsed various escape routes if she were caught by evildoers. Gitana thought this was overkill until Donna, who did agree with Chase on this point, had gotten hold of the architectural plans for the building. "I mean, what if there's a fire?" Donna had said.

"Or a bully," Chase added.

"She'll need to know her way around," Donna said.

"I don't think that includes air shafts and electrical closets," Gitana replied.

"You can never be too informed," Donna said as she and Chase pored over the documents.

Chase now hid in the small alcove between the banks of lockers and waited for Bud, who she had ascertained was not yet in her classroom. She's probably being harassed by the school thugs already, her lunch money stolen, maybe even her shoes, Chase thought in horror, until she remembered that she'd written

Bud's name and address inside her trainers in permanent marker and that Bud was bringing her lunch because of her dietary proclivities. Instead, Bud came down the hall with Summer and Collins, chatting away and looking quite at ease.

"Bud, come here," Chase hissed from her hiding spot.

Bud looked around.

"Over here," Chase whispered, although over the hubbub it wasn't necessary—or effective. The five-minute bell rang its warning.

Collins glanced over and spotted Chase. "Bud, your mom wants you." She pointed at Chase. "We'll save you a seat," she said.

Bud quickly came over. "What is it?" She looked worried.

"I just wanted to tell you that I love you," Chase said, kneeling down so she was eye to eye with Bud.

"Oh. I love you too."

"Okay," Chase said, getting up.

"I'd better go," Bud said, pointing her thumb over her shoulder and in the direction of the classroom. She suddenly hugged Chase's thigh and then ran into the room.

That was our first real goodbye, Chase thought. Her cell phone vibrated in her pocket and she slipped outside to answer it.

"You're standing outside her classroom, aren't you?" Gitana said.

"How did you know?" Chase said, glancing over the immaculate grounds of the school with its stately oaks and manicured lawns. At first the beauty soothed her and then she thought about how much water it took to maintain such a look.

"Because I know you. Now go home and start writing. It'll take your mind off Bud until it's time to go pick her up."

"I can't. I have to meet Lacey at Borders for coffee so we can discuss her 'I have a lesbian dream' concept and then we're going to the Main Library so Isabel can help us with the research."

"Lacey is going to the library. Wow, put this day down on the calendar of unlikely events."

"She's starting to make me nervous," Chase said as she walked to her car.

"Just don't agree to do anything."

"I won't."

"I'll see you tonight and everything will be all right."

"I know." She clicked off and climbed in her car. At least I think I'll be all right, she thought. Bud promised to call at lunchtime so she only had to get through three and a half hours. She knew she was going to have to stop being so needy. Perhaps she should make an appointment with her therapist, Dr. Robicheck, so they could discuss it.

Lacey told her about her intended plans as they sipped iced coffees, then Chase scrolled through her phone and made an appointment for the following week with Dr. Robicheck.

"I thought you were better," Lacey said.

"I was, but I think I might need a tune-up. You know how big changes sort of mess with my psyche."

"Oh, well, finish up your drink so we can get to the library. Isabel called me this morning and said she has as many lesbian books as are currently available," Lacey said, slurping the last of her iced coffee and staring imperiously at Chase's half-full glass.

"Are you going to read all these books?"

"With some help from Jasmine."

"And what is the purpose of this exercise?" Chase took several deep swallows of her coffee.

"I have to know our history. I can't point us in the right direction if I don't know where we came from," Lacey said. "I'm going to need your help."

"I'm not big on group things," Chase said, making her first attempt at extrication.

"Well, you'll just have to learn. Come on," Lacey said, getting up.

As Chase got into Lacey's car, she thought, "Strike One."

The drive to the library was an interminable ride, with Lacey running through all the contractual issues of her real estate purchase in Galisteo, of which Chase had no conceivable idea. Gitana had taken care of all those kinds of details when they bought their house and property. Chase also had to give Lacey numerous instructions as to how to get to the Main Library. Lacey had at first pulled up in front of The Library.

"This doesn't look like a library," she said, glancing up at the façade.

"That's because it's not," Chase said.

"But it says so on the sign," Lacey replied, her brow wrinkled.

"This is the Library Bar."

"They serve liquor at the library?"

"Lacey, listen to me. This is a bar with books as part of the décor and waitresses that are dressed in short skirts and tight blouses supposedly indicative of schoolgirls and it's called The Library. The real library is between Fifth and Sixth Street. Drive on." Chase refrained from saying that if Lacey had ever gone to the library before she would know this.

"Oh."

They found the library, only to discover that neither one of them had change for the parking meter. They scoured the car in search of lost change and found nothing. "Jasmine is kind of a neat freak. She details the cars once a week," Lacey said.

Chase stood looking at the parking meter. "This is New Mexico."

"And?"

"We have laws against littering, using your cell phone while driving, double fine speed zones and lots of drunk driving, all of which have hefty fines attached to them and for the most part very few of which are enforced. I don't think we have to worry about a parking meter."

Inside, Isabel greeted them and then took them to the reserved shelves where Lacey's books were being held.

"You can check out up to fifty books at a time. I've collected forty-five so you're under the limit anyway," Isabel said.

Chase picked up Djuna Barnes's *Nightwood*. "I haven't read this in years. It's really a good book."

Lacey studied the cover. "Never heard of it."

"That's because it was written a long time ago and it never made it to the classics section at Borders," Chase said, and then added, "not that you've ever been in the classics section."

Lacey frowned at her. "What about this one?" she said, referring to Radcliffe Hall's *The Well of Loneliness*.

"Absolutely essential to your knowledge of lesbian history," Chase said.

"Perfect," Lacey said as she started stuffing the books into a canvas bag she'd brought with her.

Isabel cleared her throat.

"Lacey, you have to check them out. You can't just take them," Chase said.

"Well, then I'll check them out." She looked around as if in search of a cash register. "How do I do that?"

"With your library card," Chase replied.

Isabel tactfully handed her a library card application. "Just fill it out and I'll get you one."

"You don't have a library card?" Chase yelped. Several pairs of eyes stared at her and she lowered her voice. "That's disgraceful."

Lacey shrugged. "I've never needed one before. See, this is why I need you on board. You read a lot and you know things."

Oh, no, Chase thought, "Strike Two." She hoped she wasn't going to be aboard a sinking ship. She blanched—a mixed metaphor. She chastised herself for not sticking to baseball if she was operating off the strike out theory. Life was so much more complicated than writing. At least with writing there were rules. A dangling participle couldn't bitch slap you when you weren't looking.

Lacey needed intense instruction on how to operate the self-checkout machine. Finally Chase gave up and did it herself.

"Isabel, I want to heartily thank you for putting forth such an effort in compiling this bulwark of lesbianism. I'm going to make you an honorary lesbian when we get things up and running," Lacey said.

Isabel smiled. "Thank you."

"I'm sure you'll be receiving your plaque shortly," Chase said, "along with a blender, instead of a toaster oven, and a subscription to *How to be the Best Lesbian You Can*."

"We have a magazine?" Lacey said incredulously.

"Not that one, thank god," Chase said, hoisting up a stack of books that wouldn't fit into the bag.

Isabel laughed. "Have fun, ladies."

When they reached the car, Chase checked the windshield. "See, I told you."

"I love this place."

"Yeah, until someone who is texting while driving crashes into your car."

Chase's phone beeped. She pulled it from her pocket. "Oh, my god, it's Bud."

"I thought you liked to talk to Bud," Lacey said, as she maneuvered out of the tight parking lot in her Lesbaru, as Subarus were known to the community.

It was a text message. "It's lunchtime, but no one calls their moms so I don't want to stick out. Everything is fine."

Lacey leaned over to read it.

"You're supposed to be driving," Chase said, alarmed.

"We're at a red light. Boy, for a kid, she's a pretty good texter."

"She's got a BlackBerry with a keyboard," Chase said. She wrote back, "Okay. See you soon." She thought this was the epitome of self-restraint and then she handed the phone to Lacey. "You'll need to keep this for half an hour while Bud's at lunch."

"Why?" Lacey said, taking the phone.

"Because I can't control myself."

"Is this like the Mentos thing?" Lacey said as she got on the freeway and headed uptown.

"Yes. Speaking of which, do you have any?"

"You told me not to."

"Since when do you listen to what I say?" Chase stared out the window morosely. She wouldn't see Bud for another two and a half hours.

"Let's go to my place and we'll look at the books until it's time for you to pick up Bud. It'll take your mind off it," Lacey said.

"All right."

"We'll stop at Smith's and get a Papa Murphy's pizza for lunch and some Mentos. It'll be fun."

"Pizza usually does cheer me up," Chase conceded.

"Great," Lacey said.

At two o'clock, Chase's car was the first one in the queue

for student pickup. She had meticulously studied the system of child pickup and delivery, which had a one-way entrance and was sectioned off by traffic barriers. If you weren't early, it could take some time to maneuver through the line. She had brought her laptop but was unable to concentrate as she kept looking at the clock in the corner of the screen. Finally, she heard the bell ring and waited anxiously for Bud to spill forth. It seemed like an eternity before she saw her. Bud was jostling between Summer and Collins. She waved and smiled at Chase. The three girls did some kind of funky handshake thing and then Bud got in the car.

"What was that about?" Chase asked, resisting the urge to hug her really tight because she knew it would embarrass Bud.

"It's our special handshake signifying eternal devotion to our newfound friendship," Bud said, pulling a granola bar out of her backpack.

"I saved you a piece of pizza," Chase said, pointing to the backseat.

"Really," Bud said, leaping for it.

"Now, about this handshake, I mean, eternal devotion is kind of a big step for people you just met today."

"Don't worry about it. It's just Collins' histrionics. It's entirely possible we won't like each other in a month, but if it makes her happy, what does it hurt?" Bud took enormous bites of her pizza.

"Be careful, you'll choke," Chase said as she maneuvered the car through the traffic barriers until she reached the street, which was heavily patrolled by crosswalk guards in brown and orange outfits. This was another time-consuming endeavor. "Didn't you eat lunch?"

"I had to share, that's another part of the eternal devotion thing. Collins wants to be a vegetarian, but her mom won't let her so I gave her half of my lunch because she said she couldn't possibly eat her cow meat sandwich."

"Tomorrow I'll pack enough lunch for the two of you. What about Summer?" They were finally free of the school zone cluster fuck. Chase breathed a sigh of relief as they approached Indian School and the freeway entrance ramp.

"She only eats tomato sandwiches with peanut butter crackers."

"Every day?"

"Apparently, she's been heavily influenced by *Harriet the Spy* and is mimicking some of her behaviors. She feels that to truly experience literature one must adopt some of the protagonist's proclivities. She wants to be a theatrical performer when she grows up."

"Harriet didn't eat peanut butter crackers."

"Summer doesn't really like tomato sandwiches so she brings along the peanut butter crackers."

"And I thought we were weird," Chase said as they drove for home.

"Apparently not." Bud leaned her head against Chase's shoulder. "I missed you."

"Ditto."

Chapter Twenty-One—Beginnings
Learn to make a body of a limb.—Shakespeare

"Do you realize this is the first time we've been alone in the afternoon for the longest time?" Chase said. She and Gitana were sitting on the deck of the writing studio admiring Chase's jewel garden, an elaborate display of flowers that had gotten larger and larger each year so that it covered almost half an acre and was still a work in progress.

"That is because I'm playing hooky and Bud is at school and you've just finished your latest lesbian novel to the outstanding cheers of the Pink Mafia," Gitana replied.

"I had to send them every chapter to see if it met their approval. I've never had a counsel of beta readers before."

"Donna told me that you had to make some of the sex scenes more tasteful," Gitana said.

"Yeah, we'll see what Ariana has to say about that. The evil editor was the one who made me write graphic sex and the Pink Mafia disapproves of it. Go figure."

"I think the publishing world might want to do a series of focus groups on what kind of sex scenes lesbian readers like," Gitana said, sipping her lemonade.

"Don't say that in front of Lacey." Chase pinched off another piece of tortilla and threw it to the mountain jays. She'd been feeding them when Gitana arrived. "She'll have us all doing another panel discussion and it's taken me the entire month of August to get over the last one."

"I think you did beautifully. In fact, I'm sure your lezzie has officially returned."

Chase reached over and took her hand. "And how do you figure on that one?"

"I don't know. You just seem more lesbian. For awhile there you were getting a bit suburban."

"What!"

"Well, you were. Your clothes have also improved," Gitana said playfully, pulling at Chase's cream-colored silk shirt and coffee-colored linen Capri pants.

"My mother took me shopping. I can't look like a bag lady at the coffee klatch. I would embarrass Bud."

Gitana squeezed her hand. "I don't think Bud cares."

"She does. She clandestinely got Stella to suggest a shopping trip, mentioning that as a writer of prominence I might need a bit of a spruce up."

"No more khaki shorts and Thrift Town cast-offs?"

"Well, I can't swear off that. I just have to look more presentable to pick her up at school. Bud says it's like having a uniform. I still get to have play clothes. Speaking of which, I need to pack my bag for yoga and then Lou wants to talk to me about something so we're taking the kids to the park afterward. We should be home about seven thirty. Will that be all right?"

Gitana checked her watch. "I'll help you pack." She got up.

"I don't have much, just my yoga outfit and then my play clothes," Chase said.

"We've only got a couple hours," Gitana said, pulling on Chase's hand.

"It's not going to take two hours to pack," Chase said, following Gitana back to the house.

"You're thinking suburban again. I want to spend the next hour and forty-five minutes fucking your brains out between the Wonder Sheets."

"Oh, but I still have to pack."

Gitana was pulling Chase's T-shirt off as they went upstairs. "Think lezzie," Gitana said as she slid out of her panties.

It didn't take much persuading for suburban thoughts to subsume to thoughts of lesbian delights.

After yoga Chase and Lou hung upside down on the monkey bars while Bud and Peter designed their own game of Frisbee golf using smashed up cans they'd retrieved from the recycle bin. After Chase had disinfected them with the can of Lysol she always had on hand, Bud had smashed the cans flat using the hammer from the tool kit Chase always kept in the trunk, wired various small rocks to the center of the cans that were now discs and then put electrical tape around the edges so they wouldn't cut themselves.

Peter watched her intently but did not appear to be amazed, only interested in how the whole thing would turn out. Lou, on the other hand, stood in wonderment. "The kid is like MacGyver."

"Well, you know..." Chase trailed off. She didn't want to go into Bud's intellectual abilities.

Somehow or another they'd ended up on the monkey bars. "I think these things really do straighten out your spine," Lou said.

"It's definitely along the lines of an inversion table," Chase said.

Lou sighed. "I've got a problem."

"Anything you need," Chase offered up. "What is it? A babysitter, a car tune-up, plumbing issue, financial...I don't do gynecological work, but I do have a good therapist."

"You have a therapist?"

"Let's just keep that between us."

"It's nothing to be ashamed of. Therapy is like a mind tune-up."

"That's a good way to look at it," Chase said.

"What I need is advice," Lou pulled herself up. Her face was very red. Chase did the same. They sat on top of the bars and swung their legs.

Chase bit her lip. "I can try. I'm not the soundest-of-mind kind of advice giver."

Lou laughed. "You're better than you think. Marsha asked me out."

"That was entirely my fault. When I told her to have a go at it I didn't mean you and I tried to explain to her that I didn't think you were ready. She just said she'd wait." Chase looked glum. She stared out at Bud and Peter—childhood suddenly seemed much easier.

"Don't worry. It wasn't your fault," Lou said, touching her arm. "The thing is I thought I might go out with her."

"Really?" Chase was incredulous.

"We talked and she's got a good head on her shoulders. She agreed that going slow would be prudent and if at anytime either one of us changed our mind about the direction of our friendship—that's what we're going to call it instead of relationship—we would tell the other. I think that's a rational way to approach it."

"You're probably going to go to bed on your first date."

"I know."

"Well, it's easier jumping into cold water than it is sliding," Chase said.

As she lay awake in bed, Chase thought about jumping into cold water. Hadn't that been what she and Gitana had done, having Bud, becoming parents, writing herself in and out of lesbian fiction, learning to be social or socially adapted as Lily had taught her. She leaned over to kiss Gitana, who nuzzled against her. Then the phone rang. She leapt up to grab her cell phone on the nightstand. She kept it there in case there was an emergency—what if her mother or Jacinda had a heart attack? Or there was an intruder? Or one of her friends died in a car crash and the body needed to be identified, although that probably wouldn't be an issue because the police would already know who it was by the car license plate... These thoughts blazed through her head as she clicked on her phone.

"I'm in your driveway. You need to come down."

"Lacey?"

Gitana stirred and Chase crept to the bathroom.

"I want to show you something."

"Lacey, it's the middle of the night."

"It's eight thirty."

"Oh, but everyone's asleep."

"You're not. Come down or I'll sit out here and honk until you do."

"You'll wake everyone up."

"Exactly."

"I'll be right there." She pulled on a pair of khaki shorts and a T-shirt that read SUP. Delia, with all her marketing savvy, had designed the T-shirt and was now selling them on the Internet, telling the group, "Dudes, we are not the only ones suffering from this malady and we should be willing to share the wealth." Chase slipped downstairs, grabbing house keys on the way out. She locked the front door and got in the car.

"Perfect. Buckle up."

"Where are we going?"

"To the new center of the lesbian universe. I want you to be the first to see it." Lacey glided out of the driveway like a ghost car.

"Can't it wait until tomorrow?"

"No, it's too important."

"Because..."

"The fate of our people is at stake." Lacey glanced at her as they passed the only streetlight in ten miles, the one that marked the entrance to the highway, and Chase saw the slightly crazed look in her eyes.

"Don't speed. No one knows where I am," Chase said, wishing

she had had the foresight to write a quick note, something to the effect of, "My best friend has abducted me for some midnight mission. If I don't return, I love you all."

"I'll be careful."

They drove north toward Santa Fe on Highway 41. There were no other cars on the road, and it suddenly felt like they were the only two people on the planet.

"Lacey, please tell me what we're doing."

"I want it to be a surprise." She flipped in a Lucinda Williams compilation disc and they drove in silence until they reached Galisteo. The tiny town was shut up for the night. Only a few lighted windows indicated that the place was even inhabited. Lacey turned on a dirt road and their headlights scattered rabbits and god-knows-what-else.

"You're not going to murder me, are you?" Chase asked.

"Not unless you get in my way," Lacey said, pulling up slowly to a gate. "I'm kidding. Could you get the gate?"

Chase obediently complied.

Lacey parked the car in front of an enormous building with four wings, each one ending in a tower that looked like a small observatory. They got out.

"What is this place?" Chase asked.

"I'm not exactly sure. The roofs of the four observatories fold back, but it doesn't appear they had telescopes in them. I'm thinking they used these rooms for ceremonies. There are signs of Wicca activity."

"Wicca?"

"I haven't found any dead chickens. There were chalk circles, but the property company went to great pains to remove them after I bought the place."

"This is the property you were talking about?"

"Yeah. Look at the stars out here and listen, no noise."

A series of high-pitched yelps rang through the night. "See, just natural sounds, the coyotes singing and..."

A hellacious cry rang out as if something was being ripped to pieces. "What's that?" Lacey said, fishing keys out of her pocket.

"That coyote singing noise you heard is the sound they make

when they have savagely caught and killed something and are celebrating."

"Oh, well, see, this is a place of celebration," Lacey said brightly.

As they entered the great hall, as Lacey called it, Chase said, "Are you and Jasmine planning to live out here by yourselves?"

"With about two hundred other people," Lacey said, switching on the light. The place was hollow and enormous. "Admittedly, the place needs work."

"Two hundred people? Is this going to be like a refugee camp?" Chase gazed around. The great hall had arched doorways leading off in intervals of five feet. A second story that ran the length of the hall had larger openings.

"A refugee camp of sorts—a place for our people to conjoin, comingle and cavort." Lacey looked around with the glow of one imagining the end product with little or no knowledge of the immediate requirements of the here and now.

Requirements like the services of a good pest control company, Chase thought, hearing things scuttling around.

"So what exactly is the plan here?" Chase said as she followed Lacey down the massive stone hallway toward one of the observatories that wasn't really an observatory, but rather, as Chase imagined it, the place where ritualistic appendectomies were performed while Orion looked on and the moon covered her face in abject horror.

"This," Lacey put her arms out majestically, "is going to be the Lesbian Illumination Institute, a place where lesbians can come to embrace their inner lesbian strengths, gain knowledge and go out and conquer the world, basically."

"Conquer the world?"

"Well, at least control major portions of the world's commercial interests, gain political office and manipulate the course of human history. Think of it as the Skull and Bones of the lesbian world."

"Are you feeling okay?"

"I have never been better. And now we're going to celebrate." She pulled out of her enormous purse a bottle of chilled champagne ensconced in a cooler bag and two glasses wrapped in tissue paper. She popped the cork expertly. Chase was impressed. "A toast, to new beginnings."

Chase raised her glass. "You are truly amazing."

"Does that mean you'll help?" Lacey gazed at her fondly. "Because I'm going to really need you."

"This is insanity." Chase sipped her champagne and thought of trust funds. She'd used hers to finance her early writing career and help Gitana start the orchid nursery—both dreams that normal people would have thought nonsense. Now Lacey was going to use hers to finance the most impractical of ideas, but the first important enterprise Lacey had ever been involved with. This was her friend, whose largest interests to date were clothes, hair and interior design. Lacey had never had a mission in life before. How could Chase let her down?

"Just think what this could do for your writing career. You'll have a microcosm to study human nature." Lacey looked at her pleadingly.

"All right, I will help you, but it must not interfere with my family life or my writing."

"I can work with that." Lacey gave her a bone-crushing hug. "I wish we could have sex right now. That would make it perfect."

"What!"

"Just testing. You are going to be surrounded by lesbians."

Chase was discomfited.

"I was teasing." Lacey poured her another glass.

When Chase crawled back into bed, Gitana rolled over and opened her eyes. "Where have you been?"

"Drinking champagne with Lacey in the middle of nowhere and selling my soul for the sake of our people."

Gitana pulled her to her. "Let's have sex."

"Funny, that's what Lacey wanted to do, but I declined."

"You must have made her very happy. She equates getting her heart's desire with clitoral stimulation."

"I agreed to help her change the world along with two hundred other lesbians."

"We better really celebrate," Gitana said as she kissed her way down Chase's stomach.

"Hmm."

Chapter Twenty-Two—End

Respice finem:
Consider the end.—Latin proverb

Chase clicked on the speakerphone, dreading who was on the other end. Myra's disembodied voice in the kitchen was more tolerable than her voice going directly into your ear, Chase had discovered. Myra had been on safari in Africa for three weeks and had just got back. Chase pitied the animals who had had the misfortune to cross Myra's path. She must have seen the webcast, Chase thought. It had to be faced, though. As Lily always said, as if it were the SUP motto, "Looking the other way when the lorry is coming will not prevent it from running you over." The word "lorry" had to be explained to Delia. The statement would then be followed by a series of possible approaches. Lily seemed to feel that with enough repetitions, like muscle memory for a sport you'd given up and then taken up again—the proverbial bicycle—the group could be trained to see a situation and quickly assess and adjust accordingly, like soldiers who despite chaos would always remember what to do.

"Hello, Myra, I hope all is well in your world and that the weather is fine," Chase said. She sat abruptly on one of the kitchen stools and put her head on the cool ceramic surface of the kitchen island. So much for muscle memory and approaching lorries, she thought, recalling that a lot of foreign pedestrians were killed each year in Great Britain because they failed to realize that the truck would be coming from the reverse direction and stepped into the oncoming traffic when crossing the street. How did negligence of customs figure into Lily's scheme?

"Kid, you were fucking great! You looked fantastic in that suit. We should have fucking gone for that kick-ass look before. It never crossed my fucking mind. It's bohemian, quirky and fucking outlandish. It's like Tom Fucking Wolfe wearing that white suit. Everyone remembers the fucking guy even if they don't like his stuff."

Chase perked up. She reached around for a notepad and pencil. She began making scratch marks. Six for seven—not bad, every sentence except one had a swear word in it—this was a perfect example of Tom Wolfe's fuck patois. During all her conversations with Myra, Chase ran a tally of the swear words because it kept her calm while she pretended to listen to what Myra was saying. Donna would reiterate it for her and Donna didn't have an expletive in almost every sentence.

"Son of a bitch, that Jew tailor is my new fucking go-to-guy. Get him to make five more. I'll fucking send him a check. And Christ on a bike that no shoes look was fucking brilliant. You better have had some clean ass toenails. Those web creeps can blow shit up and toe jam would be a cock-sucking pixel nightmare."

Chase winced. When Myra was truly pissed or excited her level of cursing ascended to new heights.

"We'll schedule pedicures before any appearances. We don't want any of those cunt interviewers and prissy ass readers at book signings getting a load of anything, shall we say, fucking untoward."

Chase wished Myra didn't talk so loud. It must be a New York thing because everything was so noisy there. Bud had walked in the kitchen and Chase madly motioned her out.

"I know she swears like a fucking sailor," Bud said.

Chase glared at her and shook her finger.

"Is that the kid? Hey, let's get her a fucking little suit and she can go barefoot too—kind of like that Austen Powers mini-me fucking gig and what about the blue bear book? Can she draw? That would be the best. That would outdo that fucking Marley kid who painted abstracts. Bud could be an artist and a writer."

"Who told you about that?"

"Who else? The ever-vigilant Donna, my eyes and ears."

"It's just a short story." Chase looked in alarm at Bud, who was getting her breakfast out of the fridge. She shrugged.

"Donna said the fucking kid worked it into quite the kick-ass quest story and what was the short fucking story is now the mother-fucking end. How sweet is that?"

"Bud, is that true?"

She nodded nonchalantly as she filled the dog bowls with kibble. She took the food out to Annie and Jane, who were waiting patiently in the sunroom for their breakfast.

"So here's your instructions, no shoes, get more suits made, and have a pedicure and get the mini-me to send me some picture ideas for her new book. You'll have to sign the contract as she's a minor. All right then, ta-ta. Oh, p.s., kid, you're doing a good job, maybe this dancing to your own accordion thing is working—I know it's supposed to be drum but in your case accordion is more apt."

"Where'd you hear about that?"

"Lacey told me."

"How do you know Lacey?" Chase was puzzled and concerned. Lacey, as far as she was concerned, was a loose cannon.

"She had Donna run an idea for a radical lesbian anthology gig by me and I'm going to run it by you-know-who. Lacey might fucking be onto something. I didn't fucking really give this lesbian culture thing any credence until now. You dyke bitches might be onto something here. Nothing like drumming up some kick-ass business. I didn't think you mother fuckers had it in you."

"Dyke bitches? Myra, that's not exactly a politically correct description."

"Relax, it's a term of endearment."

Chase clicked off as Donna came running in the kitchen door.

"Look at this!" She was waving a printed e-mail at Chase. She danced something that resembled a hip-hop move and the Cabbage Patch hula-hoop hip swirl. "You won!" She grabbed Chase and kissed her cheek. "You won!"

"I won what?" Chase poured herself more coffee. "You want one?"

"Yes, please, with lots of milk. Of course, we'll have to plan a celebration."

Chase handed Donna her coffee.

"I knew you had it in you. I have to get you a plane ticket."

Chase sat on a kitchen stool. She'd had enough surprises for one dyke bitch in a day and it was only seven thirty in the morning. That was the problem with dealing with New Yorkers—a three-hour time difference. Myra could ruin your day before it ever got started. She gave Donna the stink eye, silently demanding elucidation.

"The Best Lesbian Novel of 2010," Donna shouted. "The judges loved it."

"What do I have to do?" Chase felt sulky and perhaps a little ungrateful.

"You're not happy?" Donna said.

"That panel thing really wore me out. I'm not good at stuff like this." She got up.

"Where are you going?"

"To talk to the Divine Vulva and Commercial Endeavor. I need some guidance."

"Oh, well, I'm going to call Gitana. She'll be excited about it."

"Can you take Bud to school? I don't think I can face the queue today."

"Sure. Bud will be thrilled about your award. Have you seen her scrapbook and wall of recognition? She's very proud of you."

"Great."

Chase walked through the jewel garden, picked a few weeds and studied the condition of the path. It needed edging. Then she went to her writing studio.

"Isn't it fabulous?" Divine Vulva said, swirling around in Chase's desk chair. They'd obviously heard the news.

Commercial Endeavor said derisively, "I think it's going to hurt your career as a mainstream author."

Divine Vulva threw a cocktail sauce-covered shrimp in her direction. It hit Chase's writing mascot, Curious George, square in the forehead. "You're such a party pooper."

"And why is that?" Chase asked Commercial Endeavor, flouncing down on the couch and scrubbing the cocktail sauce off Curious George's forehead with a corner of her T-shirt. She ate the shrimp, figuring it fell under the five-second drop rule.

"Because it will only serve to encourage you to pursue this senseless path of moist-mound sagas when you have real work to do," Commercial Endeavor said.

"That's not true." Divine Vulva flung another shrimp, which landed several feet short of Commercial Endeavor.

"Will you stop throwing shrimp?" Chase said petulantly.

"Sorry. But getting this award means that this work does have value." Divine Vulva retrieved the shrimp and ate it.

"That's disgusting," Commercial Endeavor said. "You don't know where that floor's been."

"Five-second drop rule," Divine Vulva said.

Chase looked at her fondly.

Divine Vulva sat down next to her and swung her legs onto Chase's lap. "We rock," she said.

Chase studied Commercial Endeavor, who was brooding in the corner. "Come sit by us. We're a family. I've proved I can do both so maybe we could all just get along."

Commercial Endeavor sat on the other side of Chase, pushing Vulva's legs to one side so she could put her own legs on Chase's lap. "I'm just looking out for you because I love you."

"I know you do," Chase said.

"How about we put a lesbian in the mystery novel and some mystery in the lesbian novel, then we could work together. I think we'd make a good team, except," Divine Vulva pointed a finger at Commercial Endeavor, "you have to stop being so homophobic."

"I'm not homophobic. I'm just not attracted to you."

"Why not?" Vulva pouted.

"Because you dress like a prostitute and you eat entirely too much shrimp," Commercial Endeavor said.

Vulva looked down as if seeing herself for the first time. She was wearing a sequined black miniskirt and a low-cut white frilly blouse with cocktail sauce stains on the front.

"She does have a point," Chase said.

"Okay, hold on." She disappeared into the bathroom.

"I can't wait to see this," Commercial Endeavor said.

"Me either."

Vulva came out wearing khaki shorts and a black T-shirt that read "I like girls."

"Now, that is an improvement. She looks just like you," Commercial Endeavor said.

"I promise to eat more vegetables," Vulva said.

"I'm going to do some gardening," Chase said, "and then we'll go over the galley proofs for the mystery novel, all three of us."

Later that afternoon there was a tap on the door and Lacey, Bud, Gitana and Donna came in. Now this really was a surprise, Chase thought, looking up from her computer.

Lacey had a bottle of champagne, a bottle of sparkling cider and five glass flutes. "Congrats!"

Bud was wearing a green suit with black pin-stripes and a black mock turtleneck. Gitana was holding its equivalent in grown-up size.

"We went shopping at Thrift Town. I think it must have been some theatrical costume," Gitana said.

"Bud wants to go onstage with you," Lacey said, trying to open the champagne bottle. It wasn't going as well as it had at the Lesbian Illumination Institute.

"You better let Donna do that before someone loses an eye," Gitana said.

"We can't wear shoes, though," Bud said, climbing on Chase's lap and snuggling.

"Isn't she perfectly adorable?" Vulva said to Commercial Endeavor as they watched from the corner of the room.

"So are you," Commercial Endeavor said, putting her arm around Vulva.

"Where is this awards ceremony, anyway?" Chase asked.

"It's in San Fran, baby, and we're all going," Lacey said, taking a glass of champagne from Donna.

"And there's a two-story Thrift Town there," Bud said, her eyes lighting up.

"Well, in that case, count me in," Chase said as they toasted.

"I thought that might serve as an incentive," Bud said.

"So since my first plaque of achievement was a Vulva, is this award going to be some kind of gold-plated clitoris?" Chase inquired.

"Let's hope not," Gitana said.

Lacey gave her a bone-crushing hug. "See, now you'll have the perfect credentials to be the writing instructor and vice president of the Institute when it's up and running. We're having some plumbing and electrical and roofing issues."

Chase smiled insincerely and glanced over at Commercial Endeavor, who said, very quietly, "We'll blow the place up before we let that happen."

"You can do a lot with fertilizer," Vulva added.

That was what Chase liked about her muses—they never ran out of ideas. She wondered how they were going to take it when they found out she'd already agreed to help. But if the place went up in smoke...well, just as long as no people or animals were harmed in the process.

Lacey raised her glass, "To the Revolution!"

Chase raised her glass with the others and thought about marching with her accordion to somewhere very far away like the Antarctic until this whole thing blew over, or she could take Bud to the Smithsonian and they could stay until they had explored the entire museum—that would take awhile.

Gitana took her hand and whispered, "I love you and I'm proud of you."

Chase smiled and knew her travel plans were moot.

**Publications from
Bella Books, Inc.**
Women. Books. Even Better Together.
**P.O. Box 10543
Tallahassee, FL 32302
Phone: 800-729-4992
www.bellabooks.com**

CALM BEFORE THE STORM by Peggy J. Herring. Colonel Marcel Robicheaux doesn't tell and so far no one official has asked, but the amorous pursuit by Jordan McGowen has her worried for both her career and her honor.
978-0-9677753-1-9

THE WILD ONE by Lyn Denison. Rachel Weston is busy keeping home and head together after the death of her husband. Her kids need her and what she doesn't need is the confusion that Quinn Farrelly creates in her body and heart.
978-0-9677753-4-0

LESSONS IN MURDER by Claire McNab. There's a corpse in the school with a neat hole in the head and a Black & Decker drill alongside. Which teacher should Inspector Carol Ashton suspect? Unfortunately, the alluring Sybil Quade is at the top of the list. First in this highly lauded series.
978-1-931513-65-4

WHEN AN ECHO RETURNS by Linda Kay Silva. The bayou where Echo Branson found her sanity has been swept clean by a hurricane—or at least they thought. Then an evil washed up by the storm comes looking for them all, one-by-one. Second in series.
978-1-59493-225-0

DEVIL'S ROCK by Gerri Hill. Deputy Andrea Sullivan and Agent Cameron Ross vow to bring a killer to justice. The killer has other plans. Gerri Hill pens another intriguing blend of mystery and romance in this page-turning thriller.
978-1-59493-218-2

SHADOW POINT by Amy Briant. Madison McPeake has just been not-quite fired, told her brother is dead and discovered she has to pick up a five-year old niece she's never met. After she makes it to Shadow Point it seems like someone—or something —doesn't want her to leave. Romance sizzles in this ghost story from Amy Briant.
978-1-59493-216-8

JUKEBOX by Gina Daggett. Debutantes in love. With each other. Two young women chafe at the constraints of parents and society with a friendship that could be more, if they can break free. Gina Daggett is best known as "Lipstick" of the columnist duo Lipstick & Dipstick.
978-1-59493-212-0

BLIND BET by Tracey Richardson. The stakes are high when Ellen Turcotte and Courtney Langford meet at the blackjack tables. Lady Luck has been smiling on Courtney but Ellen is a wild card she may not be able to handle.
978-1-59493-211-3